DIRTY
Thirty

By Janet Evanovich

The Stephanie Plum novels

One For The Money
Two For The Dough
Three To Get Deadly
Four To Score
High Five
Hot Six
Seven Up
Hard Eight
To The Nines
Ten Big Ones
Eleven On Top
Twelve Sharp
Lean Mean Thirteen
Fearless Fourteen
Finger Lickin' Fifteen
Sizzling Sixteen
Smokin' Seventeen
Explosive Eighteen
Notorious Nineteen
Takedown Twenty
Top Secret Twenty-One
Tricky Twenty-Two
Turbo Twenty-Three
Hardcore Twenty-Four
Look Alive Twenty-Five
Twisted Twenty-Six
Fortune and Glory (Tantalising Twenty-Seven)
Game On (Tempting Twenty-Eight)
Going Rogue (Rise and Shine Twenty-Nine)
Dirty Thirty

DIRTY Thirty

JANET EVANOVICH

REVIEW

First published in the United States by Atria Books,
An imprint of Simon & Schuster Inc., 2023

First published in Great Britain in 2023 by
HEADLINE REVIEW
An imprint of HEADLINE PUBLISHING GROUP

1

Cataloguing in Publication Data is available from the British Library

ISBN 978 1 0354 0198 7 (Hardback)
ISBN 978 1 0354 0197 0 (Trade Paperback)

Offset in 11.76/18.9pt Sabon LT Std by Jouve (UK), Milton Keynes

Printed and bound in Great Britain by Clays Ltd, Elcograf S.p.A.

MIX
Paper | Supporting
responsible forestry
FSC
www.fsc.org   FSC® C104740

Headline's policy is to use papers that are natural, renewable and recyclable
products and made from wood grown in well-managed forests and other
controlled sources. The logging and manufacturing processes are expected
to conform to the environmental regulations of the country of origin.

HEADLINE PUBLISHING GROUP
An Hachette UK Company
Carmelite House
50 Victoria Embankment
London EC4Y 0DZ

www.headline.co.uk
www.hachette.co.uk

CHAPTER ONE

I'm Stephanie Plum. Jersey girl. Rutgers graduate. Successful underachiever working for Vincent Plum Bail Bonds as a recovery agent, hunting down losers who've skipped out on their bond.

A half hour ago, I heard police chatter about Duncan Dugan exhibiting erratic behavior in an office building downtown. Dugan is a big-ticket bond who failed to show for his court appearance. He's been accused of robbing a jewelry store on King Street at gunpoint, almost running over a crossing guard in his effort to leave the area, and leading seven police cars on a high-speed chase before running out of gas. Since I'd been assigned the task of finding Dugan and dragging his sorry butt back into the legal system, I rushed to the scene with my coworker Lula. Dugan was standing on a fourth-floor ledge. He was a little chubby with short brown hair and his eyes were hidden behind aviator shades. I knew from his arrest sheet that he was five foot ten and thirty-six years old, but he looked younger up there on the ledge. He looked like Charlie Brown, possibly because he was wearing a yellow and black Charlie Brown–style three-button knit shirt. He was flattened against the front of the building, and he was looking down at the crowd that had gathered below him.

"He's gonna jump," Lula said to me. "I got him pegged for a jumper."

There was a large police presence in the area. There were fire trucks and ambulances, and a satellite news truck was parked not far away. It was lunchtime, and the outdoor eating area attached to the building's café had been cleared of diners.

"I'm thinking this might be partly your fault on account of he knows you're after him," Lula said to me. "He probably don't want to go to jail. You should yell up to him and tell him jail isn't so bad. Tell him he'll get free room and board and he'll have a chance to make new friends."

"I'm not yelling that up to him," I said. "That's crazy talk."

"Yeah, but is it true?" Lula asked.

"Technically, yes."

"Hunh," Lula said. "There you have it."

It was a nice October day in Trenton, New Jersey. The sky was as blue as sky gets in Trenton and the sun was shining. I was wearing jeans and sneakers and a hooded sweatshirt over my V-neck, fitted T-shirt. Lula was wearing spike-heeled, thigh-high boots, and as usual she'd managed to squeeze her plus-size body into a spandex dress designed to fit a much smaller person. Her hair was frizzed out into a big puffball and her fake lashes were furry black caterpillar quality. Lula is a person of color and I'm a person of less color.

My eyes are blue. My hair is brown, naturally curly, and shoulder length. I'm lacking the patience to iron my hair into straightness or blow-dry it into luxurious waves, so it's almost always in a ponytail. I make up for this by wearing lip gloss and smiling. Lula justifies the small dress and large lashes by being Lula. The fact is that it all works for her, and on a good day, she's spectacular.

A woman pushed her way through the crowd and stepped out onto the street. I was guessing that she was in her midthirties, and if Duncan was Charlie Brown, then this woman was Charlie Brown's friend Lucy. Her hair was dark brown, almost black, and cut medium short with short bangs. She was wearing a blue shirtwaist dress and blue running shoes.

"Duncan, you moron!" she yelled up to Dugan. "What the heck are you doing?"

"I'm gonna jump," Dugan said. "I screwed up. It's over. I'm jumping to my death."

"Well, you better take a header then, because you're only on the fourth floor. If you don't fall right, you could just end up with a bunch of broken bones or maybe paralyzed."

"I don't like heights. Four is as high as I can go."

"You need to crawl through that window next to you and get down here," the woman yelled up to him.

"I'll go to jail."

"Big deal. My uncle Fritz went to jail, and he said it wasn't so bad. He got free room and board and he got to make a bunch of new friends."

"Fritz said that?"

"More or less. Anyway, it won't be for so long, and in the meantime we can talk."

"What would we talk about?"

"Stuff."

He looked over at the window. "I don't want to get broken bones."

"You see?" Lula said to me. "You could have been the hero if you'd been the first one to tell him about making friends in jail. Although the business about broken bones was a good addition."

Dugan turned to get to the window, his foot slipped, and he fell off the ledge. There was a collective gasp from everyone watching as Dugan crashed through the yellow and white awning that stretched over the sidewalk café and landed like a sack of wet cement on the pavement.

I'm not normally a fainter, but I came close to fainting when I heard him hit. I bent at the waist, sucked in air, and fought the nausea. When I straightened up, Dugan was surrounded by paramedics and police.

"Do you think he's okay?" Lula asked.

"Not even a little," I said.

"They're bringing a stretcher over," Lula said. "That might be a good sign."

One of Dugan's arms came up and he did a little finger wave. "I'm okay," he said. "Sort of."

The crowd dispersed after the wave and message from Dugan, but Lula and I stayed. The woman who had shouted up to Dugan approached the outer rim of the first responders, hung there for a couple minutes, and left.

The paramedics finally lifted Dugan onto the stretcher and rolled him off to the ambulance. I knew one of the men. Jerry Fisher.

"Where are you taking him?" I yelled to Jerry.

He turned and waved at me. "The medical center."

I gave him a thumbs-up, and Lula and I walked down the street to my car.

———

I dropped Lula off at the bail bonds office on Hamilton Avenue and drove a couple more blocks to the hospital. The ambulance was parked in the ER drive-thru. I bypassed the drive-thru and went to the parking garage.

The bail bonds office and the medical center are on the fringe of the Burg. I grew up in the Burg and my parents still live there. It's a residential chunk of South Trenton clinging to Hamilton Avenue, Chambers Street, and Liberty Street. Houses and yards are small. Televisions are large. Secrets are nonexistent. A few people cheat on their taxes but it's okay because they're grandfathered into the mob.

I checked in at the desk in the ER, showed them my papers for Dugan, certifying that I had the right to capture him, and took a seat in the waiting room. After an hour I was told Dugan was in surgery. Three hours later, he was out of surgery and in the ICU, hooked up to a bunch of machines. I talked my way into the ICU and approached Dugan. "Hey," I said. "How's it going?"

"Okay," Dugan said, his voice barely a whisper.

"It looks like they have you all fixed up. I bet you'll be as good as new in no time."

Dugan blinked.

"You probably want to rest," I said. "I'll come back tomorrow."

He wasn't in any shape to flee, so I went back to the office.

———

"I was just closing up for the day," Connie said. "Lula told me about Dugan. How's he doing?"

"He's in the ICU. I didn't get a chance to talk to a doctor. His condition was listed as stable. He got lucky. His fall was broken by the café awning."

Connie Rosolli is a couple years older than me. She's the office manager, the guard dog for Vinnie's private office, and like Vinnie, she's certified to write a bond. She has a lot of black hair, thinks there's no such thing as too much mascara, and likes bright red lipstick and polka dots. She wears heels to work but keeps a pair of running shoes in her bottom drawer next to her Glock nine. She can shoot the eyes out of a grasshopper a quarter mile away.

She took two folders out of her top drawer and handed them to me. "Two new FTAs came in today. Nothing exciting. Both are low bonds. A repeat shoplifter. Gloria Stitch. And a low-level drug dealer. Hooter Brown."

I slipped the files into the messenger bag I used as purse and mobile office. "These two FTAs aren't going to pay my rent."

Being a bond enforcement agent has its highs and lows. One of the lows is that I don't get a salary. I get a percentage of the original bond when I make a capture. If I don't make enough captures, I'm forced to mooch food off my parents and moonlight for rent money.

Connie took a business card off her desk. "This might help. A man came in about an hour ago, looking for you. He said he had a job that required your special skills."

I took the card from her. "I don't have any special skills."

"He asked me if you were good at finding people, and I said you were our best skip tracer."

"I'm your *only* skip tracer." I looked at the name on the card. "Martin Plover. He owns Plover's Jewelry, right? That's the store Duncan Dugan got caught robbing."

"Yeah, small world," Connie said. "Plover told me he'd be in the store until eight o'clock if you were interested. He also left his cell number on the back of the card."

I dropped the card into my messenger bag.

"Are you going to talk to him?" Connie asked.

"Maybe," I said. "Probably."

I left the bonds office, got into my Jeep Cherokee, and drove downtown to Plover's Jewelry. I parked across the street and watched the store for a couple minutes. The "special skills" thing had me worried. I hoped it didn't involve anything kinky. I needed money, but not that bad.

I crossed the street and entered the store. It was five o'clock and there were no customers in Plover's. A nicely dressed man who looked to be in his late sixties to early seventies was seated at a writing desk. He stood when I walked in.

"Stephanie Plum," he said. "Sorry I missed you at the office. Thank you for coming to the store."

"Do I know you?"

"We've never officially met. I recognize you from the Leoni viewing. I was there when you put Bella Morelli in cuffs and hauled her out of the funeral home. That took guts. I don't think I could have done it," he said.

Bella Morelli is a Sicilian immigrant stuck in a Marlon Brando *Godfather* time warp. Her hair is gray. Her dresses are always black. Her posture is vulture on the attack. She's crazy like a fox, and she's my boyfriend's grandmother. She was being her usual disruptive self at the Leoni viewing and the funeral director begged me to take her away.

"Bella wasn't really all that upset about leaving in cuffs. She loves a dramatic exit," I said to Plover.

"She scares the heck out of me. She put a curse on Stu Carp, and he got shingles."

I nodded. "She scares the heck out of a lot of people. Connie said you mentioned a job."

"Yes. I thought of you because you're obviously good at finding people and surviving dangerous situations."

"Like removing Bella from the viewing."

"Exactly! Like removing Bella from the viewing."

"About the job?" I asked.

"I want you to find a former employee. I've reported him as missing to the police, but nothing has come of it."

"How long has he been missing?"

"Three weeks. He disappeared on the same day that I was held at gunpoint and the store was robbed in broad daylight by some moron."

"Did your employee disappear before or after the robbery?"

"After," Plover said. "Actually, I fired him. He was supposed to provide security. I hired him so I wouldn't get robbed, and I got robbed."

"But now you want to find him?"

"Yes," Plover said. "He stole a tray of diamonds valued at close to a million dollars."

"Seriously?"

"Duncan Dugan, the moron who robbed the store that afternoon, got low-hanging fruit. He cleaned out the cases. I don't want to trivialize that. It was terrifying. It was a smash-and-grab without the smashing. He had me dump everything into a garbage bag while he held me at gunpoint. Fortunately, all the pieces he took were insured and he left the cases intact."

I glanced around the store. "It looks like you got everything back."

"Unfortunately, no. The bag of stolen jewelry wasn't in the car when the police finally arrested the driver. Everything you see here is new. My displays are a little skimpy, but at least I'm still in business."

"How could the bag not be in the car? I thought the police were on him the second he pulled away from the curb."

Plover shrugged. "I don't know. It wasn't in the car. And it gets worse. The real loss was with the unset gemstones that were stolen separately. A large part of my business is in engagement rings. Couples come in and select a setting and a stone. So, like most jewelers, I keep an inventory of gemstones. Mostly diamonds of varying sizes and quality."

"And you think your security guy stole the unset stones."

"Yes. I do."

"Have you told the police?"

"Yes, and they said they conducted an investigation, but nothing came of it. I can't fault the police. I have no real proof that my guard took the stones. All I can say is that the gems are definitely missing."

"But you seem sure that the guard took them."

"After the robbery, when I locked up for the night it was just me and one of the police officers. Andy had left a couple hours earlier."

"Andy is the security guard."

"Yes. He always worked from noon to eight. Six days a week. He left at eight o'clock on the day of the robbery, and he never returned."

"And you haven't heard from him."

"Not a word," Plover said. "My routine is that every night I take the jewelry out of the display cases, and I put the jewelry in the safe. When I open in the morning, I take the pieces out of the safe. The morning after the robbery I opened the safe to get the few items that were left to display, and the diamond tray was missing."

"The diamond tray always stays in the safe?"

"Yes."

"Did Andy know how to open the safe?"

"I never gave him the combination, but he was there when I closed every night. If he was motivated, I suspect he could have watched me punch in the numbers. The thing is there's no other way the diamonds could have disappeared. There were no signs that anyone had tampered with the safe. Someone opened it."

"There are people who have skills when it comes to opening safes."

"Whoever took the stones came in through the front door without damaging the lock. He disarmed the alarm, opened the safe, and took the diamonds. I have a camera at the rear entrance but not at the front door. My security company suggested a front-door camera, but I didn't think it was necessary. I was trying to save money."

"Andy had a key?"

"Yes, and he knew the code to disarm the alarm."

"Have you been in contact with his family?"

"His parents don't seem to be very concerned. They said he's always been a free spirit. He doesn't have siblings, and he isn't married."

"And you want me to find Andy?"

"Yes."

"Why?"

"I want the diamonds if any are left. Truth is, they were underinsured. And I'm angry. I trusted Andy. I want him arrested and sent to jail. I believe you get paid when you find people. Find Andy and I'll give you a thousand dollars."

"Does Andy have a last name?"

"Andy Manley."

Holy bejezus. Sucker punch to the brain. I knew Andy Manley. I went to school with him. His nickname was Nutsy. He felt me up at a party when I was fourteen years old, and he told everyone I stuffed my bra with toilet paper. It was a lie, of course. I stuffed my bra with Kleenex. Fortunately, halfway through high school I managed to grow breasts that were acceptable and only required a push-up bra on special occasions.

"I might be able to find Andy for you," I said to Plover, "but I can't guarantee that he'll be sent to jail."

Plover nodded. "Understood."

———

It was six thirty when I pulled into my apartment building's parking lot. The building itself is an unimaginative three-story chunk of brick and mortar. I live on the second floor, in a one-bedroom, one-bath unit that's mostly furnished in hand-me-downs from dead relatives. I share the apartment with a hamster named Rex, and honestly, it's all very comfortable. Rex is the perfect housemate and best friend. He's nonjudgmental, he never complains, and he's ecstatically happy when he gets an occasional Ritz cracker or a corner of my Pop-Tart. He lives in a large glass aquarium, he sleeps in a Campbell's soup can, and he runs all night long on a hamster wheel, going nowhere. I feel like his life mimics mine.

I saw that lights were on in my apartment and Joe Morelli's SUV was parked in my lot. Morelli is a Trenton cop working plainclothes. I have a long history with him and possibly a future. For as long as I've known him, no one has ever called him Joe. His mother, his grandmother, and my mother call him Joseph. Everyone else has always known him as Morelli. At present, for lack of a better word, he's my boyfriend. He has a key to my apartment, and I keep a couple T-shirts and a toothbrush at his house. I parked next to Morelli, bypassed the unreliable elevator in the lobby, and took the stairs.

Morelli's dog, Bob, lunged at me the instant I opened the door to my apartment. Bob is big and orange and overly friendly. Morelli and I don't know for sure, but if we had to pick a breed, it would be rogue golden retriever.

He put his two massive paws on my chest, knocked me flat on my back, and gave me Bob kisses. Morelli shooed Bob away and pulled me to my feet.

"Sorry about that," Morelli said. "Are you okay?"

"Yeah, he caught me by surprise."

Bob was still in front of me, tail wagging, eyes bright.

"Who's a good boy?" I said to Bob. "Who's a good boy?" I gave him a hug and scratched him behind his ears. He snuffled me for food, didn't find any, and went back to his place on my couch.

"This is a surprise," I said to Morelli. "I don't usually see you on a Monday."

Joe Morelli is six feet of lean muscle. His hair is black and wavy. His eyes are soft brown and expressive when he's feeling romantic, and they're laser focused and unreadable when he's being a cop. He was wearing his usual outfit of running shoes, jeans, and casual cotton knit sweater.

We were standing in the small foyer that led to my kitchen. I flicked a glance into the kitchen and saw a thirty-five-pound bag of dog food resting against a cabinet. This might have suggested that either Bob or Morelli or both were moving in with me.

"Oh boy," I said.

Morelli grinned. "I'm guessing the 'Oh boy' is about the dog food in your kitchen. I need to go out of town for a few days. I was hoping I could leave Bob with you. Last time I left him at home with a dog sitter he knocked her down when she opened the front door, and he ran away. It took half the force to find him."

"Sure," I said. "How many days are a few?"

"I don't know. Police business. I've been tagged as a witness in the Wisneski trial."

"I read about that. It was a drug bust gone bad in Miami."

"Yeah. I'm not supposed to talk about it. I heard you were babysitting Duncan Dugan this afternoon."

"He's FTA. Lula and I were there when he fell. I followed the ambulance to the medical center and waited for him to get out of the OR. I'll check up on him tomorrow."

"Dugan was operating above his pay grade when he robbed Plover," Morelli said. "He's a quality control inspector for one of the lines at the button factory. No priors. From what I hear, this was totally out of character for Dugan. The gun he was using turned out to be a toy. If bad guys were ranked by skill level, Dugan wouldn't even make amateur."

"That could all be true, but if I had to stand around all day making sure buttons were round, I might decide to rob a jewelry store. Were you one of the guys investigating?"

"No," Morelli said. "I only investigate when there's a lot of blood. I learned about it from my mom, because Plover also accused Nutsy Manley of stealing a tray of diamonds the same day. She heard about it at bingo. Jonesy is the principal on both thefts."

"Plover came to the office today. He hired me to find Nutsy."

Morelli's eyes narrowed ever so slightly. "You're kidding, right?"

"No. He hired me to find Nutsy. He said he reported his suspicions about Nutsy to the police, but they haven't had any luck locating him."

"Walk away from it," Morelli said. "Let the police do their thing."

"I need the money."

"Do you get paid by the hour or do you only get paid if you find him?"

"I get paid when I find him."

"Then you're wasting your time. Chances of you finding him are slim to none," Morelli said. "The police can't find him, and Ranger can't find him."

Ranger is the other man in my life. Carlos Manoso, a.k.a. Ranger. Former Special Forces. Tall, dark, and dangerous. More muscle than Morelli but not so much that he doesn't look good in or out of clothes. I've seen him both ways and he's not a man you can easily forget. He was my mentor when I first became a bond enforcer. He was a bounty hunter then. Now he's the owner of a high-end security business.

"Why is Ranger looking for Nutsy?" I asked Morelli.

"Don't know. It's street chatter. Nutsy was a private hire, but Rangeman installed and monitored the security equipment for Plover. Maybe Ranger's just protecting the Rangeman brand. Maybe there's something more."

"Plover didn't share that information with me," I said.

"This robbery smells bad. The initial robbery was almost a joke. The fake gun. Dropping the bag of jewelry. The prime suspect trying to commit suicide. And then the follow-up of a second robbery that had to have been done by a professional. For sure not Dugan, since he hadn't been bonded out at the time of the alleged theft."

"Could Dugan have been working with someone? Maybe even Nutsy?"

"Anything is possible. I'm sure Jonesy looked into it. He's a good man. I haven't talked to him lately, but he's probably digging around, looking for a connection. There could also be a mob connection here since the second theft was so professionally executed. It wouldn't be good for you to poke the bear if it's mob. You don't want to get involved," Morelli said.

"It's all good. I can partner with Ranger."

"My worst nightmare," Morelli said. "I'll be stuck in Miami, and you'll be doing God knows what with Ranger. He's built a premier security company, but he's a threat as a human being.

He's fearless. He plays by his own rules. And I don't like the way he looks at you."

"Like I'm lunch?"

"Yeah," Morelli said. "Plus, he has skills and resources to back him up when things get bad. You have Lula."

All this was true.

Morelli leaned in and gave me a quick kiss. "I have to run. I'm catching a plane out of Newark and I'm late. Bob's leash is on the counter. Probably you want to stash that bag of food up somewhere high, so he doesn't binge-eat it and throw up on your couch."

I locked the door after Morelli left and I looked at Bob, sprawled on my couch. "Just you and me," I said. "Have you had dinner?"

Bob's eyes popped open at the mention of dinner.

I got his bowls out of the cabinet and filled one with water and the other with kibble. Bob rushed into the kitchen, snarfed down the kibble, and went to the door. I liked Bob a lot and I didn't mind him living with me. I wasn't so excited about the walking and picking-up-Bob-poop part.

It was seven thirty when we got back from the walk. I made myself a peanut butter and olive sandwich, washed it down with a bottle of beer, and had a Butterscotch Krimpet Tastykake for dessert. I gave a chunk of the Krimpet to Rex. He shot out of his soup can, almost exploded with joy when he saw the Krimpet, and hauled his treasure back into his can. Another reason why hamsters are the best. No agonizing over how fat their ass will be if they eat a Krimpet. Just snatch it up and hide it in your soup can before it goes away.

This is pretty much the extent of my skills in the kitchen. I usually eat at the sink, and I never have dinner guests. Since I don't have a second bedroom to use as an office, I work at my otherwise unused dining room table.

Bob and I moseyed over to the table. I opened my MacBook and tapped *Andrew Manley* into a search engine. Seconds later I started getting information.

Manley had enlisted in the army when he graduated high school. After his stint in the army, he went to a clown school in Florida, graduated with honors, and got a job at Rent-A-Clown in Des Moines. After six months he returned to Florida and drove a cement truck. He migrated back to Trenton two years ago and moved in with his parents. According to his online information, he was still living there. He'd been working as a security guard for Plover for almost a year. Prior to that he was a box store bagger. He owned a Yamaha SR400 bike. No car. His parents owned a white Toyota Corolla. They lived about a half mile from my parents. I knew the neighborhood, but I didn't know the senior Manleys.

I was guessing my grandma Mazur knew them. Grandma moved in with my parents when my grandfather went to the big bacon buffet in GodLand. She's hooked into the Burg gossip network, and she knows everything about everyone. A large percentage of it is even true.

"I have a plan," I said to Bob. "First thing tomorrow we'll go to my parents' house to talk to Grandma about the Manleys. This has the added advantage of getting breakfast."

Bob looked happy about this. He might not have been able to put it all together, but he knew the word *breakfast*.

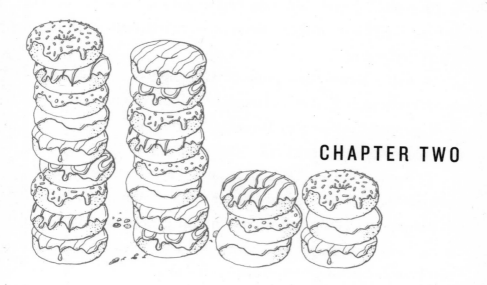

CHAPTER TWO

It's not necessary to set an alarm when you sleep with Bob. At the crack of dawn, he was a heavy weight on my chest, his nose inches from mine, breathing hot dog breath at me.

First priority was to walk Bob. Second priority was to feed Bob and Rex and give them fresh water. Also high on my day's to-do list were talk to Grandma and check on Duncan Dugan.

It was almost eight o'clock when I parked in front of my parents' house, and Bob and I went to the front door. I opened the door and Bob shoved me aside and galloped through the house, looking for my mom and Grandma. I heard a shriek and a crash that sounded like glass breaking, and I knew Bob had found his target.

By the time I reached the kitchen, my mom was picking up chunks of crockery and Bob was getting hugs from Grandma.

"He caught me by surprise," my mom said. "I wasn't expecting him. Is Joseph here, too?"

"Just me," I said. "Morelli had to go out of town, so I'm babysitting." I looked at the pieces of white porcelain in her hand. "Was that a dish?"

"It had a Danish pastry on it," Grandma said. "Bob took a header into your mother and the dish, and the pastry went flying. Bob snapped the pastry up before it even hit the floor."

I narrowed my eyes at Bob. "Bad dog."

"It was an accident," Grandma said. "He gets excited when he sees us. And he's always had a sweet tooth. It runs in the family."

Bob was as close to a grandson and great-grandson as my family was going to get from me in the near future. So, the fact that he was a dog was sometimes overlooked.

"Do you want breakfast?" my mom asked me. "I was just making some breakfast sausage and eggs for your grandmother."

I helped myself to coffee and took a seat at the table. "Sausage and eggs sound great."

Grandma brought the bakery box to the table and sat across from me. "We got more pastries. I got them fresh this morning."

I took a cheese Danish. "Any new gossip?" I asked Grandma.

"Nothing worth repeating," Grandma said. "This neighborhood is getting boring. Most of the mob has either died or moved away, and the young people just sit home frying their brains with their eyes glued to their smartphone screens. If you ask me, they'd be better off going out and stealing cars. At least they'd be learning a trade."

"Do you remember Andy Manley?"

"Nutsy? Sure, I remember him," Grandma said. "Double Dare

Nutsy. He was a whack-a-doodle in school, but he turned out to have talent. He graduated with honors from clown school. His mother went to Florida for the graduation. She was real proud of him. It's a shame it didn't work out long-term. He had his heart set on traveling with a circus, but there's not a lot of circuses anymore. I talked to his mother at bingo a while back, and she said the rent-a-clown job wasn't emotionally rewarding to him."

"So, he's home now, right? He's living with his parents?"

"Last I heard," Grandma said. "Are you looking for him? I didn't hear anything about him being arrested. Not lately anyway."

"He was working as a security guard for Plover's Jewelry and he disappeared after the robbery. Plover would like to talk to him, but he can't find him."

"And Plover hired you to find Nutsy?" Grandma asked.

I nodded.

"Hah!" Grandma said. "There's a story here." She leaned over the table at me and lowered her voice. "Are you going to come clean with me?"

"No," I said.

"Well, that's a bummer," Grandma said. "I'm dying a slow death of boredom here."

"Tell me about his parents."

"Not much to tell. His father works at the personal products factory. Office job. Accounting or something. Isn't Nutsy's biggest fan. Didn't go to his graduation in Florida. His mother, Celia, is sweet. She never wins at bingo, but you can't hold that against her. It's on account of she only plays two cards. She says she can't keep track of more than that, but I think her husband is a cheapskate and has her on a tight budget."

"Does she talk about Nutsy?"

"Not so much lately. I didn't know he was working for Plover."

"Does Nutsy have brothers or sisters?"

Grandma shook her head. "He's an only child. It's just him and the cats."

"Cats?"

"Celia takes in cats. She fosters them from the shelter until they get forever homes."

I took a plate of sausage and eggs from my mother. "And you haven't heard anything about Nutsy going missing?"

"I didn't hear anything about that," Grandma said. "There's been no talk at the bakery, and Celia hasn't said anything at bingo. I imagine it isn't unusual for Nutsy to go missing."

My mother set her plate of eggs and sausage on the table and went to get coffee. Bob swooped in, snatched up the sausage, and ate it.

I snapped a leash to Bob's collar and tied the leash to my chair. "Sorry," I said to my mom. "You can have my sausage."

"Not necessary," she said. "There's more in the fry pan, but honestly, he could use some table manners."

"What are you doing today?" Grandma asked me. "Do you have any big-ticket bond jumpers?"

"Just Duncan Dugan. He's the guy who held up Plover's and got caught. He slipped and fell off a ledge yesterday and almost killed himself."

"I saw it on the news last night," Grandma said. "He crashed through the restaurant awning."

"I'm going to check on him after breakfast. Is it okay if I leave Bob here for a few minutes while I go to the hospital? I don't want to leave him in my apartment. Last time I did that he ate my couch."

"I'll keep my eye on him," Grandma said. "I won't let him near our couch."

———

I finished breakfast and explained to Bob, who was still on the lookout for unattended sausages, that he had to be on his best behavior. I drove the short distance to the medical center, parked, and went to the front desk to get a status report on Duncan Dugan.

"He's stable and out of the ICU," the woman at reception said, handing me a visitor's pass. "Second floor. The elevators are down the hall to the right."

I grew up in the shadow of the hospital but for most of my life I only knew it from the outside. Now that I'm working for my cousin Vinnie in the bail bonds office, I've learned my way around the hospital innards. Mostly the prison ward and the ER.

I found my way to Dugan's floor, bypassed the nurses' station, and tracked down the room number I got at the downstairs desk. The door was open, and the room was empty. The bed was rumpled. An untouched breakfast tray was on the overbed table.

I retraced my steps to the nurses' station and discovered Mary Jane Sokolowski at one of the computers. I went to high school with Mary Jane. She was now married and had two kids.

"Hey," she said to me. "What's up? Haven't seen you since my sister's baby shower."

"I'm checking on Duncan Dugan. He's not in his room."

"Yeah, we made the same discovery about a half hour ago.

He's MIA. He left a note saying he felt better and he was going home."

I went stupefied for a beat. "Excuse me?"

"I know," she said. "He had a laundry list of injuries plus a compound fracture of the tibia and two cracked ribs. And he was zonked out on painkillers."

"When was the last time someone saw him?"

"Not sure, but he was here at seven o'clock this morning. That was his last chart entry."

"Do you think someone snatched him?"

She shrugged. "Don't know. I can't imagine him just walking out of here. We turned it over to security for follow-up."

"No one saw him leave?"

"None of the nurses at this station saw him leave, and we checked all the other rooms on the floor. Security would know more."

I went downstairs to security.

"I'm looking for Duncan Dugan," I said to the uniform at the desk.

"Let me know if you find him," he said. "We aren't having any luck."

I went back to my car and called the number Dugan had listed on his bond application. No answer. I banged my forehead against the steering wheel several times. "Stupid, stupid, stupid." I should have handcuffed him to the bed. I should have had him transferred to the prison ward.

My phone buzzed with a text message from my grandmother.

Bob just ate your father's going to church shoes. Are you almost done at the hospital?

Ten minutes later, I was in my car, on my way to the office, with Bob sitting in the seat next to me.

"You shouldn't have eaten the shoes," I said to him. "That was really bad behavior."

Truth is my father would probably be happy to have the shoes destroyed. The shoes were only worn at my mother's insistence. Funerals, weddings, and Mass. My mother and grandmother went to Mass regularly. My father preferred to find God in places with more comfortable seating. Hence, the shoes were seldom out and about.

I parked behind Lula's red Firebird, and Bob and I went into the office.

"Yo," Lula said. "What's the occasion with Bob?"

"I'm babysitting," I said. "Morelli's out of town for a couple days."

"What's the word on Plover? Did you go see him last night?"

"He wants me to find Andy Manley."

"Nutsy?" Connie asked.

"Yes. He was working as the security guard when the robbery went down. Short story is that Nutsy left after the robbery and hasn't been seen since. When Plover opened the shop the morning after the robbery he was missing a tray of diamonds that had been left in the safe. He thinks Nutsy took them."

"Nutsy did some weird stuff," Connie said, "but I can't see him stealing diamonds."

"He might if someone dared him," I said.

"That was high school," Connie said. "Did Plover report it to the police?"

"Yep. So far, they haven't had any results."

"That's a real bummer to get robbed twice on the same day," Lula said. "What are the chances?"

"Maybe the robberies were connected," Connie said.

"Who's this Nutsy guy?" Lula asked.

"I went to school with him," I said. "He would do anything on a dare. He went to clown school after graduating. He wanted to travel the country with a circus, but it turned out there aren't very many traveling circuses anymore."

"Was he a happy clown or a creepy clown?" Lula asked. "It makes a big difference in my opinion of a clown. I wouldn't mind talking to him. I've got a bunch of clown questions. Like, can they breathe through that big red clown nose? And what kind of makeup remover do they use? I think we should go find this guy."

"He lives with his parents. I thought that would be a place to start."

"I'm all about it," Lula said. "We don't get a lot of chances to go hunting down clowns."

"What's happening with Duncan Dugan?" Connie asked. "Has he been transferred to the prison ward?"

"He's sort of missing," I said. "He disappeared this morning and the hospital hasn't been able to locate him."

"Say what?" Lula said. "How'd he go missing? He must have broken every bone in his body."

I shrugged. "He left a note saying he felt better and he was going home."

"He had to have help," Lula said. "I bet it was that woman who tried to talk him down."

"What about medical?" Connie asked. "Can he manage without nursing care?"

"Mary Jane Sokolowski was the charge nurse on Dugan's floor. She said Dugan's leg was in a cast, and he had a couple cracked ribs. He was on painkillers and antibiotics."

"I guess you could manage that at home," Lula said. "These days they don't keep you in the hospital very long anyway."

"Can we hack into the hospital's security cameras?" I asked Connie.

"I don't have that ability," Connie said, "but you know someone who can hack into anything."

Ranger. If I couldn't get a lead on Dugan by the end of the day, I'd ask Ranger for help. And I wanted to talk to him about Nutsy Manley, anyway. Bonus.

"What are we doing first?" Lula asked. "I've got an interest in both these cases."

"I'm starting with Nutsy. His parents are only five minutes away. We can do a fast stop, talk to his mom, and move on to Duncan Dugan."

Lula stood and hiked her massive tote bag purse onto her shoulder. "That's a good choice. What are you going to do with Bob?"

"Bob is going with us."

"Like he's a K-9 bounty hunter," Lula said. "This would be a good television show. Two badass women and a killer dog. I bet Netflix would snap it up in a second. It could be a reality show and we could star in it."

This was wrong on several levels, not the least of which was that Lula and I weren't badass, and Bob wasn't a killer dog. Bob was a goofus.

We walked to my car, Lula opened the front passenger-side door, and Bob pushed past her and jumped in.

"Hey," Lula said to Bob. "I get to sit in the front. Dogs sit in the back."

Bob pretended not to hear.

Lula grabbed Bob by the collar and Bob growled at her.

"He's pulling attitude on me," Lula said. "That don't work with Lula. I've been around the block. It's not my first rodeo." She leaned in at Bob. "Get your furry orange ass out of there."

Bob held his ground.

I ran back to the office, got a doughnut out of the box on Connie's desk, returned to my car, and threw the doughnut into the back seat. Bob jumped into the back and ate the doughnut.

"Problem solved," I said to Lula.

My research listed the Manley house at 170 Greentree Street. I left Hamilton Avenue, found Greentree Street, and idled in front of 170. It looked a lot like my parents' house. Two stories. Single-car detached garage. Postage-stamp front yard. No white Corolla parked in the driveway. No sign of the Yamaha bike.

"This here's a nice neighborhood," Lula said. "It looks real conservative. You wouldn't think a clown could come from a neighborhood like this. Not that I'm thinking something derogatory about clowns, but they're out of the box, if you see what I'm saying."

I pulled to the curb and cut the engine. "Stay here," I said to Lula. "Keep your eye on Bob."

"I'm not staying in the car," Lula said. "What if Nutsy is in the house? You might need backup."

"I won't need backup."

"You always need backup," Lula said. "You don't even carry a gun. And anyway, I want to talk to Mrs. Manley. I want to know what it's like to have a son who's a clown."

"Forget the clown thing. We're going to focus on finding Nutsy. If you're coming with me, we have to get information fast. Bob will start eating upholstery if he gets bored."

I gave Bob a stern warning and cracked the window for him. Lula and I walked to the Manleys' front door and rang the bell.

A pleasant-looking woman answered.

"Mrs. Manley?" I asked.

"Oh, my goodness," she said. "Stephanie Plum. This is a surprise."

She reminded me a lot of my mom. Brown hair cut into a bob. An inch or two shorter than me. Average weight. Wearing a neat blue untucked shirt and jeans.

"I'm looking for Andy," I said. "Is he home?"

"No," she said. "I'm sure he'll be disappointed when he finds out he missed you."

A black cat tried to sneak out the door and Mrs. Manley reached down and snagged it.

"Come in, and close the door before my kitties escape," she said.

Lula and I stepped inside and closed the door. I looked around. There were cats everywhere. Orange, calico, black, tiger-striped, gray.

"Wow," I said. "You have a lot of cats."

"I don't usually have this many," she said. "There seemed to be an explosion of cats at the shelter, so I took as many as I could manage."

"When do you expect Andy to be home?" I asked her.

"Goodness, you never know about Andy," she said. "He goes off on his adventures."

"What does he do on these adventures of his?"

"I don't know exactly," she said.

"Maybe it's clown related," Lula said. "Like he could go on clown cruises, or he could be part of a secret clown society."

"He's never mentioned anything like that," Mrs. Manley said.

"I haven't seen Andy in a while," I said to Mrs. Manley. "Is he still friends with Steven Palmer and Jason Wiggs?"

"No. I believe Steven is living in North Carolina and Jason has a young family."

"So, who's his new friends?" Lula asked. "Are they clowns?"

"Lula is impressed that Andy used to be a clown," I said to Mrs. Manley.

"He was a wonderful clown," his mother said. "It's a shame it didn't work out. He's been struggling to find himself ever since."

"I understand he was a security guard at Plover's Jewelry," I said.

"Yes, but Martin Plover turned out to be a terrible person. He accused Andy of stealing. He even got the police involved. Nothing came of it, of course."

A fluffy white cat was rubbing against Lula's leg.

"Isn't that nice," Mrs. Manley said to Lula. "Sugar Cookie has taken to you."

"Yeah, but I'm more or less allergic to cats," Lula said.

"These cats are all up for adoption if either of you would like to give one of them a forever home," Mrs. Manley said.

A second cat came over to investigate Lula.

"I feel hives coming on," Lula said. "I'm getting all stuffed up."

"I'd really like to talk to Andy," I said to Mrs. Manley. "Is there any way I could get in touch with him?"

"He has a cell phone, but he doesn't always answer it. I'll give you the number. Sometimes it works if you text him."

"My eyes are itchy," Lula said. "I can feel my throat closing over. Are my lips swollen?" She had her hand on her forehead. "I'm sweating. That's a bad sign. I could be going into heart failure or something. I gotta get out of here."

She ran to the door, wrenched it open, and ran out.

"No!" Mrs. Manley shouted. "Close the door. These are indoor cats. They can't go out. They'll get lost."

A bunch of cats rushed for the door and escaped before Mrs. Manley could stop them.

Mrs. Manley slammed the door shut and ran after the cats. "My kitties! My babies!"

Lula reached the car and opened the door, and Bob bounded out. He was in cat heaven. He didn't know which cat to chase first. He had crazy eyes. He chased a calico up a tree and ran down a tuxedo cat that arched its back and hissed at him. I scooped up the tuxedo cat and it swiped at me, leaving bloody claw lines on my hand.

"I need some Benadryl. I need an antihistamine," Lula said. "Anybody got an EpiPen?"

Mrs. Manley took the tuxedo cat from me. "You have to get Rusty," she said. "He can't get lost. He has a leaky heart valve. He needs his meds."

"Which one is Rusty?" I asked.

"He's sort of rust colored, and he only has one eye," Mrs. Manley said.

Bob ran past me, and I grabbed his leash. He yanked me off my feet and dragged me halfway across the yard, but I held tight.

I stood up, grabbed his collar, and muscled him to the car. Lula was inside checking herself out in the mirror.

"Do I look puffy?" she asked me. "Is my face red?"

Lula has skin the color of a Hershey's Kiss. It was hard to tell if it was red.

"Maybe a little," I said. "I'll be right back. I have to look for Rusty. Don't let Bob out of the car."

I walked around the outside of the Manleys' house and found Rusty and a small tiger-striped hiding under a bush. I carried them to the front door and handed them over to Mrs. Manley.

"Are you missing any more cats?" I asked her.

"These were the last two," she said.

"Sorry about Bob."

"Dogs will be dogs," she said. "Say hello to your mother and grandmother for me."

I got behind the wheel and looked over at Lula. "Are you okay?"

"I didn't have any antihistamine, but I found some Tic Tacs. I think they're helping."

"Do you want to go to the ER?"

"No. I'm starting to feel better. I'm just gonna roll my window down and get some air."

"Maybe you had a panic attack."

"No way. People of my persuasion don't get panic attacks," Lula said.

"What's your persuasion?"

"I'm big and bold. I used to be Presbyterian, but I decided to change over when I was in high school."

"So big and bold is like a religion?"

"You bet your ass," Lula said. "It's a belief, you see what I'm saying?"

"What about God?"

"I'm pretty sure he's big and bold," Lula said. "He'd have to be in order to take care of the universe, not to mention everything else that's going on."

I pulled the file on Duncan Dugan, my official FTA, out of my bag and paged through it. "I'm putting Nutsy on the back burner for the moment. Duncan Dugan is thirty-six years old. He's originally from New Brunswick. Never married. He dropped out of Mercer County Community College halfway through his first year and started working at the button factory. He's worked there ever since. He owns a silver Kia Rio. For the past six years he's rented a small house near the button factory."

"Who posted the bond for him?"

"His parents put up security for the bond money. They're in Fort Myers, Florida. It looks like they moved there about ten years ago."

"Any brothers or sisters?"

"He has an older brother in Alberton, Maine."

"No priors?" Lula asked.

"No. Zip. Nothing." I stuffed the file back in my bag and pulled away from the curb. "Let's see if Dugan is home."

Faucet Street is a block away from the button factory. It's one of several streets of small cottages that are smushed together row house style. Most of them are occupied by button factory employees.

Seventy-two Faucet was a single-story, yellow clapboard house in the middle of the block. Cars were parked on the street, but none of them was a Kia Rio, and none of them was directly in front of number seventy-two.

I parked across from the house, and Lula and I sat and took the temperature of the area.

"There's nothing happening on this street," Lula said. "Everybody's working. Are we gonna do a B & E? 'Cause this would be a good time for a B & E. Just sayin'."

"No breaking and entering," I said to Lula. "I'm going to ring his bell and with any luck he's recovering at home."

"Yeah, but what if he isn't home? Can we do a B & E then?"

"No."

"How about if we smell a decomposing body?"

I looked at Lula. "Do you really want to break down a door and find a decomposing body?"

"You got a point," Lula said.

We walked across the street, and I rang the doorbell. No answer. We looked in the front windows. No indication that anyone was at home.

"Now what?" Lula asked.

"These row houses have small backyards that back up to an alley. We can check out the alley."

We returned to my car, and I drove down the narrow one-lane road that cut the block in half. I counted off houses and parked behind the yellow clapboard. The Kia Rio was parked in the small backyard.

We got out and knocked on the back door and looked in the rear windows.

"His kitchen looks clean from here," Lula said, peering through the window next to the door. "I don't see dirty dishes or anything on the table. Since he probably can't walk on his own yet, much less make breakfast, I'm betting he's not here."

I called Connie. "I'm at a dead end on Duncan Dugan. He's not home but his car is here. Can you check hospitals and walk-in medical clinics for me? He's going to need serious medical care."

"No problem," Connie said. "I'll get right on it."

I disconnected from Connie in time to see Lula bump the lock on Dugan's back door.

"Look here," Lula said. "The door just flew open."

We stepped inside and I shouted, "Bond enforcement," to make it legal.

"Crickets," Lula said. "Only sound I hear is the refrigerator running."

"I'm going to search the house," I said to Lula. "Stay in the car with Bob, and don't let him escape. I won't be long."

Ten minutes later I was back behind the wheel.

"Well?" Lula asked. "Did you find anything?"

"He's very neat. Everything in the refrigerator is perfectly lined up with the labels facing out. No mold on anything. The handle on the refrigerator door wasn't even sticky. Everything is color coordinated in his closet and all the hangers face the same way. His bed was made with the corners tucked in. No wrinkles anywhere."

"I bet he presses his linens," Lula said. "A man like that is hard to find. It's a shame he had to go break all his bones. It's gonna be a while before he can hold a steam iron."

I drove down the alley to the cross street. "He seems to be living alone. One electric toothbrush in the bathroom. The second bedroom is furnished as an office. The desk had a dock with plug-ins for a laptop, a tablet, and a phone. The plug-ins are all labeled."

"You'd expect that from a man who keeps an orderly refrigerator. A man like that would have a label maker. And I'll tell you another thing, you wouldn't expect a man like that to attempt a half-assed robbery of a jewelry store. He'd plan ahead. He'd make a risk assessment. And now that I know this individual, I can't see him involved in a badly orchestrated suicide. At the time of maximum desperation, he must not have been thinking clearly. I didn't see signs of any drugs, so he had to be severely organically and without-substance-abuse depressed."

"That's your official opinion, Doctor?"

"I studied this shit for a semester at the community college," Lula said. "I didn't actually finish the semester, but I read the chapter on the psychology of the criminal, and I watch *CSI* all the time. Did you find anything good on his laptop?"

"I didn't see any electronics. No laptop. No tablet. No phone."

"Did you look in his drawers?"

"I looked everywhere."

"I'm thinking someone came in and scooped those devices up," Lula said.

"Yeah. Someone with a key or someone who has better B & E skills than we possess. There was no sign that the lock had been forced open until you jammed a screwdriver in it and whacked it with a hammer."

"On the other hand, if Duncan Dugan had plans to off himself, he might have removed his laptop from the premises," Lula said. "He might have given it to a friend or hidden it in a dumpster. Did he leave any clues regarding friends or activities?"

"No. Nothing. No framed photos. No bowling league trophies. The bookcase in his office was empty. No notes-to-self on his desktop. Just a blank pad. There was a *Jeopardy! Brain Games* book and a crossword puzzle book on an end table in the living room."

"Most likely he's too busy organizing his refrigerator to have much of a social life," Lula said. "There's only so many hours in the day. You can't do it all."

"Dugan didn't have a lot of pots and pans. His kitchen looked a little like mine, except no hamster. There were two take-out containers in the trash. They were both from Mortin's Deli. I'm guessing he eats takeout a lot."

"I know Mortin's Deli," Lula said. "It's excellent. It's only two blocks from here. When you live two blocks from Mortin's Deli there's no reason to cook for yourself. I think we should investigate it to see if anyone knows Dugan. And while we're there I could get some potato salad and a pastrami sandwich. They make a killer pastrami sandwich."

Minutes later I parked in the small lot that was attached to the deli.

"We're going into the deli," I said to Bob. "You have to stay here. If you're a good boy, I'll bring you a treat."

Bob gave me a steady stare.

"I wouldn't take that as a definitively positive answer," Lula said. "I don't think he understands English."

"He understands," I said. "Don't let that dumb look fool you." I pointed my finger at Bob. "Listen, mister. I'm serious. If you so much as lick a piece of upholstery there's no treat."

I cracked a window, and Lula and I exited the car.

"Boy, you're tough," Lula said. "You even had me convinced for a minute."

"Only a minute?"

"Yeah. I know you'll cave. He could eat his way through the entire back seat, and you'll still give him the treat if he gives you that *I'm sorry* look with his big brown eyes. You're a sucker for brown eyes. I bet you never slept with a man with blue eyes."

"My ex-husband had blue eyes."

"Well, I guess that explains a lot."

Mortin's Deli had a few booths, but the bulk of their business was takeout. Cold cuts, cheeses, hot and cold entrées, salads, sides, sandwiches, soups. Carrot cake, cheesecake, decadent chocolate cake, and lemon meringue pie were displayed under glass domes on the counter. Two women were drinking coffee in a booth. An elderly man was checking out at the register. Lula and I went to the back of the deli, where the offerings of the day were written on a chalkboard attached to the wall.

"I want a tub of the egg potato salad," Lula told the woman behind the counter. "Give me some with the little bacon sprinkles on top. And then I want a pastrami sandwich and a piece of the chocolate cake."

The woman looked at me. "Would you like something as well?"

"Nothing for me," I said, "but I was wondering about a friend. I know he got takeout here. Duncan Dugan. I went to his house just now and he wasn't at home."

"He's a regular here," she said. "Kale salad with grilled chicken. I haven't seen him in a couple days."

"Does he ever come in with anybody?"

"Sometimes he was with a woman. I think she might be his

sister. At least, he calls her Sissy. She gets chicken salad on a croissant."

"Dark brown hair cut short, medium build, and medium height?" I asked. "Kind of reminds you of Lucy from the *Peanuts* cartoon?"

"Yeah. They pay separate. Duncan pays with a credit card and the woman pays cash."

"I don't suppose you know her full name?"

"No. Like I said, she pays cash."

"You better get something for Bob," Lula said to me. "You promised him. He might like some of those big meatballs."

"Two meatballs," I said to the woman. "No sauce."

Bob had his nose pressed against the window when we returned to the car. I gave him his treat and backed out of the parking space.

"I'm going to drop you and Bob at the office, and then I'm going to Rangeman. I want to talk to Ranger about Nutsy Manley," I said.

"Are you gonna do a nooner with Ranger?"

"No! I'm going to talk to him."

"Just sayin' on account of if it was me, and my boyfriend was out of town, and I had the opportunity, I'd definitely squeeze in a nooner."

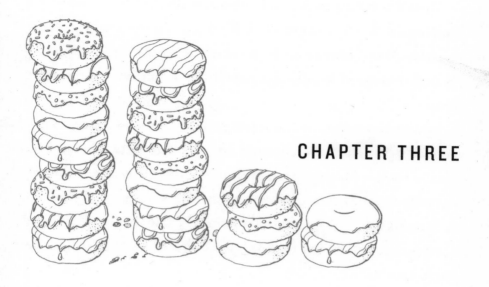

CHAPTER THREE

Rangeman is located on a quiet side street in downtown Trenton. On the outside it's an inconspicuous seven-story building with a gated underground garage.

On the inside it's pleasantly slick, intimidatingly secure, filled with cutting-edge technology and a highly skilled workforce. Ranger has a private one-bedroom apartment on the top floor. The fifth floor is dedicated to offices, a café, and the control room. The other floors serve various purposes. A gym, a shooting range, dorm rooms, conference rooms, and more offices.

I flashed my key card at the garage gate and found a parking space by the elevator. This key card is priceless. Ranger's mother doesn't have one. Only trusted Rangeman employees have key cards . . . and me. I'm not sure why I've got one, but I suspect it has something to do with Ranger's deciding it was easier to give me the keys to the candy store than it was to stop me from trying to break in when I needed help.

There's constant audio and video surveillance throughout the building, with the exception of Ranger's lair on the top floor. I waved at the camera in front of the elevator, and the doors opened. I stepped inside and punched the button for the fifth floor.

I walked past the control room and the café and followed the hallway to the end, where Ranger has an office suite. I found him relaxed back in his desk chair, waiting for me. He was in the black everyday fatigues that all Rangemen wore.

"I guess you saw me on the monitor," I said.

"Yes," he said. "Plus, the front desk alerted me, and so did the control room."

There are no secrets at Rangeman.

I sat in one of the two chairs in front of his desk. "Do you have time to talk?"

"Will it be a long conversation?"

"Word on the street is that you're looking for Nutsy Manley."

"And?"

"And I am too. Plover hired me to find him."

"You have my attention," Ranger said.

"Plover thinks Manley stole a tray of diamonds."

"This isn't breaking news."

"Do you think he took the diamonds?"

"I don't know," Ranger said. "There's something that feels off about the robbery."

"Which robbery? The Duncan Dugan robbery in the afternoon? Or the safe robbery that Plover accused Nutsy of executing?"

"Both of them."

"Morelli's advice was that I don't get involved."

"But you are involved?"

"Yep. Plover hired me to find Nutsy, and Vinnie needs me to find Dugan, who skipped."

"Babe."

Depending on the inflection, *babe* can mean many things in Ranger-speak. This *babe* was said with a smile. So, here's another possible reason why I have a key card. Ranger finds me amusing.

"Why are you looking for Nutsy?" I asked him.

"Rangeman installed and maintains the security system for Plover's Jewelry. The robbery wasn't the result of a system failure, but I still feel a certain responsibility. And I'm curious. Neither the stolen jewelry nor the tray of diamonds has been recovered. Duncan Dugan said he panicked and dropped the garbage bag with the stolen jewelry on the street, but the bag hasn't been found."

"And then Nutsy disappeared, much like the garbage bag, and the tray of diamonds," I said.

"Yes."

"Are you having any luck finding him?" I asked Ranger.

"No, but I haven't made a serious effort. It hasn't been a priority."

"I went to school with Nutsy. He was sort of a misfit in an interesting kind of way. He'd do anything on a dare."

Ella brought a tray of sandwiches into Ranger's office and set them on his desk. "Nice to see you," she said to me. "Let me know if you need anything."

Ella and her husband managed the Rangeman building, and

Ella managed Ranger. She prepared many of his meals and made sure his clothes were perfectly laundered and folded, his apartment was immaculate, his toiletries were always in place, and his towels were fluffy.

Ranger chose turkey on wheat, and I took egg salad. Ella made amazing egg salad.

"I can run some searches on Manley," Ranger said.

"That would be great. And speaking of searches, I have another favor to ask."

"I'm running a tab," Ranger said. "You don't want to owe me more than you're willing to pay."

This prompted a short stare-down. We both knew what Ranger wanted in payment. This was a game we'd been playing for a while, and truth is, we both enjoyed it.

"I could use some help accessing video on Duncan Dugan," I said.

"I heard he jumped off a ledge."

"More like he slipped and fell. I thought he was safe in the medical center, but he's disappeared."

"When did this happen?" Ranger asked.

"This morning between seven and nine. No one saw him leave. I just came from his house. He wasn't there. He has a compound fracture of the tibia and two cracked ribs for starters. He wasn't in shape to walk out on his own. I'd like to know who helped him."

Ranger called his control room and asked one of his technicians to get a video of Dugan's hospital floor between the hours of seven and nine this morning.

"Plover told me he refused to install security cameras in the front of his store. I'm sure he regrets it now," I said to Ranger. "Are there city or private cameras that you can tap into on that street?"

"It's in a one-block dead zone. I can tap into the feeds on both cross streets, but there are no security or surveillance cameras on the seven hundred block of King Street. Not even a Ring doorbell."

"And Plover only had a camera on his rear exit?"

"He was adamant about not having a front camera. Didn't want the expense. Didn't feel it was necessary. Didn't have any interior cameras. He thought it would be uncomfortable for his customers."

"I'm surprised his insurance company didn't demand cameras."

"He would have gotten a better rate with cameras," Ranger said. "He complained about it all the time. He said he was being penalized for being old-school. He said it was generational discrimination. He compromised by hiring Manley as a security guard."

"I did a fast check on Nutsy. I didn't see anything that would qualify him to be a security guard."

"He was working as a bagger at one of the box stores. He helped Plover to his car with his groceries, struck up a conversation, and Plover hired him to do security. He doesn't have a license to carry and I'm pretty sure he doesn't own a gun. At least not legally."

"That sounds like Nutsy. He had a gift for convincing people he could do anything. And mostly he could. He'd jump off a bridge, seduce the librarian, eat cat food, streak the length of a football field during halftime in thirty-degree weather."

A message appeared on Ranger's monitor that the hospital

video was ready to view. Ranger brought it up, fast-forwarded through the first hour, and stopped the action.

"This looks promising," he said.

Two figures in scrubs and surgical gowns and masks rolled an empty stretcher out of the service elevator and pushed it into Dugan's room. Four minutes later the stretcher was rolled out of the room and down the hall, and disappeared into the elevator. A person roughly the size of Dugan appeared to be on the stretcher.

Ranger called his technician and told him to access all exit cameras between eight o'clock and eight thirty.

"Is it possible these are hospital people and Dugan was taken off somewhere for a medical procedure?" I asked Ranger.

"Not likely. It would have been in his chart."

"I'm thinking these are both men. It's hard to tell under the scrubs and gowns and masks and caps, but they move like men."

Ranger replayed the video two more times.

"The smaller of the two might be female," he said. "Beyond that there are no recognizable features. I'll have one of the technicians enhance the images and we might get something."

The exit videos came up and Ranger displayed them all on his monitor. He isolated the feed from a back door that opened into a parking lot reserved for medical examiner and mortuary vehicles. The stretcher carrying Dugan appeared in the doorway where a white panel van was backed up to a short ramp. The stretcher was rolled into the van. The shorter person wearing scrubs stayed in back with Dugan and the taller one drove the van out of the lot.

The van was filthy, and the license plate was obscured in mud. It was a Jersey plate with only the first number partially visible. A three or an eight.

"Someone stole Dugan," I said.

"If the police don't already have this information, I'm sure they will shortly," Ranger said. "They should be able to spot the van if they get right on it."

"Maybe not," I said. "Dugan left a note saying that he was going home. This might not immediately be considered a crime."

My phone dinged with a text from Connie. *Bob ate Lula's new Star magazine.*

"I have to go," I said to Ranger. "Emergency at the office. Let me know if you come up with anything."

———

Bob was sprawled on the faux leather couch when I rolled into the office.

"He ate my magazine," Lula said. "And I wasn't done with it. I never got to find out what the big secret is with Jennifer Aniston."

I slouched into the plastic chair that was in front of Connie's desk. "Did you have any luck finding Dugan?"

"Nothing," Connie said. "Despite all his injuries, he hasn't checked into any of the medical centers or urgent care facilities. Jeannie Swick works in records at the medical center here on Hamilton. I talked to her a half hour ago and she said the official word is that Dugan signed himself out."

I showed Connie and Lula a screenshot taken from Ranger's monitor. "Two people dressed in surgical scrubs loaded Dugan into a van and took off with him."

"I bet they aren't even real doctors," Lula said. "I wouldn't be surprised if one of them was that woman at the jump-off. Sissy."

"Dugan's shift at the button factory is done at four o'clock," I said to Lula. "I thought we could hang out at the main gate and see if we spot her leaving."

"I'm up for that," Lula said. "Do you think she's really his sister?"

"According to our files, he doesn't have a sister."

I took Bob for a walk, and then I drove everyone to the button factory. I parked in an area reserved for visitors, and we all walked halfway around the block to the employee exit and adjoining parking lot. At precisely four o'clock, the doors opened, and people began pouring out. Lula stood at the pathway that led to the sidewalk. Bob and I watched the people heading for the parking lot. After a half hour the parking lot was almost empty and there were only a few stragglers exiting the building.

Lula walked over to Bob and me. "I didn't see Sissy," she said. "How about you?"

"I didn't see her," I said, "but there were a lot of people rushing to their cars all at once and it would have been easy to miss her."

Truth is, I'd only seen her very briefly that one time, and I wasn't sure I would even recognize her. There were a lot of women with short brown hair working at the button factory.

A text message from Ranger popped up on my phone. *I'll pick you up at 7:15 tonight.*

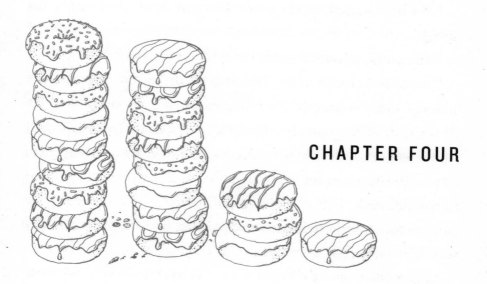

CHAPTER FOUR

"**S**ometimes Ranger is a man of too few words," I said to Bob. "I'm assuming this isn't a dinner date, but beyond that I haven't a clue."

I knew it wasn't a dinner date because Ranger didn't date. He seduced. He rescued. He tended to business.

At 7:10 I hooked Bob up to his leash and went downstairs to wait for Ranger. At precisely 7:15 the lights on his black Porsche Cayenne flashed at the entrance to my parking lot and Ranger pulled up in front of me. I opened the back passenger-side door, tossed in a dog biscuit, and Bob jumped into the back seat. I sat next to Ranger.

"Babe," Ranger said, still idling at the building.

"Morelli had to go on a business trip, and he asked me to take care of Bob."

49

Ranger glanced in the rearview mirror at Bob. "Why is he in my car?"

"If I leave him alone in my apartment, he gets bored and he eats things . . . like my couch. You didn't say anything about the night's activities, so I thought it might be okay for Bob to ride along."

"I want to search Andy Manley's room, so this afternoon his parents were lucky enough to be chosen at random by the local radio station for dinner for two at Trattoria Romano. Drinks and dessert included. Reservation at seven o'clock. I thought you would want to join me."

"Absolutely."

Ranger flicked another glance at Bob. "Is Bob going to be an asset?"

A mental video of Bob running down a bunch of crazed cats flashed through my head. "No," I said, "Bob wouldn't be an asset."

Ten minutes later a black Rangeman Ford Explorer parked next to us. Rodriguez was driving and Hal was riding shotgun.

I handed Bob over to Hal. "Behave yourself," I said to Bob.

"Don't worry," Hal said to me. "We'll take good care of him. I've got two dogs of my own."

"What kind of dogs do you have?" I asked him.

"Chihuahuas. Mindy and Killer."

Hal was built like a rhinoceros and was the size of a stegosaurus. He barely fit in the Explorer. Hal walking down the street with a Chihuahua on a leash would stop traffic. It would cause chaos. There would be laughter-induced medical emergencies.

"Chihuahuas are small dogs but they have big personalities," Hal said.

"That's so true," I said.

Ranger put the Porsche in gear and took off.

"I guess you aren't a dog person," I said to Ranger.

Ranger cut a sidewise glance at me and turned onto Hamilton Avenue. "I like dogs," he said. "It's people I'm not so sure about."

We parked in front of the Manley house and sat for a couple minutes, making sure the house was vacant. Lights were off. The white Corolla wasn't visible.

"Let's do it," Ranger said.

We got out of the car, walked to the front door, and Ranger took thirty seconds doing something with the lock to get us in. We shut the door and a herd of cats rushed over. They were meowing and rubbing against us, and a large tabby tried to climb up Ranger's leg.

"This wasn't in my briefing," Ranger said.

"Andy's mom is a foster cat mother for the humane society. And I think she has some of her own."

"If you get the fat one off my leg, I'll do something nice for you later tonight."

Oh boy. I had a pretty good idea what my reward would be.

I pried the tabby off his leg and set it on the floor. "Are you flirting with me?"

"I don't flirt," Ranger said. "I make promises that I'm very good at keeping."

So, here's what Morelli was talking about when he said this would be his worst nightmare. Ranger is walking and talking sex. He's totally ripped. He's Cuban-American with some Spanish ancestry. He's perfectly put together and is skilled in combat and foreplay. He's also smart, and I like him. I might even love him. Trouble is I also love Morelli, and at the moment, I'm supposed to be committed to him. Since I don't want to be labeled a slut, I'm going to try to honor that commitment. Ranger doesn't make it easy.

We moved through the house to the kitchen. Ranger found a bag of cat kibble and poured some on the floor, and the cats abandoned us for the kibble. We finished searching the lower level and moved upstairs to Andy's room. It was easy to find. It was the room with the photographs of clowns, mimes, and women who were mostly naked. The sign on his door said STAY OUT! DISASTER ZONE!!

The bed was a rumpled mess. Clothes were scattered across the floor. There were two empty bags of chips and two empty beer cans on his nightstand. There was a small wooden desk under the one window in the room. There was a large monitor and a Nintendo Switch with controllers on the desk but no computer or tablet.

Ranger went through the desk drawers, and I went through the dresser drawers. There was a small bathroom en suite. We both looked in at it. Bath towel on the floor. Toothpaste globs in the sink. The necessities of civilized life were all in place. Deodorant, razor, toothbrush, and floss.

"How old is this guy?" Ranger asked.

"He's my age. We graduated from high school at the same time."

"It's like he's frozen at fourteen."

"He was always unique. Did your room look like this when you were fourteen?" I asked him.

"No. I had pictures of soccer players on my walls, and I had to hide the pictures of naked women. If I'd left my clothes on the floor my mother would have given them away to the church and I would have had nothing to wear."

"It looks to me like Andy left in a hurry. He took his computer but left everything else. I don't see anything missing in the bathroom. Did you find anything in his desk?"

"A USB flash drive and a lot of candy wrappers. He likes Snickers bars."

"The flash drive could be good."

"Did you find anything in the dresser?" Ranger asked.

"Nothing I would ever want to remember."

We left Andy's room and went downstairs. The cats were everywhere. Sitting on end tables, perched on chair backs, climbing up the fake tree in the foyer, sprawled out on the foyer rug.

"Looks like the cats ran out of kibble," I said. "Be careful when you open the door. If any of them escape, we have to retrieve them. They aren't outside cats."

"Do you have any ideas on cat containment?"

"I'll sneak out while you keep the cats away and then you can get out while I keep watch."

I slipped out and there was a lot of cat screeching and growling. Ranger came out and closed the door.

"Pepper spray?" I asked him.

"Water from the vase on the foyer table."

"They rushed you, right? It was self-defense?"

Ranger grabbed the front of my sweatshirt and pulled me flat against him. "If you breathe a word of this to anyone, I'll round those cats up and dump them in your apartment."

I looked up at him. "That would be really rotten."

Ranger loosened his grip on my sweatshirt, stared into my eyes for a beat, and kissed me.

"My lips are sealed," I said.

"I noticed," Ranger said.

"It's Morelli."

"Babe," Ranger said.

The inflection was the equivalent of an eye roll. Ranger had respect for Morelli as a cop, but he wasn't impressed with him as a boyfriend. Possibly because he'd never slept with him or watched a hockey game with him or scarfed down Morelli's mother's lasagna.

"Anyway," I said, "this isn't a good place to . . . you know."

"Kiss you?"

"Yeah."

"Babe, that barely counted as a kiss." He wrapped his hand around my wrist and tugged me forward, toward his car. "I want to see what's on the flash drive. I'll call to have Bob brought to your apartment and we can use your computer to access the drive."

Fifteen minutes later Ranger parked in my building's lot and a Rangeman car pulled up next to us. Hal got out and handed Bob over to me.

"Thanks for Bob-sitting," I said to Hal.

"No problem," Hal said. "He was great."

"He ate my hat," Rodriguez said from behind the wheel.

"We took our dinner break at Joey's BBQ," Hal said. "Rod sat in front of the smoker and his hat smelled like cooked cow. If Bob hadn't eaten it, I would have ripped it off his head and thrown it out the window."

I walked Bob around the parking lot until I thought he was empty and then the three of us went upstairs. I said hello to Rex and gave him half of a Ritz cracker. I gave a whole Ritz cracker to Bob. I gave a bottle of water to Ranger.

I went to the dining room table and opened my laptop. Ranger pulled a chair up next to me and inserted the flash drive, and a list of files appeared on the screen.

The first file was titled "Big Below." It was a short story by someone named Emmett. There were a few other short stories and two screenplays, also by Emmett. The last three files were storylines for a video game.

"At first glance it doesn't seem like we got a lot out of this night," I said.

The beginnings of a smile twitched at the corners of his mouth. "I could turn that around."

"I'm talking about Nutsy."

Ranger pushed back in his chair. "Does the name Emmett mean anything to you?"

"No."

"Emmett Kelly was a famous clown, Weary Willie. He wore old clothes, and he had a sad face, and he depicted the hobos of the depression. I'm guessing Emmett is Manley's pen name."

"How do you know about Emmett?"

"I grew up in a multigenerational household in a Spanish-speaking neighborhood in Newark. My grandparents loved the circus and they loved Emmett the clown. On our living room wall, next to the television, there was a picture of Emmett. He had equal billing with a crucifix and a picture of Jesus Christ."

"Wow, I have a whole new insight into you now."

"Fortunately, I know you're being a wiseass."

"Okay, so moving along, Andy is writing short stories and screenplays and maybe video games."

"Maybe," Ranger said. "I'll take a closer look at his story and his screenplays tonight. If you want to really improve the evening, we can do it together."

"Tempting, but no."

"Right now, it's only tempting," Ranger said. "In the not-so-distant future it will be all-consuming." Ranger stood and kissed the top of my head. "Think about it."

Jeez. Truth is, it was pretty consuming *now*, but I was a good Catholic girl. Okay, so I never went to church, and I wasn't sure about God. I mean, who was he anyway? What I had was fear of eternal damnation and a set of values that were burned into my soul. Mostly they were the ten commandments and the Constitution of the United States. I couldn't repeat verbatim what any of them were, but they were stuck in the dark recesses of my brain, keeping me on the straight and narrow . . . most of the time. At least some of the time.

Ranger pocketed the flash drive and looked at Bob sprawled on the couch. "Where does he sleep?"

"In bed with me," I said.

"How long is he going to be here?"

"I don't know. Until Morelli returns."

"Babe," Ranger said. And he left.

Maybe Morelli knew exactly what he was doing when he left Bob with me.

CHAPTER FIVE

It took me a couple beats to wake up enough to realize my phone was ringing. I snatched it off my nightstand and squinted at the caller ID. Ranger.

"Yuh," I said.

"I'm coming in," Ranger said. "I didn't want to startle you."

"Wait. What?"

I looked at the time. It was five thirty . . . in the morning. It was dark out. Bob was still asleep. And the man of mystery was breaking into my apartment. I had a bump-proof lock, a dead bolt, and a chain. None of this stopped Ranger from popping in. It was as if he could slide under the door like smoke.

My bedroom light switched on and Ranger walked in. He was in black Rangeman fatigues and wide awake. I was snuggled

under the covers in a T-shirt and pajama bottoms and barely
awake. Bob half opened his eyes and went back to sleep.

"Not now," I said, sliding farther under the covers.

Ranger was standing alongside the bed. "We can do this the
easy, more politically correct way where you get out of bed on
your own, or we can do it the fun way where I drag you out."

"My lips are still sealed," I said.

"I didn't come to unseal your lips," Ranger said. "I want to
check out Dugan's house and you have a legal right to enter."

"Now?"

"Yes."

"It's the middle of the night. It's still dark out. Bob isn't even
awake."

"It's the perfect time to do an enter and search."

"Why are you interested in Dugan? I thought you were
looking for Nutsy."

"Did you read the stories and screenplays on Nutsy's hard
drive?"

"No, not yet."

"One of them is about a man who worked in a button factory
for twenty years. He has an epiphany that he's boring and
cowardly, running away from having a full life."

I sat up in bed. "So, he robs a jewelry store?"

"Yes."

"You're kidding. Does it end well?"

"He turns into a suave, professional jewel thief—like David
Niven in the old *Pink Panther* movies."

"I didn't know you were a *Pink Panther* fan."

Ranger pulled a T-shirt and a pair of jeans out of my dresser and tossed them at me. "It's mentioned as a footnote. I googled it." Underwear followed the T-shirt and jeans. Pink lace. No doubt Ranger thought this was daytime wear.

Bob was on his feet on the bed. He gave himself an ear-flapping shake and jumped down.

I gathered my clothes up. "Take Bob for a walk while I get dressed. His leash is on the hook by the door."

I took a five-minute shower, towel-dried my hair, and didn't waste time with makeup. I was in the kitchen when Ranger returned with Bob. I had coffee already poured into a travel mug. I grabbed a couple protein bars and shoved them into my sweatshirt pocket.

"Okay," I said. "We're ready to go."

"There's no *we*," Ranger said. "Bob is going to sit this one out."

"If I leave him here alone, he'll eat my couch."

"I'll buy you a new couch."

It was difficult to argue against the offer of a new couch. I scooped some dog kibble into Bob's bowl, gave him fresh water, and followed Ranger out of the building to his Porsche Cayenne.

"Were there any other interesting stories on the flash drive?" I asked him.

"'Big Below' was about a subterranean civilization of devil worshippers that was being threatened by fracking."

I buckled myself in beside Ranger and unwrapped my protein bar. "I like the devil-worshipper part, but fracking is kind of yesterday."

"Other than 'Big Below,' the stories and screenplays all featured the button-factory worker, Dwayne Dreary."

"Jeez."

"His jewel-thief pseudonym was Duncan Dare."

"I went through 'Duncan Dare's' house yesterday. He's very neat. The opposite of Nutsy. The one thing their places have in common is the complete absence of electronic devices. It's hard to imagine these two guys being friends, they are such polar opposites. But they must know each other pretty well if Nutsy is writing stories with Duncan as the lead."

"Unfortunately for Duncan Dugan, he doesn't seem to have the skills of the fictional Duncan Dare. Duncan Dare succeeded at everything. He got the jewels. He got the beautiful women. His true identity was never revealed."

"And he never fell off a ledge and broke all his bones."

"Not in the material I read," Ranger said. "While we're on the subject of Nutsy Manley, someone blew up his parents' car last night. We picked it up on the police band. No one was hurt."

"Do you know who exploded the car?"

"No. And the police don't seem to know either."

Ranger drove down Faucet Street. Lights were on in a few houses. Early risers getting ready for work. No activity on the street. Seventy-two Faucet was dark. Ranger turned at the corner and drove down the alley so we could see Dugan's house from the back. No cars parked in his yard. No lights on in his house. Ranger pulled to the side of the alley several houses away and we walked back to Dugan's house.

"What exactly are you hoping to find here?" I asked Ranger.

"A more solid connection between the two men. A lead on their locations. Motivation for the robbery."

The back door was closed but the lock hadn't been repaired

after Lula's whack with the hammer. I opened the door and shouted, "Bond enforcement," and we did a fast walk-through to make sure no one was in the house.

"Stay in the kitchen and watch the back door while I look around," Ranger said. "If someone approaches, don't let them get away."

I wasn't sure how I was supposed to accomplish this, but I gave him a thumbs-up.

The sun wasn't visible, but the sky was getting brighter. I had no idea where Ranger was in the house. He moved like a cat. Silent and stealthy. I could imagine his value in Special Forces. He didn't speak a lot about those years or why he left. One of Ranger's many secrets.

I prowled through the kitchen in the morning light, imagining Duncan Dreary coming home after a day of examining buttons, making his dinner, wondering if there was more to life than buttons.

Headlights appeared in the kitchen window and were immediately extinguished. Moments later, I heard a car door slam shut. Someone had parked in Dugan's small yard. I flattened myself against the wall beside the back door. If someone entered, I'd kick the door closed behind them and yell for Ranger. I heard someone fumbling with a key and then the doorknob turned. The door opened and a man walked in. I let him get halfway into the kitchen, I kicked the door closed, and I shouted for Ranger. The man turned and rushed at me. He shoved me away from the door and was about to run out. I didn't have a gun, and I don't have a lot of muscle, but I have boobs. So, I picked my T-shirt up and flashed my lacy pink bra at him.

"Hey!" I yelled. "Look at this!"

He stopped and stared, and Ranger stepped around me and pinned the man to the wall.

"Nice work," Ranger said to me. "I like your weapon of choice."

I straightened my T-shirt. "Might as well use 'em if you got 'em."

The corners of his mouth tipped up in a smile. "We need to talk," he said.

The guy pinned against the wall was shorter than Ranger. Maybe five foot ten. Slim. Brown hair pulled back in a ponytail. I would guess he was in his twenties. Looked like he was about to mess his pants.

Ranger took his hand off the man's chest and stepped back. "It's okay," Ranger said. "I'm just going to ask you a few questions."

"Sure," the man said.

"Your name."

"Jeff. I live down the street." He held up a key. "I have a key. I feed Marty when Duncan works late."

"Who's Marty?" Ranger asked.

"The fish. Duncan's fish."

"Is that why you're here now?"

"No. Duncan called and asked if I'd clean out his refrigerator and take out the trash. He said he wouldn't be home being that he was in the hospital. He's very neat."

I introduced myself and told Jeff that I was looking for Duncan because he was overdue for his court date.

"Oh wow," Jeff said. "Okay. That's a relief. That was scary for a minute there. I didn't know what to think. You should look for him in the hospital. I don't know which one."

"When did you talk to him?"

"This morning. He knows I'm up early. I work the early shift."

"Did Duncan sound okay?" Ranger asked.

"No," Jeff said. "He didn't sound like himself, or maybe it's that he sounded sort of out of it. From what I hear he broke a bunch of bones and I guess he's kind of doped up."

"We just walked through the house, and we didn't see a fish," I said.

"Sissy has him. Duncan said Sissy stopped by for Marty right after Duncan's accident when he fell off the ledge."

"Who's Sissy?" I asked.

"I don't know exactly except that they're friends. I've never met her. Duncan talked about her sometimes. He couldn't understand why she always ate chicken salad on a croissant. He thought it was unhealthy with the mayonnaise and the butter croissant."

"Did you hang out with Duncan?"

"No. We just have a neighbor thing. Like, we talk sometimes but we don't do social stuff. I met him at Petco a couple years ago and we bonded over fish. We're both partial to goldfish. They aren't very exotic, but they have wonderful personalities."

"Do you have a goldfish?" I asked him.

"Yes," he said. "She's a beauty."

"What's her name?"

"Goldie the Twelfth."

"Good name," I said. I gave Jeff one of my business cards. "I'd appreciate a call if you hear from Duncan."

"Okay, but I don't expect to hear from him. He said he wouldn't be home for quite a while."

Ranger and I moved toward the door.

"We're done here," Ranger said to Jeff. "Lock up when you leave."

"The lock seems to be broken," Jeff said.

"I'll send someone to fix it," Ranger said.

Ranger and I left and walked to the Cayenne. We waited in the car until we saw Jeff leave Dugan's house, put a plastic bag in the trash, climb into his car, and drive away.

"What do you think?" I asked Ranger.

"He seems benign, and his body type doesn't fit either of the two people who wheeled Dugan out of the hospital."

"Did you find anything interesting in the house?"

"Nothing specific," Ranger said. "You were right. The house is clean, it says a lot about his personality. I'm going to put surveillance cameras on his front and back doors. He's a creature of habit. He's not going to be comfortable using someone else's choice of shampoo. He's going to want his pillow, his razor, his crossword puzzle book. He's going to send someone to get these things if he's still in the area."

The neighborhood was waking up. Lights were on in all the houses and dogs were barking. Ranger put the Porsche in gear, drove the length of the alley, and turned toward the center of the city.

"I have morning meetings," Ranger said. "I'll take you home and get back to you later in the day."

CHAPTER SIX

Bob rushed up to me when I let myself into my apartment. I gave him hugs and did a quick look around. All upholstered pieces seemed to be intact, and he hadn't chewed through any table legs.

"Who's a good boy? Are you a good boy?" I asked him, ruffling his ears.

I pulled the remaining protein bar out of my sweatshirt pocket and gave it to Bob. It was oats and coconut. No raisins. Okay as Bob food.

I shuffled off to the bathroom, pulled my out-of-control hair into a ponytail, applied a light smudge of eyeliner, dusted some highlighter and blush on my cheeks, and glossed up my lips with pink lipstick. I looked at the woman in the mirror and wished I'd taken the time to look like this for Ranger. Omigod. Mental slap in the face. Get real, Stephanie. You're two inches away from cheating on your boyfriend and going straight to hell. You don't want to look better for Ranger. You want to look worse. You need pimples. Bad breath. Hairy legs. I hooked Bob up to his leash and we headed off to the bail bond office.

Lula was pacing in front of Connie's desk when I walked in. She had a butterscotch glazed doughnut in one hand and a chocolate cake doughnut in the other. Connie was looking like she needed a vacation. The door to my cousin Vinnie's inner office was closed.

"Hey," I said. "How's it going?"

"I'll tell you how it's going," Lula said. "It's not going good. I didn't get no sleep last night. And I didn't get no sleep the night before that. I didn't say nothing because I don't like to complain. I'm not one of them whiners, you see what I'm saying?"

I knew I was going to regret asking, but I had to ask anyway. "What's the problem?"

"I'm getting stalked," Lula said. "And it's no normal stalking. I'm getting stalked by Grendel."

Connie pantomimed stabbing herself in the eye with her fine-tipped Sharpie.

"Who's Grendel?" I asked Lula.

"You don't know Grendel?" Lula said. "He's a famous demon. He's a man-eater. He lives in the land of the Spear-Danes and attacks King Hrothgar's mead hall every night. Supposedly he was killed by Beowulf but clearly, he wasn't."

"Oh," I said. "That Grendel."

"He's stalking Lula," Connie said to me, holding out the doughnut box. "Do you want a doughnut? There's a maple glazed and a vanilla frosted with sprinkles."

I took the maple glazed. "What about the daily mead-hall attacks?"

"He must have given them up," Lula said.

"In favor of stalking you?"

"I don't have an explanation for it. All I know is I got this ugly big growly ogre ruining my sleep," Lula said.

"How do you know it's Grendel? Did you just read *Beowulf*?"

"You can read about Beowulf?" Lula asked.

"It's a book," I said.

"I didn't know that," Lula said. "I learned all about him in this video game I downloaded. It's a total kick-ass video game, I can't stop playing it. I thought it was made up except that don't seem to be the case."

Bob was drooling, standing in front of Connie. She gave him the doughnut with the sprinkles, and he swallowed it whole.

"Why do you think it's Grendel?" I asked. "Have you actually seen him?"

"He's always in the dark," Lula said. "He's the shadow walker. That's what they call him. He brings darkness, chaos, and death. I mean, I don't like none of that. I especially don't like death. You know how I feel about death."

"But have you seen him?"

"Hell yeah. Sort of. He's big and hairy like Sasquatch. I mean, huge! And he's got a little shrunken head. The whole package is nasty. Mostly I hear him shuffling around and making grunting sounds. By the time I get the light on, he's gone. From now on I'm sleeping with the light on. It's not good for your melatonin production, but a girl's gotta do what a girl's gotta do."

"I have my own problems," I said. "I can't find anybody."

"A new FTA just came in," Connie said. "Vinnie is in a state over it. He should never have written the bond. The guy is high risk, and the bond was six figures." She handed the file to me.

I paged through it. "Farcus Trundle. Charged with armed robbery and kidnapping."

"That's a terrible name," Lula said. "No wonder he had to turn to a life of crime."

"He's fifty-eight years old and unemployed," I said.

"Technically that's not true," Lula said. "He's self-employed as an armed robber. He might be misguided, but at least he's trying to be self-sufficient."

"He kidnapped a seventy-three-year-old woman."

"Hunh," Lula said. "He shouldn't have done that. I hope he treated her good."

"It says here that he chained her to a doghouse in his backyard."

Lula finished off the chocolate cake doughnut. "Was it a nice doghouse? Some of those doghouses have heat and carpeting and everything."

"He has a bunch of priors," Connie said. "Career criminal, sex offender and anger-management issues. You don't want to underestimate him."

I found his photo. "He's six foot two and weighs two hundred forty-five pounds. Dark brown hair, thinning at the top, beady brown eyes, day-old beard, not smiling."

"What do beady eyes look like?" Lula asked.

"Like eagle eyes but without eagle eyebrows," I said. "He has normal eyebrows."

I showed her the picture attached to the file.

"Yeah," Lula said. "He's got beady eyes. We need to go investigate this. I want to see the doghouse. I'm wondering if the old lady had to share it with a dog. It had to be a big doghouse if it was shared."

I went speechless for a couple beats, processing the mental image of a woman and a dog huddled together in a Snoopy-style doghouse.

"You might want to go in armed on this one," Connie said.

"I got us covered," Lula said. "I'm ready to rock and roll."

"Okay," I said. "Let's do it."

Lula rushed outside to my Jeep Cherokee and claimed the front passenger seat before Bob had a chance to get in. Bob didn't look like he cared too much. He jumped into the back and snarfed around, looking for yesterday's crumbs.

"Where's this loser live?" Lula asked.

"Carlory Street."

"That's just past the junkyard," Lula said. "There's some good real estate possibilities there if you don't mind living by a junkyard on one side and the power substation on the other."

For the most part, Trenton is chockablock with houses. Carlory Street not so much. It's a little over a mile long and it's sprinkled with empty lots and houses in various stages of neglect. The vegetation is overgrown, the street is dotted with potholes and abandoned cars. Feral cats outnumber humans by about ten to one.

"If you're going to kidnap some woman and chain her to a doghouse, Carlory Street is a good place to do it," Lula said. "I imagine nobody there pays a lot of attention to dogs barking or people yelling."

I bypassed the center of the city and came at Carlory Street from the substation side. There were no names or numbers on driveways, but Google Earth gave me a picture of the dirt drive leading to Trundle's house, and the GPS lady told me I was at the right spot.

"I guess this would be considered rural in Trenton," Lula said, "only it's not the scenic kind of rural. It's not Vermont, if you see what I mean."

The house was hidden from the street by a weathered privacy fence and small shed. Vines grew over the fence and tangled in brush that was partially obscured by weeds. I slowly drove down the short driveway. A cat streaked across the driveway in front of me and Bob sat up in the back seat and woofed.

I stopped just short of the house. It was all on one level with mold on the roof and rot in the wood window trim. No car on the property. No sign of activity.

"He could be hiding out in there pretending nobody's home," Lula said. "We could be walking into a dangerous situation. Good thing we brought an attack dog with us. I say we send him in first to scope things out."

I checked Bob out in the rearview mirror. His big brown eyes were focused on me. His soft, floppy ears were perked up, listening. No way was I sending Bob into the house first.

"It looks deserted," I said.

"Yeah, but what if it isn't deserted?"

"We'll have a reasonable conversation with Mr. Trundle."

I didn't really believe anyone could have a reasonable conversation with Farcus Trundle, but it was one of those things you told yourself, so you didn't prematurely hyperventilate.

Lula, Bob, and I walked to Trundle's front door, and I knocked. No one answered, so Lula looked in the front windows.

"I don't see anyone in there, alive or dead," Lula said. "There's a roach, sneakers up, on the window ledge. Are we going to bust the door down and look around?"

"I don't think that's necessary," I said.

"Good call," Lula said. "I only want to see the doghouse anyways."

We walked around the side of the house to the backyard. A rusted-out Weber grill was next to the back door. The yard was mostly hard-packed dirt. A prefab igloo-type doghouse was at the back of the area designated as yard.

"That dome thing must be it," Lula said. "It doesn't look big enough for an old lady and a dog. And I'm thinking that it had to be a *little* old lady. Even then she'd have to curl herself up in it."

"The police report said the woman was chained to the dog-house, but I don't see a chain," I said to Lula.

"There's also no dog."

Bob was beside me, looking bored, leading me to believe that there hadn't been a dog here in a long time.

I looked in the windows in the back of the house. I tried the back door. Unlocked. I hadn't intended to do a house search, but this was tempting. I stepped inside and shouted for Farcus. No answer. I was in the kitchen and there wasn't a lot to see.

"This house smells old," Lula said. "And the kitchen doesn't look like it gets a lot of use." She opened the refrigerator door. "He's got an onion and a squeeze bottle of mayo in here. There's not even any beer. Hard to believe a man with a name like Farcus could get along without beer."

We did a quick walk-through and left.

"He didn't even have a lot of clothes there," Lula said. "A winter jacket and some boots. So, what's up next?"

"I want to talk to the victim."

"The doghouse lady? I like that idea. I got some questions. I want to know what it's like to live in a doghouse."

I called Connie and asked her to get me an address for the kidnapped woman. Minutes later the text message came into my phone.

"Her name is Marjorie Katz," I said to Lula. "She lives on Miran Street."

We plugged the address into my GPS and in a half hour we were in another world. Large professionally maintained lawns, perfectly paved circular driveways, large colonial-style houses, shiny expensive cars lounging in front of four-car garages. I pulled into the Katz driveway and parked behind a black Mercedes.

"This is a long way from a doghouse," Lula said.

A slim woman answered the door. Her silver hair was cut short and styled in soft waves. Her nails were lavender and beautifully manicured. She was wearing a dress I could never afford and her low heels had the Chanel logo on them.

I introduced myself and asked if Marjorie Katz was at home.

"I'm Marjorie Katz," she said. "What is this about?"

"I'm looking for Farcus Trundle. He's in violation of his bond agreement. You were listed on his booking sheet."

"It said you were robbed and kidnapped," Lula said. "And chained to a doghouse."

Marjorie Katz closed her eyes for a beat. "Hideous, horrible, awful man. He's a disgusting human being." Her eyes narrowed. "He chained me to a doghouse. It was terrible." She lowered her voice. "He dropped his pants and showed me his one-eyed snake."

"Omigod," Lula said. "He had a snake in his pants? That's sick."

"No," Marjorie said, "I'm talking about Willy Winky."

Lula was blank faced. "Say what?"

Marjorie rolled her eyes. "His wiggle stick, baloney pony, wrinkle beast, *tadger*."

"His dick," I said to Lula.

Lula went wide-eyed at Marjorie. "Seriously? Where'd you learn all those words for a dick?"

"I was a librarian," Marjorie said.

"Well, I was a ho," Lula said. "And we never called it any of those things."

"We just came from Trundle's house, and it didn't look like anyone was living there," I said to Marjorie.

"I assumed he was, but I don't really know. He chained me up, waved his chubby at me, and left."

"Chubby," Lula said. "That's another good one. I've gotta remember these."

"Is there anything else that you could tell me about Trundle?" I said. "What kind of car did he drive?"

"He drove *my* car," Marjorie said. "I withdrew money from the ATM on Willow Street and when I went to my car, he walked over to me, put a gun to my head, and took my purse with the money in it. It was such a shock that I just stood there. I didn't shout for the police. I didn't run. I didn't do anything. It was like my brain went numb and my heart stopped beating."

"Understandable," Lula said. "It's obvious you're a refined

lady and not used to dealing with scumbags threatening you with deadly force."

"Yes," Marjorie said. "I suppose that's it."

"Stephanie and me are professionals, and we're used to these sorts of things," Lula said.

Marjorie nodded. "After he took my purse, he walked away. Just a couple steps. And then he turned around and pointed the gun at me again and told me to open the trunk. I opened the trunk, and the next thing I knew, I was in the trunk and the car was moving. The car stopped, he opened the trunk and dragged me out. And we were in his backyard. He drove my Mercedes into his backyard. He didn't have a driveway or anything. It was just dirt."

"I bet he stun-gunned you," Lula said. "That's what I would do if I wanted to get someone into a trunk."

"Honestly," Marjorie said. "What's this world come to? What's wrong with people that they think it's okay to throw a woman in the trunk of her Mercedes and drive off with it? People like that should be locked away."

"I totally agree," Lula said. "And if you don't mind my asking, what was it like living in a doghouse?"

"I didn't live in the doghouse," she said. "There was a chain attached to a big eye screw that had been screwed into the ground in front of the doghouse. He wrapped the end of the chain around my ankle and padlocked it. He said he was originally just going to rob me, but he got to thinking that anyone who drove a Mercedes and had diamond earrings would be good to ransom. Then he made me give him my earrings and he drove away in my car. As soon as he was out of sight, I started working to get free."

"How did you do that?" Lula asked. "Did you have a secret cell phone on you?"

"No. The eye screw wasn't cemented in. I was able to work it loose."

"Did it take you days to get it loose?" Lula asked.

"No," Marjorie said. "About twenty minutes, I think. I was motivated to get out of there before he came back."

"Lucky for you that you had a stupid kidnapper," Lula said. "He wasn't smart enough to know that someone with hands instead of paws would be able to get that screw thing out of the ground."

"I couldn't get the chain off my ankle, so I carried it with me, and I walked out to the cross street, where I was able to flag someone down," Marjorie said.

"Awesome," Lula said. "You're like your own hero. Did you feel empowered?"

"No," Marjorie said. "I felt like a ninny. Like a stupid victim. It was terrifying and embarrassing. I was sobbing when the car stopped to help me. Sobbing! It was horrible. Not my finest hour."

"What was your finest hour?" Lula asked.

"I made popovers for a dinner party once and they were perfect," Marjorie said.

"Did you get your car and your earrings back?" I asked her.

"My car, yes. Not the earrings. He said he had a girlfriend down the street. He said he was going to trade them off for a good time. That was when he took it out and waved it at me."

We left Marjorie Katz and returned to my Jeep Cherokee and Bob.

"I expected Marjorie Katz to be an old lady," Lula said. "She didn't even look that old. Mostly she looked rich."

"Seventy-three is the new fifty-three," I said.

"Does that make thirty the new ten?"

"No. Thirty is the new forty-five," I said.

I got behind the steering wheel and saw that it had some tooth marks in it.

"What's with the tooth marks in my steering wheel?" I asked Bob.

Bob played dumb and looked happy to see me.

"No dog treats for you, mister," I said.

Bob still looked happy to see me, so I pulled a couple dog biscuits out of my bag and gave them to Bob.

"That's rewarding bad behavior," Lula said to me. "How's he gonna learn what's right and what's wrong if you keep giving him biscuits?"

"It was a wash because he looked happy to see me."

"Okay, I get that," Lula said. "That's a validating condition."

"We need to take another look at Carlory Street."

"Trundle's girlfriend, right?"

"Right."

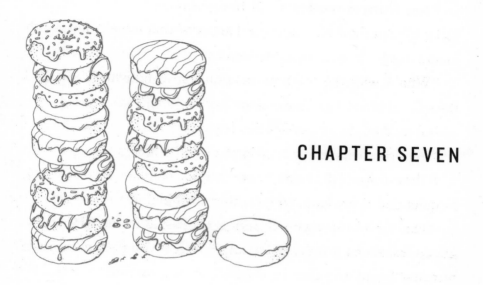

CHAPTER SEVEN

I drove past Trundle's property and went a quarter mile down the road, heading toward the junkyard. I picked out a black Range Rover parked in a driveway that led to a gray bungalow. I pulled to the side and grabbed Trundle's file out of my bag. He'd listed his personal vehicle as a black Range Rover. I scanned the file and found Trundle's license plate. It matched the plate on the SUV in the driveway.

"I don't know if we're so happy about this," Lula said. "He doesn't sound like such a nice guy."

"True. But we know he's not especially smart, so that gives us an advantage."

"Yeah," Lula said. "We're totally smart. We got smart in spades. And I got a gun."

I turned into the driveway and parked behind the Range Rover.

"You're parking behind him so he can't drive off," Lula said to me. "That already shows how smart we are."

I had a dilemma now. What to do with Bob. I didn't want to bring him to the house and put him in harm's way. I also didn't want to leave him alone in the car one more time.

"This is the plan," I said to Lula. "You take Bob and stay behind me when I go to the door. I don't want to bring Bob into the house."

"Yeah, but what if Farcus is in there and things get dangerous?"

"Then I especially don't want Bob involved."

I handed Bob's leash to Lula, and I walked to the bungalow's front door. I rang the bell and a woman answered. She was midforties with a mess of red hair and a nose ring. She was wearing a tank top that showed off some gym muscle and a lot of tattoos. She had diamond studs in her ears that were about two carats each.

"What?" she said.

"I'm looking for Farcus," I said. "I saw his Range Rover in the driveway."

"And?"

"I owe him some money," I said. "He wasn't at his house."

"He isn't here."

"His car is here."

The woman leaned to one side and looked behind me. "What's with the dog and fatso?"

"Excuse me?" Lula said.

"No insult intended," the woman said. "I happen to be a personal trainer and I could get that fat off you, in case you're interested."

"I'm not fat," Lula said. "I'm a big voluptuous woman and you're a skinny bitch. No insult intended."

"None taken," she said, "but you've gotta get the dog out of here. My Sally Belle doesn't like other dogs."

"What kind of dog is Sally Belle?" Lula asked.

"She's a purebred poodle doodle," the woman said. "And she's very sensitive."

"This here is Bob," Lula said. "And he's very orange."

"About Farcus," I said to the woman.

"I told you. Farcus isn't here."

"Then you wouldn't mind if I look around."

"Freaking A, I'd mind," she said. "Take your orange dog and get your ass off my property."

I showed her the badge I bought on Amazon and told her I was representing Vincent Plum Bail Bonds and that I had a right to search her house.

"Over my cold dead body," she said.

"Hunh," Lula said. "Do the world a favor."

"You want a piece of me?" the woman said to Lula. "You think you got what it takes?"

"I got more than what it takes," Lula said. "You'd be a puddle of rancid grease when I was done with you."

"No rancid grease puddles," I said. "Let's keep this civil and professional."

The woman tried to shut the door, but I got my foot in the way. Lula put her weight to the door and muscled it open. I stepped in first, the woman sucker punched me in the face, and Lula let go of Bob and took the woman down to the floor. The poodle doodle ran in to see what was going on and Bob lunged at the poodle doodle.

"Run, Farcus," the woman yelled. "Run!!"

I caught a glimpse of Farcus heading for the back of the house and I took off after him. I chased him around the house and saw him jump into his Range Rover. The woman ran out of the house and barely got in the Rover before Farcus put it in reverse and rammed my Cherokee into the road and out of his way. Under more normal circumstances I might have been able to catch him, but I was hampered by the blood dripping out of my nose.

I pinched my nose shut, tipped my head back a little, and walked into the house. Lula was on her feet, arranging the girls and tugging her tiny spandex skirt over her plus-size ass. Bob was in the middle of the room humping the poodle doodle.

"Oh crap," I said.

"Yeah," Lula said. "Bob's doing the nasty with Sally Belle. He's not just fooling around either. He's doing some impressive thrusting."

"We should try to separate them."

"That don't seem right," Lula said. "He's banging his brains out. Seems like he should at least get to finish."

"He's neutered. How much of a finish can he get?"

Lula found her cell phone in her giant handbag and went to Google. "It says here that he can finish. He just can't make puppies." She turned her attention from Bob to me. "You're a mess. You got blood all over you."

"It's my blood from when Trundle's girlfriend hit me in the nose."

"She got away from me and ran out of the house, and while I was getting myself up off the floor, I heard a car crash. What happened out there?"

"They rammed my Cherokee out of the way and took off."

Bob had stopped thrusting, but he was still attached to the poodle doodle.

"Now what?" I said. "Is he done, or what?"

Lula went to Google again. "Sometimes this happens, and they stay stuck together. Good thing this don't happen with people. When I was a working ho it would have cut into my profit margin if I had to delay my exit. I guess I would have had to go to an hourly rate."

"How long do they stay stuck? Should we take them to a vet?"

"Google says you just have to wait for Bob to shrink."

I left Lula to keep an eye on the dogs and I went to the bathroom to wash the blood off my hands and face. Most of the bleeding had stopped, but there were still some dribbles, so I stuffed some tissues up my nose to help things along. Not much I could do about the blood on my sweatshirt and T-shirt.

The dogs were apart when I returned to the front room.

"Are they okay?" I asked Lula.

"Yeah," Lula said. "The poodle doodle's walking a little funny, but we've all been there."

So true.

We locked the doors, I gave the poodle doodle fresh water and left her a dog treat, and we vacated the house. The front of my Cherokee was bashed in, but the car was still drivable.

"Are you sure you can see okay with all that tissue stuck up your nose?" Lula asked.

"No problem," I said. "My eyes are fine."

"They don't look fine," Lula said. "They're turning black and purple and they're looking puffy."

———

I dropped Lula off at the office, and Bob and I went back to my apartment. I changed my clothes, pulled the tissue out of my nose, and made myself a peanut butter and olive sandwich for lunch. I made a peanut butter and deli ham sandwich for Bob because he doesn't like olives. I knew I should put ice on my nose, but I was lacking motivation. I was debating taking a nap when Morelli called.

"I only have a few minutes before I have to get back to court," he said. "I just wanted to check in. Is everything okay?"

"Yep. Bob's doing great. He had an amorous adventure with a poodle doodle today."

"How amorous?"

"As amorous as a dog could get."

"He's neutered," Morelli said.

"Apparently, some dogs can overcome that handicap."

"Bob actually did it with the poodle doodle?"

"Yep."

"All the way?"

"All the way and then some."

"That's my boy. Any other good news?"

"That's as good as it gets," I said. "While I have you on the phone, were you aware that Duncan Dugan and Nutsy knew each other?"

"I didn't know that. I've only seen Nutsy a couple times since high school, and I'm not really involved in the Plover case. You might want to share that with Jonesy since he's the principal. I have to go. They're waving at me. I'll call you tonight."

I shuffled into the bathroom and looked at myself again. Two black eyes and a slightly swollen nose. Not my finest hour, and I had no hope of ever making a decent popover.

"What do you think?" I asked Bob.

Bob looked up at me as if I were pretty. And that's why I'd take a bullet for Bob.

"When the going gets tough, the tough get going," I said to Bob. "Let's go to the office and see what we can dig up on someone. *Anyone.*"

Bob was all for it. He followed me out of my apartment and down to the parking lot and jumped into my crumpled Cherokee. When we walked into the office, Connie was cleaning her gun and Lula was on the couch reading *Star* magazine.

"I like the way you coordinated your black and purple eye with a poison-green T-shirt," Lula said to me. "It totally works but you need to change your nail polish. I'd go with black."

"I have some information on the girlfriend," Connie said. "Maxine Polinski. Works as a personal trainer at Manny's Gym. Forty-seven years old. Owns the house on Carlory Street. Divorced three times. Currently single. Operates as a pimp for three girls working Stark Street."

"I didn't recognize her," Lula said. "I'm out of the Stark Street loop. I don't even know who's working my corner now."

"She throws a good punch," I said.

"She'll be going back to the house," Lula said. "The poodle doodle is there and anyways, it's her house. Probably Trundle will be going back with her. He has to shack up somewhere and her house is better than his house."

"I might want to take Ranger with me next time," I said.

"Yeah, that would be a good idea," Lula said. "Taking Ranger anywhere is a good idea, but maybe you want to wait for the eyes to calm down first."

"Not attractive?" I asked her.

"Horror movie," Lula said.

I took Oakley mirrored wraparounds out of my bag and put them on. "Better?"

"Freakin' A," Lula said.

"Do we have anything new on Duncan Dugan?" I asked Connie.

"Zero," Connie said. "It's like he dropped off the earth since he left the hospital. But I heard a disturbing piece of news at Giovichinni's. I went to get lunch and ran into Shirley Greeley. She lives next door to the Manleys, and she said last night someone blew up the Manleys' Corolla. Fortunately, the Manleys weren't in it. It was an IED that detonated a little after midnight. Shirley said the Manleys are pretty shook up and their cats are completely freaked out."

"I heard about the bombing from Ranger," I said to Connie. "I saw him this morning."

"Shirley didn't know much, so I called my cousin Lorraine," Connie said. "She's working dispatch. She said as far as she knew there were no persons of interest."

The Manleys weren't the sort of people who got car bombed. They weren't controversial. They weren't activists. They didn't object to anything, and they didn't alienate anyone. They fostered cats. I guess if you really hated cats you might want to bomb the Manleys, but other than that, I couldn't see it.

"I'm thinking this might be clown related," Lula said. "There are people out there who have real strong feelings about clowns. Not everybody likes them. If you look close at a clown, they could be creepy. I think this could be an act of clown terrorism. There's all kinds of terrorists running around out there these days. The terrorists I'm talking about would be anti-clown. Only thing is, they would be low on the terrorist top ten since they weren't smart enough to know the Corolla belongs to Nutsy's parents and not Nutsy."

"You have to worry about your own sanity when Lula's rantings start to make sense," Connie said.

I didn't think clown terrorists had blown up the Corolla. I thought the bombing was related to Nutsy and the robberies. A logical assumption would be that Duncan Dugan and Nutsy were friends. It was an unlikely alliance, but opposites are supposed to attract, right? And the next logical assumption would be that the two robberies were connected. That Duncan Dugan took the merchandise out of the cases and Nutsy went back and took the uncut stones. And somehow this resulted in someone getting pissed off enough to blow up Nutsy's parents' Corolla. It was a lot of assuming but it was all I had. Problem is, while my brain was telling me this reasoning was logical, my gut was telling me that it felt wrong.

I hiked my messenger bag up on my shoulder. "I'm going to visit Mrs. Manley."

"Gee, I'd like to go with you," Lula said, "but I've got something to do. I've got plans."

"What kind of plans?" I asked.

"I've got plans to stay here where there are no cats," Lula said.

"Good thinking," I said. "I'll leave Bob with you."

———

I parked across the street from the Manleys' house and checked out the crime scene. The Corolla had been taken away, but the driveway was smudged with black soot and the grass on either side of the driveway was scorched. The small front yard was dotted with chunks of tire. It brought back memories of some of my own traumatic events. My apartment's been firebombed. I've had multiple cars destroyed. I've been kidnapped and stalked, and I've survived three days of having Lula as a roommate. All horrible at the time. Scary and confusing. Now just a part of my history. As it turns out, I'm resilient. Go figure.

My mom wishes I had a more boring history. She's been given the role of Family Adult in Charge of Worrying. It's not a job I'd want, but my mom is pretty good at it. When the job is overwhelming, she goes to Jim Beam for help.

I crossed the street and rang the bell. Mrs. Manley opened the door and immediately looked to see if I was alone.

"Bob is back at the office with Lula," I said.

"It's just that the cats are a little on edge after last night."

"Understandable. How about you? Are you okay?"

"It doesn't seem real," Mrs. Manley said. "These things happen to other people and in the movies."

"Have you heard from Andy?"

"He showed up right after the fire trucks. He said he heard about it on the police band. He was here for just a few minutes and then he left. I think he might have a girlfriend."

"I imagine he was worried about you."

"He was very upset. He wanted us to leave. To take a vacation until the bomber was found. I can't do that of course, but it was sweet of him to be concerned."

"He must be in the neighborhood if he got here right after the fire trucks."

"I don't know. I didn't think to ask. I was having a hard time getting a grip with everything going on. I tried calling him this afternoon, but he didn't pick up. He's terrible about answering his phone."

"I just thought I should stop in to see if there was anything I could do, but it looks like you have everything under control here," I said.

"I couldn't help noticing you have a nice big SUV," Mrs. Manley said. "I could really use a ride to the vet clinic tomorrow afternoon. Iris, Snuggles, Red Cat, and Mr. Meow Meow are supposed to get shots, and our only car got blown up."

When she got to the part about the car getting blown up, her eyes filled with tears. She blinked them away and pulled herself together.

Getting sucker punched in the face had been less painful than the prospect of taking a car full of cats to the vet. I'd made the offer of help because that's the sort of thing you're supposed to say, but it had been completely insincere.

"Sure," I said. "No problem. What time do you want me to pick you up?"

"One o'clock."

I called Ranger on my way back to the office. "Have you learned any more about the Manley car bombing?" I asked him.

"The house across the street has a Ring doorbell and it captured someone dressed in black. Black hoodie, black COVID mask. Black slacks. The doorbell angle wasn't great, but it shows the figure approach the Manleys' Corolla at the appropriate time.

Appears to be a man. If he came in a car, it's out of the frame, and it doesn't drive past the Ring camera before or after the man shows up. He disappears behind the Corolla and then reappears and leaves."

"Does this man look like one of the people who snatched Dugan out of the hospital?"

"It's possible but there's no point of reference on size. My gut tells me no."

Ranger's instincts were flawless. If his gut said no, then I was on board with no.

"Where do we go from here?" I asked.

"I have a dinner meeting tonight with a new client. Are you free to have dinner with us?"

"Omigod, are you asking me out on a date?"

"I'm asking you to join us for dinner. What we do after dinner will be up to you."

"Can I bring Bob?"

"Babe," Ranger said. And he disconnected.

A beat later I got a text message. *I'll pick you up at six thirty. No Bob.*

———

Morelli called at six o'clock. "Just checking in," he said. "I'm going out for burgers with Ed Mallow in a couple minutes. He got sent down here with me."

"Do I know him?"

"He's FBI. Trenton office. Short bald guy. I think you ran into him when you went after the truckers who were doing human trafficking."

"Have you testified yet?"

"No. This thing is going to drag out. How are you doing? Did you find Nutsy?"

"Not yet."

"Are you working with Ranger?"

"Maybe a little."

"What's a little? What does that involve?"

"He wanted to snoop around Duncan Dugan's row house, and I had a legal reason to enter."

"Did he find anything?"

"Nope."

"You know the deal with the bag of jewelry, right?"

"Just that it wasn't in the car with Dugan when they arrested him."

"He said he panicked when he ran out of the store. Changed his mind about wanting to rob it and dropped the bag of jewelry on the sidewalk. So far as I know, the bag still hasn't been found."

"Do you think Nutsy took it?"

"It's possible. He was there, but so were a lot of other people. My understanding is that a small crowd had gathered in front of the store when the alarm went off and the police arrived."

"The plot thickens."

"Yeah, that's only the half of it. I have to go. You and Bob are okay, right? No disasters?"

"Why? Did you hear something?"

"Should I have heard something?"

"No. Definitely not. Nothing to hear. We're great. Bob hasn't even eaten my couch."

"Good to know," Morelli said.

———

I was waiting outside my building when Ranger pulled his shiny black Porsche 911 Turbo into the lot. I was wearing heels, a black dress with a scoop neck, and a short red jacket over the dress. My hair was brushed out and hung in waves to my shoulders. My lip color was natural and glossy. I didn't need eye shadow since my eyes were already purple. I thought I looked classy and moderately sexy, as long as you were willing to overlook the fact that I'd been punched in the face.

I slid in next to Ranger, placed my black clutch on my lap, and buckled my seat belt.

"Babe?" Ranger said.

"Yep."

"Is there something you want to tell me?"

"Morelli called."

"That's nice, but I don't care. I'm talking about your face."

"Farcus Trundle's girlfriend sucker punched me. Then he smashed his car into mine and they drove away. That's the short version."

"This is the same Farcus Trundle who chained Marjorie Katz to a doghouse?"

"Yes."

"Rangeman runs security on her house. Next time you feel inclined to visit with Farcus, let me know and I'll tag along."

"That would be great," I said. "He's FTA. Where are we going for dinner?"

"We're eating at a hotel restaurant in Princeton. The client chose it. He's in town for two days, talking to his architects and designers."

"And you."

"Yes. And me."

"What's my purpose?"

"I start my day at five in the morning and I go straight through until Tank takes over the night shift. I like what I do. Almost always. I help to keep people safe. I protect their property. I provide jobs for good people. I'm good at it. It's rewarding. Dinner with Ralph and Brenda Seward isn't rewarding or enjoyable. I have dinner with them because this is the way Ralph does business. And I'm doing business with him because I like the project. So, to make this evening tolerable, I've invited you. Someday I'll take the time to figure out why I like you so much, why you amuse me, why you intrigue me, why you're so desirable. Tonight, I'm just happy you're here to save me from being alone with the Sewards."

"Wow. Holy cow."

That got a rare full-on smile from Ranger. His teeth were white against his dark skin, in the dark car. The smile reached his eyes, where he had a few crinkle lines that I thought were from squinting, not smiling.

"I don't like that you were hit in the face," Ranger said, "but it should improve the dinner conversation."

"I could put dark glasses on and say I had surgery."

"It's your story. Tell it however you want."

———

The Sewards were already at the table when we arrived. They were enjoying cocktails. Dirty martinis with multiple olives. I was guessing they were in their late sixties. They were pleasantly plump with faces that reflected an excellent cosmetic dermatologist and surgeon. They were appropriately dressed for dinner at a Four Seasons–equivalent hotel. They were smiling and gracious. Ranger, in a perfectly tailored black Tom Ford suit and dress shirt open at the collar, fit right in. Me, not so much with two black eyes and a slightly swollen nose.

"Isn't this nice," Brenda said. "We finally get to meet Mrs. Ranger."

"You can call me Stephanie," I said.

Ranger looked like he was enjoying himself. He ordered a seltzer water from the waiter and a glass of champagne for me.

"You're probably wondering about my bruises," I said.

"Oh no," Brenda said. "I didn't notice them, but now that you mention it. Have you had work done?"

"No," I said. "It was just one of those job-related incidents. I was trying to make an apprehension and I got sucker punched."

Brenda and Ralph sucked in some air.

"Oh my gosh," Brenda said. "I didn't realize you were in law enforcement. Ranger is very private. We hardly know anything about you."

"He's very protective," I said. "He's such a sweetie pie."

Brenda and Ralph looked at sweetie pie Ranger.

"Ralph is like that too," Brenda said. "We've been married for forty-six years, and he still holds my hand when we go for a walk after dinner."

"She tends to wander away," Ralph said.

"Only that one time when I saw the squirrel," Brenda said. "He looked injured."

"He was rabid," Ralph said. "Fucking rabid squirrel. Anybody could see that he was rabid."

"You don't know that for sure," Brenda said. "He might have been injured. Maybe he had a stroke like your brother Bill."

"Bill didn't look like that when he had the stroke," Ralph said. "He couldn't use one side. His arm just hung there. And he couldn't talk. He kept saying *rub-a-dub* and *bingo bango bongo*. Totally different from the squirrel."

I chugged my champagne and ordered another. Ranger's smile was small but constant.

It was a little after nine when the valet brought Ranger's Porsche around. We were in front of the hotel and Ranger pulled me close against him and kissed me, giving me a rush that stopped just short of orgasmic.

"I should explain about my unsealed lips," I said. "It's a temporary condition resulting from drinking three glasses of champagne."

"I thought it might be because you were Mrs. Ranger."

"That role ended when we left the table."

His voice was soft. His lips skimmed across my ear. "Would you consider staying in the role a little longer?"

I put a couple inches of space between us and looked up at him. "You're thinking about taking advantage of me in my three-glasses-of-champagne condition, aren't you?"

"I am."

"It has some appeal but don't think for too long. The amorous stage of inebriation has a short shelf life for me. I'm afraid I'll be asleep in ten minutes. I'd hate to miss the grand finale."

Ranger kissed me again. Long and slow and hot. He broke from the kiss and stuffed me into his Porsche, holding my head cop style so I didn't give myself a concussion.

"I'm going to give you a rain check on the grand finale," he said, sliding in behind the wheel. "What I want to do to you is going to take longer than ten minutes, and you're going to want to remember all of it."

CHAPTER EIGHT

Lula was already in the office when Bob and I walked in. She was in sneakers and gray sweats, and her hair was pulled up into a topknot ponytail that looked like a Dr. Seuss Truffula tree.

"I didn't get any sleep again last night," Lula said. "I could hardly pull myself together this morning. I just put on the first thing I saw. Look at me. I'm wearing sneakers. *Sneakers.* They aren't even bedazzled."

"Grendel again?" I asked.

"It's horrible. I left the light on, but I fell asleep. I woke up at two o'clock, my light was off, and I could hear him breathing and growling. A big black blob. I just about wet myself."

"Omigod," I said, "what did you do?"

"I reached for my gun. It was under my pillow. I was all prepared for an incident like this. Only thing I hadn't counted on was the adrenaline factor. When I grabbed my gun, I squeezed one off prematurely and blew my pillow apart. It was a good pillow too. It was made in America by the smiley guy on television. It was one of his generation-two pillows that keep you from getting all sweaty."

"What about Grendel?"

"He left. Disappeared. Poof!"

"Have you reported this to the police?"

"I told them about Grendel days ago, when he first appeared."

"And?" I asked.

"And a couple police officers came to my apartment and talked to me, and when I told them about Grendel, they asked me if I indulged in recreational drugs."

"What did you tell them?"

"I said, 'Hell yes. Doesn't everyone?'"

"How'd that go over?" Connie asked.

"I thought they were being conversational, but turns out that was a sneaky cop trick question. They got all Officer Picky on me and said they were gonna have to search my apartment. My personal opinion is that they just wanted to look through my underwear drawer."

Lula rents a couple rooms in a colorful Victorian house in a marginally safe neighborhood. It had been a one-bedroom apartment with a sitting area and a kitchenette, but Lula's extensive wardrobe didn't fit in the one small closet. So Lula elected to sleep on the couch and turn the entire bedroom into a closet.

"Has anyone else in your house seen Grendel?" Connie asked Lula.

"No one will admit it, but I can't see how they don't hear him stomping around. I'm on the second floor. He has to go up the stairs, and it's not like ogres are dainty. And he's a real heavy breather. And there's the growling."

"Maybe it's just a large dog," Connie said. "Dogs growl."

"No way," Lula said. "It's ogre growling. Big difference. Huge difference. I know all about this because I googled it."

"How does he get into your apartment?" I asked. "Don't you lock your door?"

"I always lock my door. And my windows are closed, too. The thing is, he's not just an ogre. He's also a demon. They didn't say a lot about the demon part in the game instructions, but I'm thinking he has some nasty superpowers. Like he might be able to turn himself into slime and ooze under the door."

Connie cut her eyes to Lula. "You don't really believe any of this, do you?"

"The slime part is speculation," Lula said.

I hitched my messenger bag higher onto my shoulder. "I'm heading out. I'm going after the two low-bond FTAs. I promised to take Mrs. Manley and the kitties to the vet this afternoon, but I've got the morning."

"I'll ride along for the FTAs but I'm gonna pass on the vet," Lula said.

Lula, Bob, and I got into my bashed-in Cherokee and I pulled the files out of my bag.

"We've got Hooter Brown, the drug dealer, and Gloria Stitch, the shoplifter," I said to Lula. "Who do you want to snag first?"

"I don't know Gloria Stitch," Lula said, "but I know Hooter Brown. We go way back. I wouldn't mind saying hello to Hooter."

I handed her Hooter's file. "Give me an address."

"He's probably working now," Lula said. "He'll be hanging in front of one of the coffee shops by the government buildings. He's not high on the food chain of drug dealers but he has a decent piece of real estate on account of the big guys pushing the good stuff don't want to bother with the a.m. trade. Hooter fills in that spot and helps the bureaucrats get through the day with a little coke and a lot of weed."

I took Hamilton to State, headed across town, and cruised the area around the government buildings.

"There he is," Lula said. "He's on the corner, in front of the office building with the scaffolding."

I pulled up next to him and Lula rolled her window down.

"Hey, Hooter," she yelled. "How the hell are you?"

Hooter looked over and grinned. "Hey, ho," he said. "What's up? You want some blow?"

"I don't do any of that," Lula said. "I get high on life. Get in the car. I want to talk to you."

"You giving out for free?"

"You wish," Lula said. "I don't do any of that anymore either."

"Well what good are you then?"

"Get in the car and you can find out."

Hooter sauntered over and got into the back seat.

"Whoa, bitch," he said. "There's a dog back here. That's out of my comfort zone."

"That's Bob," Lula said. "He's cool. And you don't be feeding him anything bad. Anything bad happens to Bob on your account and I'll hold your ugly stump of a nose until you're dead."

Hooter was smiling. Lots of incredibly white teeth against very dark skin. "I've missed you," he said. "Where've you been? I heard you were working on the wrong side of the street."

"You mean the cop side?"

"Yeah."

"Stephanie and me are working for Vincent Plum Bail Bonds."

"That kind of straddles the line," Hooter said.

"You missed your court date," Lula said.

Hooter gingerly patted Bob on the head. "It was at an inconvenient time. I'm a wage earner. I gotta make a living. Besides, the poor dumb bastards who work in the big gray building across the street count on me. How they gonna get through the day without Hooter's help?"

"I hear you," Lula said, "but you have to reschedule."

"Yeah, I know the drill," Hooter said. "Give me another hour to work and then I'll go to the courthouse with you."

"No way," Lula said. "We'll come back in an hour, and you'll be gone."

"Girl, you got mean when you stopped being a ho," Hooter said.

Hooter opened the car door, jumped out, and took off down the street. Bob jumped out and took off after Hooter.

"Damnation," Lula said, wrenching her door open, hitting the ground running.

I cut the engine and ran flat out after Lula. I followed Lula around the corner and almost crashed into her.

"I can't run in these stupid sneakers," she said. "I'm used to running in heels."

I could see Hooter and Bob still running, half a block away. Hooter stopped, jumped on a Harley, revved it up, and peeled off into traffic. Bob watched Hooter for a moment, obviously decided the game was over, and sat down on the sidewalk. I whistled and Bob trotted back to me.

"I knew that was too easy," I said to Lula when we reached my Cherokee.

"Next time we'll creep up behind him and cuff him," Lula said. "I've never known him to be violent. He's just sneaky. I should have guessed he'd jump and run."

"Gloria Stitch is next up."

Lula paged through the Stitch file. "She should be home. She's eighty-one years old and she's in an assisted-living facility in Hamilton Township."

"Omigod."

"I could probably outrun her even in sneakers," Lula said. "So, this should turn out better."

This wasn't going to turn out better. This was going to be a disaster. There was no way I could apprehend an eighty-one-year-old woman and look like a hero.

"She might even be happy to see us," Lula said. "Maybe she just didn't have money for an Uber to take her to court. And now here we are giving her a free ride."

I was going to cling to that thought. It was a good thought.

I took Hamilton to Nottingham and followed the GPS directions to Sunnydale Senior Living. I parked in the visitor parking, and Lula and I entered the lobby of the four-story building. Bob stayed in the car with the window cracked.

"This is nice," Lula said. "It's real classy with the potted plants and conversation areas. And the reception desk looks like a hotel instead of an old people's home."

I checked in at the reception desk and asked for Gloria. I was told she was most likely in the dining room on the fourth floor.

"They got a dining room here," Lula said, entering the elevator with me. "And the elevator is clean and doesn't smell like a burrito and fries. I wouldn't mind living here."

We got off at the fourth floor and followed the people migrating to food. I had my file in hand with Gloria's photo. Gray hair. Caucasian. Large-frame animal-print glasses. Used a walker.

"Here's another advantage," Lula said. "If I lived here, I could beat all these folks to the buffet."

I spotted Gloria queued up at the double doors to the dining room. I eased my way through the residents and introduced myself.

"What happened to your eyes?" she asked.

"I tripped and fell," I said.

She nodded. "I see that a lot. People are always face-planting here. You reach for your walker, and it rolls away and *splat* . . . you're on the floor."

"You missed your court date," I said. "We're here to help you get a new date."

"I appreciate your offer of help, but it isn't necessary," Gloria said. "You get to be of an age where you don't need to go through all that nonsense."

"Unfortunately, that's not true," I said. "You need to go to the courthouse and get a new date scheduled. It will only take a few minutes."

"I'm so sorry," she said. "I'm sure you went to a lot of trouble to drive over here. And I know this is your job. And I don't want it to look like you aren't doing your job, but I'm going to have to decline. I get these court requests all the time, and I simply don't see the point in honoring them."

"Yeah, but you stole a bunch of clothes," Lula said.

"It wasn't a bunch of clothes," she said. "Lynette Bolger died, and I needed a new dress for her celebration-of-life event."

"I guess I could understand that," Lula said. "Except why didn't you just buy a dress?"

"I used to buy everything," Gloria said, "and then one day I found out that I could simply take what I wanted. It's much better than buying. They run a little bus once a week to the mall and we get to shop around for an hour or two and then the bus brings us back here. It's very pleasant."

"That's stealing," Lula said.

"Not stealing," Gloria said. "It's shoplifting, and if you're a senior or destitute, it falls into the RAM program. Redistribution of Available Merchandise. It supplements Social Security and Medicare. It's an entitlement program."

"I never heard of that program," Lula said, "but I know a lot of people who participate. Most of them are in jail."

The doors to the dining room opened and everyone surged forward.

"It's been lovely chatting with you, but I have to go," Gloria said. "If you aren't at the front of the line there's no more carrot cake left for dessert and Jack Hestler coughs on everything. You always want to be ahead of Jack."

I stepped away from the lunch line and headed for the elevator.

"What are we going to do with Gloria?" Lula asked. "Are you going to come back after lunch and put her in cuffs?"

"No," I said. "I'm going to leave and never come back. If Vinnie wants to apprehend her, that's his problem."

"Is that on account of RAM?"

"No. I'm walking away because she's not going to cooperate,

and I'll look like I'm abusing the elderly and I'll feel like a jerk if I put her in cuffs and drag her out of the building."

"Yeah, it could be hard to get her out of here. Not to mention, these old folks stick together. They could turn into an angry mob. And what are we supposed to do if they try to run us over with their scooters? We'd probably get into trouble if we shoot at them."

"No doubt."

CHAPTER NINE

Bob was panting and drooling on the side window when we reached my Cherokee. I let him out, he lifted his leg, relieved himself on my left rear tire, and jumped back into the car.

"We should be thinking about lunch," Lula said. "Bob looks hungry."

"What do you think Bob would like for lunch?"

"He wants chicken salad from that bakery and deli on Nottingham. We passed it on our way in. They make excellent chicken salad, and they make fries with duck fat. Duck-fat fries are the next-best thing to an orgasm."

My sex life had been skimpy lately with Morelli working overtime and flying off to Miami, so a runner-up to an orgasm had a lot of appeal.

Fifteen minutes later I parked in the lot next to the deli.

"I'll wait out here with Bob," I said to Lula. "Get chicken salad on a croissant for Bob and one for me, and make sure mine comes with extra fries."

When Lula came back to the SUV she had chicken salad croissants for everyone plus a big bucket of fries, coleslaw, chips, drinks, and a white bakery box filled with pastries.

"I had a hard time making choices in there," she said. "This is a five-star deli-bakery."

We tailgated off the Cherokee, and Bob was done with his croissant before I finished unwrapping mine. I gave him a handful of fries on a napkin and told him he had to pace himself.

"He keeps eating like that and he's going to get acid reflux," Lula said. "He's gotta learn to savor."

Halfway through my croissant I looked down at Bob. The French fries were long gone and so was the napkin.

"Can't blame him for eating the napkin," Lula said. "It probably had soaked up duck fat. I might have eaten it too."

I finished up with an apple tart and Lula grazed through the rest of the box on the way to the office.

"I'm going to leave you and Bob at the office," I said. "I promised Mrs. Manley I'd take her cats to the vet for their checkup."

"You're a good person to offer to do that," Lula said.

"I got suckered into it."

"Still, you're living up to your promise." Lula stopped eating and leaned forward. "I could swear that's Farcus Trundle's truck two cars in front of us. It's a big black truck with the back sort of dented in from where he shoved you out of his driveway."

We all stopped for a light, and when the light turned the black truck peeled off Hamilton, onto Olden Avenue.

"That's him. I can see his big bowling-ball head," Lula said. "He's going home."

This wasn't a good time to run into Trundle, but I didn't want to throw away a shot at capturing him. It was my job to take him down, but more than that, I didn't like him. He was a horrible human being. He did bad things to good people. He smashed his truck into my car. And his girlfriend punched me in the face. I wasn't crazy about her either. I followed him onto Olden, keeping a respectable distance.

"Are you thinking about making an apprehension?" Lula asked. "Should I get my gun out?"

"No gun. Let's see how it plays."

"How about if you follow him home, and when he gets out of his truck you run him over?"

It was a pleasant thought but might not go well in court.

He turned onto a side street and when I turned, he put his foot to the floor and raced down the street.

"He spotted you," Lula said.

Not hard to do with the front of my Cherokee crumpled.

"Keep your eyes on him," I said. "I'm not doing ninety on this side street."

"He's way ahead of you and he turned right again," Lula said.

I turned right when I reached the corner, but the black truck was nowhere in sight. I continued down the street, I stopped at the cross street, and I was suddenly hit from behind. BAM.

"It's him!" Lula yelled. "It's Farcus. He must have gone around the block and come up behind you."

BAM. He hit me again, bouncing my Cherokee halfway into the intersection.

"That does it," Lula said. "He knocked Bob off the seat and my pastries all spilled out. I'm going to shoot the sonovabitch."

"No! Not a good idea!"

Lula was out of her seat belt, turned around, and two-handing her gun. BANG!

Trundle laid rubber with the truck in reverse. He executed a U-turn in the middle of the block and drove away. Bob climbed onto the back seat. Lula put the pastries back into their box and fastened her seat belt. I looked at the bullet hole in my rear window and slowly drove back to Hamilton Avenue.

I parked in front of the bail bonds office, and we all got out and looked at the damage to the back of my Cherokee.

"It's not so bad," Lula said. "He hit you straight on. That's good on account of you can still drive it, being that the wheels weren't affected. It doesn't even look like you're leaking anything. You aren't going to be able to open the tailgate door, but that's okay because you got four more you can use."

"Always look on the bright side," I said to Lula.

"You bet your ass," Lula said.

I handed Bob's leash to Lula. "I have to pick up some cats."

"Not much of a bright side about that," Lula said.

I chugged off to the Manley house and parked in the driveway. Mrs. Manley answered the door on the first ring.

"We're all ready to go," she said. "I have the other kitties corralled in a bedroom. I didn't want to take a chance on them escaping when the door was open."

Iris, Snuggles, Red Cat, and Mr. Meow Meow were in cat carriers stacked up in the foyer.

We each took two carriers and carted them to my Cherokee.

"Oh, my goodness," Mrs. Manley said. "What happened to your car?"

"Minor accident," I said. "Nothing to worry about."

We put the cats on the back seat and Mrs. Manley got in next to me.

"I take the kitties to the vet clinic in the strip mall across from the diner on Route 33. It's just off Hamilton," Mrs. Manley said. "The cat rescue has an account there."

The cats were meowing and clawing at the doors on their cages.

"Are they okay back there?" I asked. "They sound unhappy."

"They aren't very good travelers, but they'll settle down in a minute or two."

"Have you talked to Andy today?" I asked her. "Did he stop around again?"

"He called this morning to make sure we were okay, and I told him you were taking me to the vet. He thought that was incredibly nice of you. He said he always liked you. He thought you were a good person."

"I'd really like to talk to him. Maybe you could help us get together. I've tried calling and texting him, but he never answers me."

"He's a terrible communicator," Mrs. Manley said. "He never returns my calls either. It's like his head is in the clouds. He's always been creative and sometimes I think he gets lost in his projects. He's been writing stories lately and putting them on his blog. I've never read any of them because they're just for his blogger friends."

This was a conversation I wanted to continue, but I was having a hard time focusing because the meowing had turned into full-on howling.

"Are you sure they're all right back there?" I asked. "They sound distressed."

"It's Red Cat. He's an instigator. Once he starts misbehaving, everyone else joins in. I'm sure they'll be fine, although it wouldn't hurt if you could drive a little faster."

I would have loved to drive faster, but something was rattling under the Cherokee and there was a vibration in the steering wheel. I was afraid if I drove faster the car would fall apart.

"Holy cow," I said. "What is that smell?"

"It might be Mr. Meow Meow. I think he made poo poo. He has irritable bowel syndrome. It flares up when he's upset or when he gets nervous."

I was counting the seconds. I had the strip mall in sight. I hit the button to open the windows and moderately fresh air poured in. A couple beats later, I was at the parking lot entrance.

"The vet clinic is to the left," Mrs. Manley said.

I turned left and found a spot in front of the clinic.

"Right on time," Mrs. Manley said. "This shouldn't take long."

I helped her carry the crates into the waiting room. There were two other people waiting. They both had cats in crates.

"I'll wait outside," I said. "I need to catch up on my email."

Mrs. Manley took a seat and smiled at me. "No problem at all."

I went outside and took stock of my SUV. Front smashed in. Back smashed in. Interior reeking of sick cat. Something very wrong with its internal operations. (Just like Mr. Meow Meow.) The windows were wide open. I tossed the key onto the driver's seat, and I stepped away. If there was a God in heaven and I had any luck at all, someone would steal the disaster that used to be a Jeep Cherokee.

A half hour later, Mrs. Manley came out of the clinic, carrying two crates. Unfortunately, no one had stepped forward to relieve me of the Cherokee, so I went into the clinic and helped carry the rest of the cats out.

"Are they okay?" I asked.

"Yes. And they all got their shots."

The cats were hunkered down, sulking in the back of their respective crates.

"They cleaned and disinfected Mr. Meow Meow's carrier," Mrs. Manley said.

No kidding. I slid it onto the back seat and my eyes were burning from the fumes mingling with the lingering stench of cat poo.

I got behind the wheel, chugged out of the parking lot, and headed for Hamilton Avenue. "About Andy," I said to Mrs. Manley. "Does he come home for dinner sometimes? Does he bring his laundry home?"

"Now and then," she said. "Tonight is meat loaf and mashed potatoes. I always make that for Thursday dinner. It's Andrew's favorite. When he was working for Plover, he always came home right away after work, and I would reheat everything for him. Last week he stopped in for a few minutes and got takeout. He took enough for two people. It's one of the reasons I think he has a girlfriend."

"Did he ever mention her name? Would it be Sissy?"

"He's never mentioned a Sissy."

"How about Duncan? He used to have a friend named Duncan."

"No. He's never mentioned Duncan. Andrew mostly worked

and spent time on his computer, playing games and writing his stories. I think he had computer friends."

"He never went out to socialize?"

"He socialized on his computer. That's how they do it now. That might be how he met his girlfriend."

I made it to the Manley house without the car dying and without a single cat meowing or pooping. I got Mrs. Manley and her cats safely inside, reminded her I'd like to talk to Andy, and vibrated and clanked all the way to the office. I parked at the curb in front of the office and there was a loud *clunk*. I got out, looked under the car, and saw something lying on the road. It was big and black with grease, and I had no clue what it was.

Lula, Bob, and Connie came out and looked under the car with me.

"That don't look good," Lula said. "That looks like an important component of internal combustion. And I think it definitely belongs stuck up in your car."

"Do you know what it is?" I asked her.

"My knowledge of cars is more cosmetic," Lula said. "I know about things like how to work the radio and choose a paint color."

"I don't know what it is either," Connie said, "but I'm pretty sure the car isn't going to run without it."

Lula sniffed at it. "This car doesn't smell good. It smells like sick doody."

"It's from Mr. Meow Meow. He got nervous. He has IBS."

"Maybe he's getting too much gluten in his food," Lula said. "I've been hearing a lot about gluten and I'm thinking of eliminating it."

"You would have to stop eating doughnuts," I said.

"Say what?"

"Doughnuts have a lot of gluten in them."

"I didn't hear about that," Lula said. "That doesn't sound right. Doughnuts are a major food group."

"What about your car?" Connie asked. "Do you want me to have it towed somewhere?"

"Have Sanchez Auto Body pick it up. They'll be able to tell me if the car is worth fixing. And if it isn't worth fixing, they'll get me scrap-metal money from the junkyard."

"Are we going car shopping?" Lula asked.

I took Bob's leash from her. "No. I'm short on cash. No captures, no cash. No cash, no new car. And I want to wait to hear from Sanchez. Bob and I are going to walk to my parents' house. We could use some exercise, and when I get there, I can borrow Big Blue."

Big Blue is a 1953 powder-blue-and-white, gas-sucking Buick Roadmaster that Grandma Mazur inherited a bunch of years ago. After numerous speeding tickets, Grandma lost her license, but she kept her car. It lives in the single-car garage at the back of the house, and I get to use the beast when I'm desperate.

Bob trotted in front of me, happy to be out and walking. I was feeling the same. I grew up in the Burg and I could walk the streets with my eyes closed and know exactly where I was at any moment. I'd been glad to leave and get out of the fishbowl, but it was good to be able to come back sometimes and get dinner or borrow a car.

Grandma was in the living room, watching television, when Bob bounded in. She was in my father's chair, and she had a bag of chips in her lap and a drink in her hand.

"Perfect timing," she said to me. "Your father is in Atlantic City with his lodge. Boys'-night-out bus trip. He won't be back until late, and your mother is grocery shopping, so I'm having hors d'oeuvres and a cocktail. Help yourself to whatever you can find in the kitchen. Truth is, it's kind of skimpy, so you need to be creative."

"What are you drinking?"

"I wanted to have something classy like a martini, but we didn't have any of the right stuff, so this is whiskey poured into a martini glass." She held the chip bag out to me. "Want some? They're spicy barbecue."

"I'll pass. I can't stay. I came to borrow the Buick."

"What happened to your Jeep?"

"It got smashed by an FTA."

"What happened to your face?"

"It got punched by the FTA's girlfriend."

"That sucks," Grandma said. "Are you sure you don't want a whiskeytini?"

"It's tempting, but no. Things to do. Places to go. People to see."

"Anybody I know?"

"I'm still looking for Nutsy."

"I heard his parents' car got blown up," Grandma said. "I can't imagine who would do such a thing to the Manleys."

"Do you have any ideas?"

Grandma sipped her whiskeytini and smiled. "I suppose I've got one or two."

"Me too," I said. "You go first."

"I think it has to do with Nutsy. It looked like Nutsy had settled into his job with Plover. He was living at home. He wasn't doing anything nuts. And then there's this robbery. And he's accused of stealing a tray of diamonds *after* the robbery. And then he disappears, but he's still in the area because people see him from time to time. Just glimpses of him. Like he's in hiding. So, there's something going on here, but the diamond robbery doesn't fit. I can't see it going down like that with Nutsy. I could see him taking something on a dare, but everyone would know about it. And he'd give it back."

I nodded. "My exact thoughts," I said to Grandma.

"There was some talk about the robbery and all in the beginning," Grandma said, "but it got old pretty fast. Nutsy's stunts aren't exactly news anymore. Now all of a sudden, his parents' car gets blown up. Now it's getting interesting again."

"Do you think someone thought it was Nutsy's car?"

"Not for a second," Grandma said. "Everybody knows Nutsy has a motorcycle. I think this was a warning. I think you're not the only one after Nutsy. Someone's trying to flush him out."

"Who?" I asked her.

"I don't know," Grandma said. "Who do you think?"

"I don't know who it is, either. Maybe someone who thinks he's got the tray of stolen diamonds."

"Plover?" Grandma asked.

"I guess that's one possibility, but I can't see him skulking around under cover of darkness, planting a bomb."

"He could have hired someone."

"Or there could be undiscovered people involved."

"I suppose you want me to help you unravel this mystery," Grandma said.

"Keep your ear to the ground," I told her.

CHAPTER TEN

Bob and I rumbled out of my parents' garage in the Buick. I drove past Morelli's house to make sure it hadn't burned down. I drove past the Manley house to make sure Nutsy's Yamaha SR400 wasn't in the driveway. I drove past the office to see if the Jeep had been picked up. Morelli's house looked fine. No motorcycle in the Manley driveway. My Jeep was still in front of the bail bonds office.

"I have a problem," I said to Bob. "It's meat loaf night at the Manleys', and I'd like to hang out to see if Nutsy shows up. Rule number one on a stakeout is to be inconspicuous, and a '53 powder-blue-and-white Buick isn't inconspicuous. Lula's fire-engine-red Firebird isn't inconspicuous either. I could borrow a car from Ranger but that could get complicated."

Bob looked like he was paying attention, but since he couldn't speak human, he wasn't able to make a contribution. I turned back into the Burg and drove to my parents' house. My mother was home from shopping and her car was parked in the driveway. It was a very inconspicuous silver Camry.

"All I have to do is talk her into letting me borrow the Camry," I said to Bob. "Easy, right?"

Bob's mind was elsewhere. He was looking at the house with big bright eyes, remembering hugs and dog treats. I parked at the curb and kept a tight grip on Bob's leash in case he remembered the treats with too much enthusiasm. Grandma was in the kitchen with my mom when Bob and I walked in.

"Back so soon?" Grandma asked. "We're deciding on dinner. We don't have to make such a big deal out of it with your father in AC. We were thinking we might get takeout."

"You and Bob are welcome to have takeout with us," my mom said. "Or we could heat up some leftover pot roast and gravy."

"I'm going to pass on dinner. I need to be someplace at five thirty. I was hoping I could borrow the Camry for an hour or two."

"Your grandmother said you came for the Buick," my mom said. "Is there something wrong with it? It hasn't been serviced in ages."

"The Buick is fine, but I need a car that blends in. I'm still looking for Nutsy, and I think he might show up at his parents' house for dinner tonight. The Buick is too recognizable. He might spot it and get scared away."

"Good thinking," Grandma said. "Do you have inside information that he's going to be sneaking home?"

"I talked to his mother, and she said that she's making his favorite meal tonight. Meat loaf."

"That's worth a stakeout," Grandma said. "And it works out perfect. We can pick up some pizza at Pino's and head for the Manleys'. We should wear hoodies, so no one recognizes us. This is going to be good. I don't even care if I miss *Jeopardy!*"

"No one is going on a stakeout," my mother said. "We'll get pizza delivered. The Manleys just got their car blown up. They don't need people parked across the street spying on them. This isn't a television show, and we aren't the police."

"Stephanie's almost the police," Grandma said. "Besides, we're trying to help the Manleys. We think someone is after Nutsy and they're trying to flush him out by terrorizing his family."

My mother stopped unpacking groceries and looked at me. "Is that true?"

"It might be," I said. "I don't want to involve you and Grandma. I thought Bob and I would sort of casually hang out and watch the house. I don't have authority to make an apprehension. I just want to see where Nutsy goes. Maybe get a chance to talk to him. I've been trying to get in touch but he's avoiding me."

"I don't like this," my mom said. "Celia is a good person. And Nutsy has always been odd, but I've never heard that he was mean or dishonest. I don't like hearing about this."

"That's why we should do something," Grandma said. "We need to do some investigating. And we could have pizza. It would be like a picnic."

"Good Lord, it's not a picnic. You're investigating a lunatic who blew up a car," my mother said.

"Okay, there's a little danger and possibly insanity involved," Grandma said, "but it's not like a zombie apocalypse or Armageddon."

My mother went hands on hips. "Someone blew up a car."

"People are blowing up Stephanie's cars all the time," Grandma said.

"Not *all* the time," I said.

"The important thing is that Stephanie needs to talk to Nutsy," Grandma said.

"If you're going to do this and you need the Camry, I'm driving," my mom said to me. "I don't know if you're still covered under our insurance policy."

———

At five thirty my mom, Grandma, Bob, and I were parked half a block away from the Manley house. We had three large Pino's pizzas. One with the works. One with barbecued chicken. One with sausage and no onions for Bob. We didn't get drinks because we couldn't pee in a jelly jar like guys do on stakeouts.

"I've got a good feeling about this," Grandma said. "I think Nutsy's going to show up. He knows it's meat loaf night and he's probably under a lot of stress, and there's nothing better for stress than meat loaf. It's comfort food. There would be less of a problem with drugs in this country if people ate more meat loaf."

At five forty-five a Nissan Sentra stopped in front of the house and Harry Manley, Nutsy's father, got out. He thanked the driver, walked to the front door, and let himself in.

At six thirty we were stuffed full of pizza, slouched back, and on the lookout for Nutsy. Grandma was in the front, next to my mom. Bob and I were in the back. Bob was stretched out on the seat with his head in my lap. Grandma was nodding off and snorting herself awake. My mom was steely eyed and vigilant.

The sun had set but it was still light enough to clearly see down the street.

I heard the bike before I saw it. Not the whine of a crotch rocket. Not the deep-throated rumble of a hog. My cousin Paul had a Yamaha SR400, and he called it a sputter putt.

The 400 approached from the opposite direction. It rolled into the Manleys' driveway and came to a stop. The driver didn't remove his helmet. It had a full-face mirrored visor, but I knew it was Nutsy. He was lanky and a little too tall for the 400. He let himself in through the front door, being careful not to let any cats escape.

"That's Nutsy," I said to my mom and grandma.

"Maybe you should go in and say hello," my mom said. "He might be happy to see you. You were school friends. You could get to talk to him."

"We weren't friends," I said. "We knew each other. I'm afraid he would be polite in front of his parents and then leave and lead us on a wild goose chase. I want to see where he's staying. There's a chance that he's with Duncan Dugan, and I need to bring him in."

Grandma was awake and sitting up. "Dugan's the man who robbed Plover's," she said. "He's the one with all the broken bones."

"Do you think Nutsy was in cahoots with Duncan on the robbery?" my mom asked.

"It's possible," I said. "They knew each other. There's a connection."

"You could get an almost-new car if you could grab Dugan and Nutsy," Grandma said to me. "It would be a twofer. Dugan is a high-money bond and Plover would give you a big bag of money for Nutsy."

"Dugan is a given," I said. "I haven't decided about handing Nutsy over to Plover."

The Manleys' front door opened and Nutsy, helmet already in place, walked out with a small insulated cooler. He strapped it onto his passenger seat, straddled the bike, and kick-started it.

"That was fast," Grandma said. "He wasn't even in there for ten minutes. He must have called ahead."

He turned in the driveway, and we all ducked down out of sight. There was the sound of the bike moving away from us, and my mom popped up with her hands on the wheel and her foot on the gas pedal.

"I got him in my sights," Grandma said. "Don't get too close. We don't want to spook him."

I was leaning forward in the back seat to get a better view. Bob was sitting up next to me, feeling the excitement, not knowing where to put it.

"He's heading across town," Grandma said.

"Where's Dugan live?"

"By the button factory," I told her.

"He could be heading there."

It was dark enough that my mom had to use her lights, making it easier for Nutsy to pick up a tail. He turned down a side street, turned again at the first corner, and picked up speed.

My mom dropped back, still keeping him in sight. He turned again, moving into a more urban area with office buildings and restaurants.

"He just cut down that alley," Grandma said. "He's going behind the big brick building."

My mom killed her lights and turned into the alley at full

speed. She was hunched over the wheel. Her grip was white knuckled.

"I'm on it," she said, eyes narrowed.

"Maybe you should slow down," I said. "This alley is single lane and there's not good visibility."

"No problem," she said. "I can see him ahead of me."

"Yes, but he's on a skinny little bike and you're in a Camry."

I could see the end of the alley just ahead. There was a U-Haul box truck parked on one side of the alley and a brick wall on the other.

"You can't fit," I said to my mom. "It's too narrow."

"He's turning right," she said. "I can make it."

"You can't make it!" I yelled.

Bang! Clank! Both side mirrors got ripped off the Camry. Bob gave a single woof, but my mom never blinked. She wrenched the wheel around and made a sharp right turn.

"Do you see him?" she asked Grandma. "Is he still in front of us?"

"He's two cars ahead," Grandma said.

My mom switched her lights on. "Let me know if he turns."

"I think that's him taking a left at the next intersection," Grandma said.

My mom turned but kept her distance. After a quarter mile the 400's lights blinked off.

"What the heck?" Grandma said.

I lowered my window and stuck my head out. "I can hear him," I said. "He's off to the right. I think he cut across an empty lot just ahead and came out on the next street."

My mom stopped at the empty lot. A small ranch house was on

the other side of the block. Lights were on in the back windows. A dog was barking.

"He must have driven between houses," she said.

She turned at the corner and drove past the houses. There was no sign of Nutsy. I thought I might have heard the 400 in the distance, but it was very faint.

"This is disappointing," my mom said.

"I thought for sure you were going to jump the curb and cut through the field," Grandma said. "You were really into it. You were kicking ass."

"I think I might have gotten a little carried away," my mom said.

"I liked the part where you barreled through the alley," Grandma said.

My mom looked out her window at the spot where the side mirror used to be attached. "We should go back to get the mirrors and leave a note in case the U-Haul truck got damaged."

"And then we're going to go home, and we'll all have a whiskeytini," Grandma said. "A big one."

————

I skipped the whiskeytini, and Bob and I motored home in the Buick. Bob loved the car with the spacious bench seat in the front. I was less enamored. It drove like a refrigerator on wheels and got about three miles to the gallon. Jay Leno might have been able to look sexy in it. When I got behind the wheel, I looked like the sort of woman who would wear cotton granny panties and a hairnet.

I was in my apartment for less than three minutes when Morelli called.

"This is crap," he said. "The trial is going nowhere. I'm in a cheesy green hotel with water savers in everything that has water. There's no room service. And I'm running out of clean clothes." There was a beat of silence. "How's Bob? How are you doing?"

"Bob is great. I'm in a slump. I can't catch anyone. I find them. I chase them down. I lose them."

"If you're referring to Nutsy and Duncan Dugan, I heard someone blew up the Manleys' car."

"Do you know who did it?"

"No," Morelli said. "Do you?"

"No. Nutsy dropped in on his parents earlier tonight. I think he picked up dinner. I tailed him across town but lost him on King Street. He cut across an open lot, and I wasn't able to follow him."

"He still riding the 400?"

"Yep."

"He's had that since high school."

"He's staying in the area, but he's hiding. I'd like to know why."

"Do you think he stole the tray of diamonds?"

"My brain says yes. My gut says no."

"Not to say anything disparaging about your brain, but I'd go with your gut."

"Bob is standing in the kitchen looking hungry. How often do you feed him?"

"Twice a day and he gets a treat at bedtime."

"That's all?"

"How often have you been feeding him?" Morelli asked.

"It varies. I guess he eats when I eat."

"Including the doughnuts?"

"Yeah. And then sometimes he eats other people's food if they aren't careful."

"He's lactose intolerant. Don't let him eat cheese."

"Does that include when it's on pizza?"

"Oh man, did you feed him pizza?"

"We were staking out the Manley house and I didn't have dog food with me."

"He'll be okay, but make sure you get him outside fast when he goes to the door."

———

I was outside with Bob when I saw Ranger's 911 roll into my building's parking lot. It was the third time in an hour that I'd had to take Bob out and we were now sitting on the curb.

Ranger parked a few feet away and walked over to me. "Are you waiting for someone?" he asked.

"I didn't know Bob was lactose intolerant and I fed him cheese. We're waiting to see if he's empty."

"I'm on my way to a break-in and robbery in Hamilton Township, and I saw your Cherokee getting loaded onto Sanchez's flatbed. What happened?"

"Do you really want to know?"

"No," Ranger said. "I see the Buick parked here. Do you want a loaner?"

"Yes. I can't sneak around in the Buick."

"I'll have something dropped off."

CHAPTER ELEVEN

I dragged myself out of bed and shuffled off to the bathroom. The sun was shining, and the day had started without me. I took a fast shower with the hopes of waking up. I got dressed in my usual uniform of T-shirt and jeans. I went to the bed and looked down at Bob. His eyes were open, but he wasn't moving. It had been a long night for both of us. It had been after midnight when Bob made his final trek down to the parking lot.

"Time to get up," I said. "We have things to do. You should have breakfast. You'll feel better."

Bob plodded after me, into the kitchen.

"Do you have to go out first?" I asked him.

Bob looked at the door and then he looked at me. He didn't move.

"Okay then," I said. "I'm going to take that as a no."

I filled Bob's bowl with dog kibble, and I stared into the refrigerator for a couple beats. Nothing jumped out at me, so I settled on a frozen waffle with peanut butter. When in doubt, there's always peanut butter.

"I'm sorry about the cheese last night," I said to Bob. "I didn't know you were lactose intolerant."

Bob gobbled his dog kibble and came to me for some ear scratches. Bob wasn't the sort of dog who held a grudge. I gave Rex fresh water and filled his food cup with hamster food and a peanut. This concluded my duties as earth mother. I hooked Bob up to his leash and we went downstairs.

The Buick was gone and in its place was a shiny black Ford Explorer. It was a Rangeman fleet car. This wasn't the first time Ranger had left a car for me, so I knew the drill. I reached under the right front wheel well and removed two keys. One for the car and one for the locked gun box under the driver's seat. The note on the passenger seat told me that Big Blue had been returned to my parents' garage. I got behind the wheel and texted a single word to Ranger. *Thanks.*

"This is going to be an excellent day," I said to Bob. "My black eyes are turning green and orange, and my nose isn't swollen anymore. In a couple days I'll be as good as new. I have a nice car to drive, and I think I'm closing in on Nutsy and Duncan Dugan."

When Bob and I walked into the office, Lula was on the couch with her iPad, Connie was at her desk, and Vinnie's door was closed.

"Is he here?" I asked Connie.

"No," she said. "He's downtown, bailing someone out."

I got coffee and returned to the desk.

"Your Jeep got picked up," Connie said. "Sanchez emailed me last night. I printed it out for you." She handed me the email. "Bottom line is that your frame is bent, there's massive bodywork to be done, and the thing that was lying on the ground was critical to the performance of the car. He also said that the car smells like nothing he's ever smelled before and doesn't want to ever smell anything like that again. He said for a lot of money, he can fix everything but the smell. He's suggesting you junk it."

I stuffed the email into my messenger bag. "Tell him to junk it."

"You don't look unhappy about your car," Lula said to me.

"I'm in a very good mood," I said. "Every single traffic light was green for me this morning. And I didn't get stuck behind a school bus. And I have a nice car to drive in place of my Jeep."

Lula looked out the front window. "I'm thinking that's a Rangeman car," Lula said. "No wonder you're in a good mood. Tell me you started your day taking care of business with Mr. Hot and Handsome."

"Sorry, there was no business. He saw the Jeep getting winched onto Sanchez's flatbed and he gave me a loaner."

"Too bad," Lula said. "It'd be good to know one of us was getting some. Grendel stole one of my dresses last night. It was from my Hawaii collection. And there's a pink rabbit-fur jacket missing too. That dress is going to look terrible with that jacket. I don't know what he was thinking. This ogre is out of control."

"How do you know it was Grendel?" I asked.

"Who else would it be?" Lula said. "Everything was in place when I went to bed, and when I got up this morning, I was missing a dress and a jacket."

"Did he wake you up with his breathing and growling?"

"No," Lula said. "I slept through the night. He must have been extra sneaky."

"So, you think Grendel is a cross-dresser," Connie said.

"I don't know what to think," Lula said. "Just now, I've been reading about ogres, and there's no mention of ogres being fashion-forward. It seems to me that the average ogre is a nasty bugger, but I think I could hold my own with one. I see them as being big but stupid with bad breath. Like, if an ogre is hungry, he could eat you, but I figure you could distract him with a sandwich or some cookies. So, I keep a plate of Oreos by me when I'm sleeping. Nobody can resist Oreos. Now, an ogre that's a demon is a whole other ball game. A demon is evil. There's no distracting evil. Not even with Oreos that are double stuffed. It's the demon part of Grendel that worries me."

"Did Grendel eat the cookies last night?"

"No, on account of I woke up at two o'clock to go to the bathroom and I was hungry when I got back to bed, and I ate the cookies."

"It's hard to imagine Grendel wearing your Hawaii dress," I said.

"Maybe he doesn't intend to wear it," Lula said. "The demon part of him could want it for some voodoo ritual. He could be interested in harvesting my DNA off it to use for evil purposes. It would be hard to do because I haven't worn that dress since it came back from the dry cleaner. Of course, Grendel had no way of knowing that."

"You don't seem to be terrified," I said. "If something was showing up in my bedroom at night and I didn't know who or what it was, I'd be terrified. What I'm seeing from you is that you're annoyed because you can't sleep and now it's taking your clothes."

"I was terrified in the beginning, but then nothing happened. I wasn't attacked or anything. And on top of that I'm real brave."

"Is it possible that you're imagining all this?" Connie asked.

"It occurred to me," Lula said. "Like maybe it was a dream. Or maybe it was too much tequila before bedtime."

"And?" Connie asked.

"And I'm pretty sure it's Grendel. There's the brown hair on my carpet. I think it must have come off his hairy foot."

"Grendel doesn't wear shoes?" Connie asked.

"I've never seen his feet but it's possible. Hobbits don't wear shoes and they have hairy feet, so maybe ogres are like that too," Lula said.

I'm used to Grandma Mazur talking about people getting beamed up into alien spaceships, getting chased by Bigfoot, and seeing ghosts march across the Morgan Street cemetery every May 23. So Lula believing in Grendel and hobbits didn't seem all that odd to me. Okay, I had my doubts about Grendel. It would be more believable if it was Grendel's American cousin. And it would be totally believable if it was some whack job dressing up in an ogre suit and creeping around in the dark.

"I'm still going with the big dog theory," Connie said. "A dog would shed on your carpet and make scratches in your door."

"The scratches were at six feet," Lula said. "And they were deep. I shouldn't be talking about this because now I'm getting a little terrified, and I decided I was going to stay calm."

"We should head out," I said. "I want to drive around the neighborhoods by the button factory."

"Are you thinking Duncan Dugan might have gone home?" Lula asked.

"No, but he might be in the area. And his pal Nutsy might be with him."

"I'm in favor of doing a ride-around," Lula said. "You got a Rangeman car, and they always smell good. Like new-car smell and testosterone."

I'd have bet money that by the end of the day the car was going to smell like Bob.

I buckled myself in behind the wheel and Plover called.

"I have to talk to you," Plover said. "I'm at the store. Is it possible for you to meet me here?"

"Sure," I said. "I'll be there in twenty minutes."

"Small change of plans," I said to Lula. "This shouldn't take long."

———

King Street was quiet at this time of the morning. Stores were just beginning to open. Not a lot of foot traffic. Plover's doors were still locked. He saw me approach and he opened the door. Lula and Bob trooped in after me.

"I brought my assistant and security dog," I said to Plover. "I hope that's okay."

"Sure," Plover said. "I just want to know how it's going."

"I'm making some progress," I said.

"What kind of progress? What does that mean? I don't want to sound cranky, but I thought you might have found him by now."

"It hasn't even been a week."

"I guess that's true. It seems longer. I just want this to be done. I want some closure. I want to know what happened to my diamonds. And why did he do this? I gave him a job. I trusted him."

"There's the possibility that Andrew Manley didn't take the diamonds," I said. "Did anyone else know your security code? Did anyone else know the combination to your safe?"

"My father and my brother. They've both passed."

"Anyone else? A former or current employee?"

"This is a small family business," Plover said. "My wife helps out during high-traffic times. Weekends and holidays. Over Christmas I have a salesclerk, Mindy Spurling. She's been with me for years, working part-time. She's never had access to the safe or had a need to know the security code. I can't think of anyone else."

"How about a cleaning crew?"

"This store doesn't require a lot. My wife and Mindy and I do daily dusting and polishing. Every Thursday night I have Tidy Cleaners come in and do floors and the bathroom. I'm always here so they don't need to know the security code."

Ranger was responsible for the security system. I knew there wouldn't be a leak there.

"Did you hear about Andy's parents' car?" Plover asked. "Someone planted a bomb. It's unbelievable. Why would someone want to blow up the Manleys? Are they part of a crime family? Is that why their son took my diamonds? I don't like being mixed up in this. I run a family business. I'm boring. I like being boring. My socks always match. I've been married for forty-two years. I have a ten-pound dog and five grandchildren. In all the years the Plovers have been in business in this very same location, we've never been robbed. We've never lost a single stone. And now this!"

"I can see it's all been a traumatic experience for you," Lula said to Plover, "but you've got nothing to worry about. We're closing in on the suspect. We've got him in our crosshairs. It won't be long now."

"That's good to hear," Plover said. "What do you know? Is he in the area? Do you have an address? Does he have an accomplice? Has he tried to fence my merchandise?"

"That's all classified information right now," Lula said. "We'll give you a full report as soon as our suspicions are verified."

"Is there anything else?" I asked Plover. "Do you have any new information?"

He shook his head. "No."

"There's a show on the animal channel that you should watch," Lula said to Plover. "It's about anxiety issues and how to control them. It's mostly about dogs and cats and it was about a chicken once, but you might find it helpful until we can get your problem resolved."

Plover was at a loss for words. If I were in his shoes, I wouldn't have known how to respond to that either.

"I need to get back to work," I said to Plover. "I'll be in touch when I know more."

CHAPTER TWELVE

Lula, Bob, and I piled into the Explorer. I pulled into traffic and headed across town.

"Are we doing our ride-around now?" Lula asked.

"Yep," I said. "We're on the hunt for the Yamaha."

"I can understand how Plover has a problem with Nutsy," Lula said. "He put his trust in him and now he feels betrayed. You don't suppose what he said about the Manleys being part of the mob is true, do you?"

"No."

At least I hadn't until Plover mentioned it. There was a time when everyone knew everyone who was mob in Trenton. Things are different now. The mob has been marginalized by the gangs. The mob still exists but it's gone low profile. The thing is, even at low profile, Celia Manley, the cat lady, wouldn't have made the cut for Mob Housewives of Trenton, New Jersey. For starters, her hair was all wrong. I'd ask Grandma about it. And Connie. Grandma knew everything about everybody, and Connie's family was connected. Connie's uncle had done wet work before someone whacked him.

I found the street where my mom lost Nutsy. I stopped at the empty lot, and in the daylight, I could see where he'd crossed the grassy field and driven between two houses one street over. I was a couple blocks from the button factory and about a half mile from Duncan Dugan's house on Faucet Street.

"I'm going to cruise a grid," I said to Lula. "Look for Nutsy's Yamaha."

It took almost an hour to get to Faucet Street. There was very little traffic at this time of day, so I was able to go slow, checking out the alleys as well as the streets.

"I don't know about this exercise," Lula said. "If I was trying to hide, I wouldn't leave my car or bike out where people could see it."

"I agree, but not all of these houses have a garage. Some of them have just driveways and some people park cars in spaces that back up to the alley. And some of the garages are filled with junk and don't have room for a car."

I drove past Duncan Dugan's house. There was no activity on the street. A few cars parked at the curb but none in front of number 72 Faucet. I drove down the alley and stopped when I came to Dugan's backyard. The Kia Rio was missing. I idled there for a while before moving on.

"Your luck is holding," Lula said. "You got no luck at all."

"It's a process," I said. "If you stick with it long enough, you get lucky."

"That's a load of baloney," Lula said. "If something good happens to you right off the bat, it's that you got lucky. If something good happens to you after you put in days of not being lucky, it's hard work rewarded. And then there's times when you gotta wait for all your stars to get in alignment."

"That's today," I said. "My stars are in alignment."

"How do you know?" Lula asked. "Did you get your chart done?"

"No. I just know. Like I said before, all the traffic lights were green this morning."

"I gotta admit, that's a sign."

I cruised two more blocks and turned down an alley that had single-car garages that belonged to the houses. Two houses in I saw a green tarp covering something that might have been a bike parked next to the garage. I sucked in some air and my heart skipped a couple beats.

I pulled to the side of the alley one house down and Lula and I walked back to the garage with the tarp. I lifted the tarp and looked at the Yamaha 400. More heart irregularities.

"Good golly, Miss Molly," Lula said.

"I want to see what's in the garage," I said to Lula. "There are windows in the doors but they're too high for me to see in them. Can you give me a boost?"

"A boost? How am I supposed to do that? It's not like I'm Ranger."

"I'm an expert," I said. "Just squat down a little so I can get my foot on your leg and then I'll get on your shoulders."

"I guess I could do that," Lula said. "It's like we're cheerleaders."

"Exactly!"

We got in front of the garage doors, Lula squatted a little, and I got my foot on her leg and climbed onto her shoulders.

"Whoa, missy," Lula said. "How much do you weigh? I feel like all my spine is getting fused together and shrunk. How do those cheerleaders do this?"

"Move over a little so I can see in the window."

Lula inched over. "What do you see?"

"Duncan's Kia Rio."

I climbed off Lula and peeked around the side of the garage. No one was standing there with a shotgun. Yay.

"How's this going down?" Lula said. "You got your stun gun? Pepper spray? Cuffs? I know you don't got a gun."

"I don't think I'll need any of that. I'm going to knock on the door and talk to Nutsy."

"Last time you said you were just gonna talk to someone you got punched in the face."

"This is different. Nutsy and I were friends. He felt me up. That has to be worth something."

"I didn't know he felt you up," Lula said. "That might make a difference if it was a good feel."

"I was fourteen. It didn't amount to much."

"In that case, maybe you should take your stun gun."

I looked back at Bob. He had his nose pressed to the window.

"Stay with Bob," I said to Lula. "I don't want him eating Ranger's car."

"His problem is that he gets separation anxiety," Lula said. "He's an insecure dog. And on top of that he gets bored and then he gets even more anxiety. That television show I told Plover about was about all this. It was about a beagle that was in therapy because his owners got a divorce. He was eating everything too, and he got fat and diabetes."

"Did the therapy help him?"

"They didn't say. The next part of the show was about a cat with eczema."

"I won't be long. I'll call if I need help."

Lula walked to the Explorer, and I went to the back door and knocked. A woman answered. She had the right hair color and cut. She was medium height and medium build, wearing a T-shirt and jeans and sneakers. I was guessing she was my age. Pleasant looking, but a little worried.

"Sissy?" I asked.

"Yes," she said. "Do I know you?"

"I'm friends with Nutsy."

"There's nobody here named Nutsy."

"Andrew Manley," I said.

"No. Sorry. You have the wrong house."

"I know he's here. His bike is outside. I need to talk to him."

"Honestly, he really isn't here."

"How about Duncan Dugan? Is he here?"

"No," she said.

I showed her my credentials. "As a representative of Duncan's bail bonds agent, I'm legally authorized to search your house."

"Okay," she said. "But they aren't here."

"Do you know where they are?"

"Not exactly."

"When will they be back?"

"I don't know," she said. "They might not be coming back."

I did a fast walk through the house. It was obvious that Nutsy and Dugan had been staying there and either intended to return or else had to leave in a hurry. Someone had been sleeping on the couch. Probably Dugan. Two pillows and a quilt were still there. A box of Kleenex, some hand sanitizer, and the television remote were lined up on a small table next to the couch. Very neat. One bedroom belonged to Sissy. The second bedroom, which was very small, was a disaster. Bed incredibly rumpled. Candy wrappers, socks, underwear, and crumpled pieces of paper were on the floor, scattered around the small room. This would be Nutsy's slob cave.

I returned to Sissy. "Talk to me," I said.

"I don't know anything."

"I saw you in the street when Duncan fell off the ledge."

"We're friends. We used to work together at the button factory, but I got fired. Duncan fired me. I missed too many irregular buttons."

"But you were still friends?"

"He was right. I didn't have what it takes to sort buttons. I'm one of those *good enough* people and buttons have to be perfect. So, I got another job, and we stayed friends. My new job is much better. I do customer service for a hospital supply company. I can work at home most of the time."

"Were you in a relationship?"

"With Duncan? No. We were just friends. I'm not perfect enough for Duncan. Everything always has to be perfect. Like the buttons."

"Is Duncan perfect?"

"I thought he was," Sissy said, "but things haven't been going right for him lately."

"Why did he rob the jewelry store?"

"I honestly don't know. It was so out of character for him."

"He's friends with Andrew Manley."

"Yes. That was a surprise. I didn't know he had other friends. Actually, that's not accurate. He spends a lot of time online. He has cyber friends. I guess originally Andrew was one of Duncan's cyber friends, and then they connected somehow. It's weird because they're like the Odd Couple. Duncan is a neat freak and Andrew is a total mess, but they like a lot of the same things. Like old movies. That's why Duncan was sleeping on the couch instead of in the bedroom. He likes to watch movies late at night on the classic movie channel."

"Does Duncan have any other interests? Hobbies? Sports?"

"He plays games with his cyber friends. And he reads people's blogs. I don't think he has his own blog, but he follows Andrew's. I don't know much about the games and blogs. I don't even Twitter. Or tweet."

"What are your interests?" I asked her.

"I'm taking cooking classes," Sissy said. "And I like the old movies that Duncan watches. I guess that's what we have in common."

"And now Duncan and Andrew are gone," I said. "You know where they're going, don't you?"

"Not exactly. They loaded up my van and took off. They put my La-Z-Boy recliner in the back for Duncan. He's still in a lot of pain."

"Is this the white van that was used to get Duncan out of the hospital?"

"Yes. I wanted a Mini Cooper when I went shopping for a car, but the van was dirt cheap, and I didn't have a lot of money."

"Why did you have to get Duncan out of the hospital?"

"Andrew found me and told me that Duncan was in danger in the hospital, and we had to get him out. I don't know what danger Andrew was talking about, but it didn't have anything to do with the hospital itself. It seemed like it was related to the robbery. Sometimes it's hard to get a grip on what Andrew is rambling on about."

"I need to talk to them," I said. "Andrew is being accused of stealing diamonds, and Duncan is now considered a felon because he missed his court date. I'd like to help them but I'm missing some important information."

Sissy pressed her lips together and went silent for a couple beats. "They aren't bad people," she said.

"I know."

"And you think you might be able to help them?"

"I'm going to try."

She blew out a sigh. "I'm pretty sure they're going to Duncan's brother's house. It's somewhere in Maine. I overheard them talking. Duncan needs medical care, and he can't get it here."

"When did they leave?"

"It was super early this morning. Around five o'clock. Do you know where his brother lives?"

"I can find out."

I gave her my card.

"Call or text me if you hear from them," I said.

"Should I tell them you're looking for them?"

"Yes. You can tell them to call me. Tell them that I'm trying to help them."

"Are you going to Maine?"

"I haven't decided. I'd rather talk to one of them on the phone."

I left Sissy and jogged back to the Explorer. I was hoping she'd call Duncan or Andrew and persuade them to call me. If that didn't happen, Bob and I were taking a road trip.

"How'd that go?" Lula asked when I got behind the wheel. "It doesn't look like you got punched out this time. That's a step in the right direction."

"I talked to Sissy, and I walked through the house. Duncan and Nutsy left in the white van at five this morning. She thinks they're going to Duncan's brother's house in Maine. Apparently, he can get medical care there."

"Oh boy, are we going to Maine? I've never been to Maine."

"I haven't decided. I'm hoping for a call. I'd rather not drive to Maine."

Lula was tapping away on her cell phone. "It says here that it's an eight-hour drive. Of course, that depends on where you're going in Maine."

"Text Connie and get Dugan's brother's address. I'm going to head for the government complex and look for Hooter Brown. If we have to go to Maine, I'd like to get Brown and Trundle off my to-do list before we hit the road."

"Sounds like you're planning on driving and not flying."

"Unless Morelli comes home immediately, I have Bob traveling with me. And I can't see Bob flying."

"Good point," Lula said. "This is an excellent time to snag Hooter. It's between the early morning crowd and the noon lunch rush. He's going to be relaxing somewhere, having a maple bacon latte, reviewing his inventory."

Twenty minutes later I spotted him. He was sitting on a bench, all by himself, in a vest pocket park. "There he is," I said to Lula.

"Yep," she said. "I see him. How do you want to do this?"

"I'm going to park on the street behind the little greenway and come up behind him."

"Take him by surprise."

"Yeah. I'm not wasting time and energy. I'm going to stun him, and we'll cuff him and carry him to the car."

"I like your style," Lula said. "No bullshit."

It wasn't so much style as desperation. I was running out of time and money. I wouldn't be on an expense account in Maine. I got paid when Vinnie got reimbursed for his bond. End of story. I'd be buying gas with my rent money. I needed the capture payout on Farcus Trundle and Hooter Brown, and I needed it now.

I circled around and parked on a side street that was adjacent to the greenway. I had cuffs in my back pocket and my stun gun in hand. Lula adjusted her girls and tugged her skirt down over her ass. I cracked a window for Bob and locked the SUV.

"Don't you dare chew, drool, or otherwise destroy this car," I said to him. "I won't be long." I turned to Lula. "Stay back until I tag him."

"Roger dodger," Lula said.

I walked straight up to Hooter, stuck my stun gun to the back of his neck, and gave him twenty thousand volts. He squeaked and crumpled. Lula moved in and took his feet, and I got him under the armpits. A couple people stopped and stared, and Lula told them we were taking a friend to get some Narcan. We loaded Hooter into the back of the SUV so he wouldn't take up Bob's room on the back seat. We cuffed him and took off for the police station.

"That went smooth as anything," Lula said. "Are we good, or what?"

Halfway to the police station, Hooter started to twitch and talk gibberish.

"Hey, Hooter," Lula said. "Don't you worry. We'll get you bailed out and back on the street. You might not make the lunch crowd, but you'll catch some of the early-shifters going home at three o'clock."

"Thish shluuush," Hooter said.

I drove to the rear door of the municipal building, and we rolled Hooter out and helped him walk inside. He was still a little frazzled, and we had to drag him part of the way, but we got him to the docket lieutenant. I filled out the requisite paperwork and was given my body receipt, and Lula and I were on our way back to the office.

"Are you going after Farcus today?" Lula asked.

"Yes."

"How are you going to do that? He's not going to be sitting on a park bench."

"No, but he's going to underestimate me. He's going to see me coming and think, 'Here comes the nitwit who works for Vinnie.' It will give me an advantage."

"I appreciate the positive thinking, but either you want to go home and get your itty-bitty gun out of your cookie jar, or else you want to make sure your stun gun has juice."

"I've got lots of juice."

"Okay then, let's roll."

I made a U-turn and drove to Carlory Street. I cruised past Trundle's house and didn't see his Range Rover. I continued down the street to the girlfriend. No Range Rover there either.

"He must be out robbing and mugging people," Lula said.

"Too bad," I said. "I was on a roll."

"I just got Duncan Dugan's brother's address from Connie," Lula said. "According to Google, he's in a small town that's about forty-five minutes out of Bangor, Maine. That's sort of in the middle of the state. I bet it's real picturesque. Like everybody's got wooden rocking chairs on their front porch. I bet it's loaded with charming doodads and stuff."

"It's a long car ride and we aren't even sure if Nutsy and Dugan are there."

I came to the cross street and turned left, and Trundle drove past me in his black Range Rover and turned onto Carlory.

"Holy cow," Lula said. "That's like an act of God. That's a cosmic sign."

"He was looking ahead. I don't think he spotted us."

"I'm telling you, it means something. That weird shit doesn't happen every day. It all started with the green lights."

I went a quarter mile down the road, U-turned, and retraced my route back to the girlfriend's house. The black Range Rover was parked in the driveway.

"Well, here's a problem," Lula said. "We have to decide if we want to park behind Farcus and have one of those déjà vu experiences with Ranger's car. If Farcus smashes Ranger's car, you know Ranger's going to come say howdy to Farcus, and that would result in Farcus getting put in your custody. Except then we wouldn't have a nice car to drive to Maine."

"I'm not going to park behind the SUV. It's too far to drag him after I stun him and cuff him."

"Are we going to engage him in polite chitchat first?" Lula said. "You always like to start off with the horse pucky about helping him to reschedule."

"I'm short on time and horse pucky. I'm just taking him down."

I gunned the motor and drove around the Range Rover and over the grass to the front door. Lula and I got out and marched up to the house. Bob guarded the SUV. I tried the doorknob and found it was unlocked, and Lula and I walked into the living room.

"Bail bond enforcement," I shouted.

Trundle came out of the kitchen with a can of beer in his hand. "What the hell?"

"We're here to take you into town to get your court date rescheduled," I said.

"Gee, that sounds like fun," he said, "but maybe some other time. I just got a beer."

"I wouldn't mind having a beer," I said.

"Help yourself," Trundle said. "We can make this a party."

"Yeah, get one for me too," Lula said. "I'm all about a party."

I walked past Trundle into the kitchen and pretended to get beer.

"Where's the little dog?" Lula asked Trundle. "The poodle doodle what's-her-name."

"She goes to work with Maxine," Trundle said.

I came up behind him and pressed the stun gun prongs against his neck. The beer can fell out of his hand, and he dropped to his knees. "F-f-f-fuck," he said.

I grabbed the cuffs out of my back pocket and struggled to get a bracelet onto his chunky wrist.

"Hey!" he said, wrenching his hand away from me.

He caught sight of the cuff dangling from his wrist, and he swatted me away, sending me sprawling onto the floor. He got to his feet and shook his head in an effort to clear the cobwebs. Lula tackled him, but he didn't go down. He took a couple steps forward and stopped and did another head shake.

Lula had her arms wrapped around his knees. "Tag him," she yelled at me. "Tag him again."

I scrambled to my feet and lunged at him, catching him on the arm. *Zzzzzt.*

"Ow," he said. "Now you're pissing me off."

Lula still had her arms wrapped around his legs. He looked down at her, grunted, and punted her halfway across the room. I was able to get the prongs on his neck and he went to his knees. I zapped him again and he face-planted. Lula rushed over and helped wrangle his arm into position so I could get the second bracelet on him.

"Done," I said, and we jumped away from him like we'd just won the calf-roping competition at the county fair.

"We might not have a lot of time to get him into the Rangeman Explorer," I said.

We rolled him over onto his back, Lula took his legs, and I got him under his armpits. We got him about two inches off the floor and dropped him.

"This isn't going to work," I said. "He's too big. He's dead weight. We'll have to drag him."

I took a leg and Lula took a leg and we dragged him across

the floor and out the door. We got him off the small front stoop, down the two steps, and onto the grass. The SUV was parked about ten feet away with Bob looking at us from the front seat, his nose pressed to the window. We dragged Trundle to the back, I opened the rear hatch, and Lula and I looked down at him. He was drooling and his pinky finger was twitching.

"He's got a twitchy finger," Lula said. "Maybe you should give him some more volts."

"No can do. Stun gun is dead. Needs to be recharged." I cut my eyes to her. "Do you have a stun gun?"

"No. I just have one of those guns that go *bang*."

A couple more fingers were twitching now.

"It's going to be impossible to get him into the SUV once he comes around," I said. "You take one side and I'll take the other, and we'll push him in headfirst."

We got him halfway in, and Lula ran around and got into the back seat and pulled while I pushed. By the time we got him all the way in I was sweating through my T-shirt. I closed the hatch and jumped behind the wheel. Lula stayed in the back seat, keeping an eye on Trundle. Bob was in front with me. I drove out of the yard and wasted no time getting to the police station. I had about a mile to go when Trundle started swearing and rolling around in the back. He managed to sit up and Lula hauled out her gun.

"Are you going to shoot me?" he said. "I'm unarmed."

"I'm not going to shoot you," Lula said. "I'm going to smash this Glock into your nose, right between your beady eyes."

"Not until I butt my head into your fat face," Trundle said.

"Excuse me?" Lula said. "Fat? Did you just say my face was fat?"

"Yeah," Trundle said. "Fat, fat, fat."

Bob climbed onto the console and squeezed himself between the two front seats. He sidled up next to Lula and growled at Trundle, lips curled back, showing his huge white Bob teeth.

"Whoa," Trundle said. "What's with the dog?"

"He's a killer," Lula said. "You want to sit back down and be real calm. He doesn't like when people are rude."

I drove through the lot where the cops parked their cars and took Trundle to the back entrance. I called inside and asked for assistance. A uniform came out and I handed Trundle over to him. I followed the uniform inside and Lula drove the Explorer to the lot across the street. I was back in the Explorer forty-five minutes later.

"Did you get your body receipt?" Lula asked me.

"Yes. It took longer than usual. They had a lot going on. Apparently, someone shot up a bowling alley. Domestic dispute that turned ugly."

"People are serious about bowling," Lula said. "I don't get it, personally. I guess it could be fun, but you have to wear those shoes. I mean, they aren't fashion-forward, you see what I'm saying? And putting my perfectly pedicured and enameled toes in a rental? Not going to happen."

Bob was sharing the seat with Lula. He had his butt on her lap and his paws on the dashboard. Bob weighs in at seventy-five pounds, so it's not like he's a lapdog.

"Is Bob going to ride like this from now on?" I asked.

"Bob can ride wherever the heck he wants," Lula said. "He's my hero."

I had to admit I was impressed. I'd never heard him growl like that. It was like he actually knew what was happening.

I cut across town to Hamilton Avenue and parked in front of the bail bonds office, and Sissy called.

"I don't know if I should be making this phone call," she said. "I just talked to Duncan. He didn't sound good. He was in a lot of pain, which I guess is to be expected. It was a long car ride. Anyway, he's seeing a doctor tomorrow. The thing is, he's talking about leaving the country. Going to Thailand. Thailand! What is he going to do in Thailand?"

"Is he in Maine?"

"He's with his brother. Wherever that is. You said you would help him. I think he needs help. He's with Andrew, and I'm not sure about Andrew. I think he means well, but Andrew seems a little . . . eccentric."

"Did you tell him that I wanted to talk to Andrew?"

"Yes. Duncan said they would discuss it, but I'm worried they'll do something silly. Like take off for Thailand."

"I'm glad you called me. I'll do what I can to help them."

"You'll keep in touch with me?"

"Absolutely."

I'd had the call on speakerphone.

"Wow," Lula said.

I nodded. "Yeah. It looks like we're going to Maine."

"When are we leaving?"

"I don't know. I have to think about this. It's almost a nine-hour drive."

"I have to go home to pack," Lula said. "It won't take me long.

I just need some travel clothes, and of course there's my daily beautification products."

My needs weren't so complicated. A couple T-shirts, some undies, and dog food.

"I don't want to drive late at night," I said. "Either we leave first thing in the morning or else we leave now."

"I wouldn't mind leaving now being that I'm not looking forward to another night with Grendel," Lula said.

"I'll have Connie book us two rooms in a dog-friendly hotel."

CHAPTER THIRTEEN

Lula was waiting on the sidewalk when I drove up in the Explorer. She had a giant suitcase and a large tote. She hefted the suitcase into the back beside my small travel duffel bag and the twelve-pack of water, two dog bowls, and Bob-proof container of kibble that I'd packed. She brought the tote up front with her and set it on the floor between her legs. She turned and said hello to Bob, and she buckled herself in.

"This is going to be awesome," Lula said. "We're going on a road trip. I brought some snacks and a book of games that you can play in the car. And I left a note for Grendel telling him to go away and haunt someone else."

"I stopped at the office and picked up a folder from Connie. It's got some information in it about Duncan's brother, our hotel reservation, and directions to Alberton. It's a small town about an hour out of Bangor. I've already plugged the address into navigation."

I handed the folder to Lula and headed for Route 29. An hour into the trip, my phone rang.

"Babe," Ranger said, "you're on the Saw Mill River Parkway heading north."

"Duncan Dugan and Nutsy are at his brother's house in Maine. I'm going after them."

"Are you alone?"

"Nope. I'm with Lula and Bob."

There was a long silence where I thought Ranger was trying hard not to laugh out loud.

"Stay in touch," he finally said. And he disconnected.

By the time we crossed into Massachusetts, we'd gone through all the food, Bob and Lula had relieved themselves multiple times, we'd stopped to refuel, and now Lula and Bob were asleep and snoring, and I was doubting the wisdom of the trip. What the heck was I going to do with Dugan if I captured him? I'd have to strap him into the recliner and drive him back to New Jersey. And what about Nutsy? My deal with Plover didn't involve capture. I just had to *find* Nutsy. This was a good thing because I didn't want to put Nutsy in cuffs. Especially since I had no legal permission to capture him.

When Vinnie writes a bail bond for someone, they sign away a lot of their rights. One of the things that they legally agree to is the right for Vinnie's representative (me) to capture them. When someone Vinnie has bonded out fails to show for their court appearance, they're considered a felon and I can pursue them and restrain them and do whatever is necessary to return them to the court. Dugan fell under this category. Nutsy didn't. Forcibly returning Nutsy to New Jersey would fall under kidnapping across state lines, and that was a very large no-no.

I was thinking through all this when Morelli called.

"How was your day?" he asked.

"Mixed," I said. "I made a couple captures and now I'm in a car on my way to Maine with Lula and Bob. Duncan Dugan and Nutsy are supposed to be there."

"Where are you now?"

"Somewhere in Massachusetts."

"And when do you expect to be in Maine?"

"Hard to tell. It depends on how many stops everyone needs to make for food and potty."

"Call me when you get to wherever it is that you're going."

"Yessir."

"I miss you," Morelli said. "Try to stay alive."

"I'll do my best."

———

I was driving in the dark, taking directions from the navigation lady.

"Keep right at the fork to continue on I-295 North," she said to me. "Follow this road for fifty-two miles."

"Fifty-two miles," Lula said. "Is this trip never going to end? My ass is asleep. I need a bacon cheeseburger with onion rings and slaw. I need coconut layer cake and ice cream. I need a drink. Vodka straight up. I need to get out of this car. Tell me we're almost there."

"We're almost there," I said. "We're in Maine."

The next time we heard the navigation lady's voice, she told me to merge onto I-95 North.

"Continue on I-95 for eighty miles," she said.

"Omigod," Lula said. "Eighty miles. Do you know how far eighty miles is? It's freaking far. It's forever. Just shoot me. Get it over with. Make this misery end. I can't feel my legs anymore. I'm numb from the waist down. I wasn't meant to sit. I'm one of those women who's gotta go. I'm a mover. Let me out of this car and I'll walk the rest of the way. Oh crap. I can't do that. My extremities are dead. I'm a cripple."

"Look on the bright side," I said. "When we get back to Trenton you can get a handicap sticker for your car."

"I always wanted one of those," Lula said. "You get good parking spaces. A handicap sticker is worth gold."

"Merge now," the navigation lady said.

"I hate this bitch," Lula said. "She's not telling me anything I want to hear. I want to hear we're at our destination."

I loved the navigation lady. She knew where we were going. This was a wonderful thing since I hadn't a clue. She never sounded tired or annoyed. Her voice was pleasant and calm and confident. It was a small piece of sanity in my currently unpleasant circumstances.

———

It was close to eleven o'clock when I cruised down the main street of Alberton. The main street was named Main Street, and from what I could see at night the town looked like a movie set. White church with steeple. Hardware store. Grocery store. Real estate office. Rosey's Bakery. The Champion Bar and Grill. There were streetlights, but that was the only sign of life. No lights in any of the businesses. Mine was the only car on the road.

"This is it?" Lula said, looking out the window. "Is it charming? I can't tell in the dark. And my powers of observation aren't as good as usual because I'm weak due to my sugar level is all off on account of I never got a bacon cheeseburger."

"We stopped for dinner, and you got the Thanksgiving in October Special. Turkey, gravy, mashed potatoes, green beans, cranberry sauce, herb stuffing, pumpkin pie, and ice cream."

"That was a long time ago," Lula said. "I'm a big girl. I need to eat at regular intervals. I have an active metabolism."

I drove past a small park with a kid playground. A gas station was across the street from the playground, and next to the gas station was the Haggerty Inn.

"This is it," Lula said, reading from Connie's notes. "The Haggerty Inn. A three-star accommodation that's dog friendly and has free breakfast. From the picture it looks like it's got three floors and it says it's got two hundred fifty rooms. It doesn't say anything about room service or a bar."

I parked in the lot, and we got out of the car and stood for a moment letting our joints adjust.

"It's frigging cold here," Lula said. "It's wintertime cold. My nipples are all shrunk up and frozen. We don't have weather like this in Trenton. I didn't bring clothes for this. I don't even own clothes for this."

I zipped up my sweatshirt, popped the hatch on the Explorer, and grabbed my duffel and Bob's food. "I'll race you to the front desk."

Lula hauled her suitcase out of the SUV, and we hustled across the parking lot to the lobby.

"We have you in two of our nicest rooms on the second floor," the desk clerk said.

"What about food?" Lula asked.

"Free breakfast starting at seven o'clock," he said.

"Yeah, but what about now?" Lula asked.

"You'll find a list of takeout places in your room. Most are closed at this hour, but Jake's Bar is open until midnight, and they deliver."

Twenty minutes later, we were in my room, waiting for pizza and beer to get delivered. I'd already called Morelli and told him I was safely locked away for the night. I didn't bother calling Ranger. He was able to follow his cars, and he knew my exact location in real time. Plus, he probably had my messenger bag bugged and a GPS tracker sewn into the pocket of my sweatshirt.

"This is a pretty nice hotel," Lula said. "I tested out the bed and the pillows, and the linens are nice too."

"I'd like to get an early start tomorrow," I said. "Breakfast at seven and then we'll check out the brother's house."

"It's okay with me. I'm an early riser. And I'm going to get a good night's sleep in my nice hotel room without Grendel."

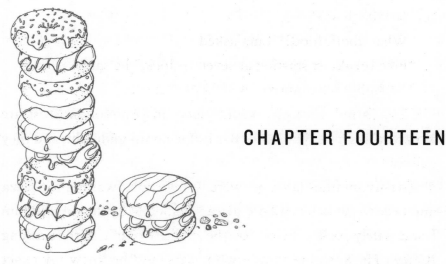

CHAPTER FOURTEEN

Bob and I got to the breakfast room a couple minutes after seven. I helped myself to coffee, a box of Frosted Flakes, a blueberry Danish, and a banana. Lula shuffled in fifteen minutes later, did a tour of the buffet, and came to my table with coffee.

"I wasn't ready for seven o'clock," Lula said. "I was worn out from the ride. How can you get dead tired from sitting all day? I barely dragged myself out of bed. I'm too tired to eat." She looked at my Danish. "Is that any good?"

"It's average."

"Average is okay. Average means good enough. And average is a lot better than lousy. I might need one."

"What about being too tired to eat?"

"Yeah, but I should force myself to eat something to get my energy up. I need to get my yin and yang balanced out."

Lula went to take a second look at the pastries and Ranger called.

"Checking in," Ranger said. "How's Alberton?"

"I haven't seen much of it yet, but I suspect there isn't much to see. Lula is laying waste to the free breakfast bar right now. When we're done with breakfast we'll head out to the brother's house."

"The brother is William Dugan. Forty years old. Manages an auto parts store. Two kids with wife number one. They're with the first wife. Wife number two is Adele. She's a dental assistant. They've been married for three years. No kids. Two dogs. They belong to the Methodist church and they're on the Alberton Knights softball team. It looks like the Alberton Knights haven't won a game in the last seven years. Adele and William have matching Honda Civics. Gray. They have a mortgage, the cars are leased, they pay their bills on time, no arrest records."

"Thanks. They sound like good people."

"There's a cousin on death row in South Carolina for killing and beheading twelve people, but he's twice removed."

"Every family has one of those," I said.

"Babe," Ranger said. And he disconnected.

Lula returned with a bunch of pastries, a sausage and egg sandwich in a paper wrapper that was soaked in grease, a bagel, and more coffee.

"I got the bagel for Bob," Lula said.

Bob's ears perked up at the mention of his name and his eyes got bright. Lula handed him the bagel and he gulped it down.

By eight o'clock we were on the road. William Dugan lived in a tidy neighborhood a couple miles out of town. The houses were modest and a mixture of ranches and small two-stories. Yards were large enough for swing sets and an occasional aboveground pool. The Dugan house was a Cape Cod with a red door and a gray Honda Civic in the driveway.

I parked in front of the house and explained to Bob that he was going to have to stay in the car, and he needed to be good because the car belonged to Ranger.

"You think he got all that?" Lula asked. "It's not like you were talking dog to him. There's a good chance he don't know what you said past *Bob*."

"Maybe you should stay with him," I said.

"Hell no. I'm not gonna miss this. From what Ranger told you, these people are softballers. They got matchy-matchy cars. I mean, this is good stuff. This is like walking into a fifties sitcom. This is *Leave It to Beaver* shit. And on top of that I can't wait to see Nutsy. It's not every day you get to see someone called Nutsy. And I got a lot of clown questions."

"Okay," I said, "but let me do the talking. I don't want to freak anyone out as soon as we walk in the door."

"When did I ever freak anyone out?" Lula said. "I'm a perfect example of decorum. I got a innate sense of saying the right thing. Are we going in guns blazing?"

"No guns. No pepper spray. No stun guns. No punching people out. Are you sure you don't want to stay with Bob?"

"Don't worry about me. Like I said, I'm full of decorum."

I rang the bell and a woman answered. Blond hair in a ponytail. Fortyish. Tasteful makeup. Wearing pink scrubs suitable for a dental hygienist.

"Adele Dugan?" I asked.

"Yes," she said.

I introduced myself, showed her my credentials, and told her I would like to talk to Duncan.

"Duncan isn't here right now," she said. "William took him to our doctor."

"Is Andrew Manley here?" I asked her.

"No. He went with Duncan and William."

"You know that Duncan is in trouble," I said to her.

"Yes. I don't know all the details, but apparently, he couldn't get good medical care in Trenton. We were surprised when they arrived. I guess they thought I could provide care, but Duncan's injuries were beyond my abilities. For goodness' sakes, I'm a dental hygienist. I clean teeth. Fortunately, we have a wonderful family doctor." She looked down at her watch. "I don't mean to be rude, but I'm a little late this morning. I need to get to work."

"Of course," I said. "Thank you for your time."

"Did you know Nutsy was a clown?" Lula asked her.

"Nutsy? That's Andrew, right?" she said. "He was a clown?"

"We don't want you to be late for work," I said to Adele. "Thank you again."

I stepped back and Adele closed and locked the door.

The upholstery seemed intact when I got back to the car. There were tooth marks on the gearshift, but they were minor.

"I thought we'd go into town and look for either the white van or the gray Civic," I said to Lula. "Go online and see where doctor's offices are located."

I retraced my route into town and Lula searched for doctors.

"It looks like there are three doctors here," she said. "One of them is an ob-gyn, so we can forget about her. One of the family doctors is on Chestnut Street and the other is in a medical building on Hoover Street. Both streets go off the main drag that we came in on."

I drove past the hotel and the little park. The Champion Bar and Grill was on the left side of the street and Chestnut Street was at the next corner. I drove one block down Chestnut and the doctor's office was on the right. It was a small gray and white house with a small parking lot on one side. There was a Toyota Corolla in the lot. No white van or gray Honda Civic.

I went back to Main Street and turned onto Hoover Street, and the medical building was one block in. The white van was parked in the lot next to it.

"Are we good, or what?" Lula said.

It seemed to me that I should have been happier. I'd found Duncan Dugan and Nutsy. Finding was huge, right? So why did I have this hollow feeling in my stomach? It was like I was facing impending doom. Or maybe I was on the verge of doing something stupid that I would regret. Doing something stupid happened to me a lot, but I didn't usually get an early warning.

I parked on the far side of the lot, away from the van.

An hour later, Nutsy appeared, pushing Duncan in a wheelchair. He was accompanied by a woman in lavender scrubs and a man I assumed was the brother. They loaded Duncan into the van, the woman returned to the building with the wheelchair, and Nutsy and the brother got into the van and drove off.

"We need one of those Kojak flashy red lights to put on the top of this car," Lula said. "Then you could pull the van over and commandeer it and drive everyone to Jersey while I followed in this SUV. Easy peasy."

"I'm going to wait until Duncan is settled in his brother's

house before I approach him," I said. "He didn't look all that great in the wheelchair. This travel has to be hard for him."

"Yeah, but it would be fun to pull someone over with our light flashing. I always wanted to do that. I even thought about being a cop, but I got discouraged with the uniform and the cop shoes. All my voluptuous beautifulness would be wasted in a cop uniform."

I gave them lots of distance on the way home. I knew where they were going. No need to spook them by riding on their bumper. They parked the van in the driveway, and Nutsy and the brother helped Duncan get into the house. After a half hour the brother left.

"All your moons are still in a row," Lula said to me. "Now there's no brother to complicate the process."

"Exactly. I was hoping he would leave to go to work or something."

I drove up to the house and parked behind the van.

"I counted the tooth marks on the gearshift," I said to Bob. "If there are any new ones when I get back there will be no treats for the rest of the day."

"You'd be a good mama," Lula said. "You're excellent at making a threat. That's one of the essential skills you need as a mother. Have you ever thought about having kids?"

"I can barely take care of a hamster."

"That's not true. I see the way you take care of Rex. He's got the good life. You keep his cage clean, and he always has fresh water and food. You don't even yell at him for running on that squeaky wheel all night. And you share all the best food with him. Pop-Tarts and such."

"Probably I should get a husband before I have a kid."

"It's not necessary. I know a bunch of women with kids and most of them don't have husbands. Not that I'm saying a husband isn't a handy thing to have in a family."

I grabbed my messenger bag and got out of the car. I still had the sick feeling in my stomach, and talking about husbands wasn't helping. Sometimes I thought I might want one, but there were scary things attached to marriage. For instance, there were two men in my life, and I wasn't prepared to choose one over the other. Not that it mattered, because neither of them wanted to marry me.

We walked to the door and rang the bell. Nutsy answered and sucked in air when he saw me.

"Oh crap," he said.

"Long time no see," I said, moving past him, into the living room.

"How did you find me?"

"It wasn't hard. How's Duncan doing?"

"He's managing. It's amazing that he didn't die when he fell off the ledge."

"I need to talk to both of you."

"Duncan's not real coherent right now. They gave him a sedative at the doctor's office to get him through the ride back here."

"He's in a lot of pain?"

"When he moves around," Nutsy said. "If he's in his recliner and watching television, he feels pretty good."

"Why did you take him out of Trenton? Surely the medical care he was getting there was as good as what he's getting here."

"It's complicated," Nutsy said. "It wasn't safe for him to stay in the hospital."

"You mean because he's a felon?"

"No. That's not it. I can't talk about it. I especially can't talk to you. You're working for Plover. My mom told me. She heard it at bingo."

"He thinks you stole his diamonds."

"He knows I didn't steal them."

"Do you ever get dressed up in your clown suit anymore?" Lula asked.

"No," Nutsy said to Lula. "The fun part about being a clown is having an audience. It's about communication."

"Like writing stories," I said.

"Yeah, I guess," Nutsy said.

"I've read some of your stories," I said.

"That's impossible," he said. "Even my mom hasn't read my stories. I post them on my personal blog, and there are only twelve followers. It's like a writers' support group."

"Is everyone in the group a writer? Even Duncan?"

"He writes poetry. How do you know about my writing? And Duncan?"

"It's not important how I know. I stumbled on it by accident. What's important is that Duncan needs to return to Trenton to get a new trial date. Right now, he's considered a felon."

"He can't go back there. It's too dangerous for him. I'm trying to fix things, but in the meantime, Duncan has to stay hidden."

"Living with his brother isn't exactly hidden."

"It was the best I could come up with," Nutsy said. "He needs help. His sister-in-law is a dental hygienist. I figure she's good with medication, at least. In a couple weeks if everything goes right, Duncan should be able to travel. Then he could get better hidden until I can straighten things out. Hell, maybe in a couple weeks, there won't be an issue anymore."

"Do you want to tell me the issue?"

"I can't," Nutsy said.

"I bet it has something to do with a clown's oath," Lula said. "Like the hypocritic oath doctors take. Did you take a clown's oath?"

"No," Nutsy said. "There's no clown oath that I know about."

"That's a shame," Lula said. "It's one of the oldest professions and seems like there should have been an oath."

"Maybe Duncan can reschedule his court date using FaceTime," Nutsy said.

Lula and I looked at each other. We'd never considered FaceTime or Zoom.

"You should call Vinnie," Lula said to me. "This here could be a game changer. Everyone would reup if they could do it on FaceTime."

I called Vinnie and got him at the breakfast table.

"Is it possible to write a bail bond any way other than physically bringing the FTA into court or the lockup?" I asked him.

"Like what?" he asked. "Maybe when he's in the prison ward at the medical center."

"How about by FaceTime or Zoom?"

"In my dreams," he said. "Where are you? Fantasyland?"

I hung up. "Great idea, but no," I said to Nutsy and Lula. "I need to bring him back to Trenton."

"He's not in any shape to travel," Nutsy said. "Give me two weeks to see if I can fix things."

"And after two weeks?"

"If he's in good enough shape and it's safe, I'll turn him over to you."

"And if he's not in good shape or it's not safe?"

"I don't know. We'll talk."

"Why are you so protective of Duncan?"

"It was my fault that he tried to rob Plover's. I'm responsible for all this mess."

"You were involved?"

"Not directly, but I wrote the story that pushed him into doing something stupid."

"The story about Duncan Dreary."

"Yeah. I thought it was just a fun thing we were doing together. You know, turning Duncan Dreary into Duncan Dare. Okay, so I'm not the most perceptive dude. I didn't see that Duncan was buying into the whole transformation thing. I guess I should have known. All those *Pink Panther* movies. He loved them. I mean, I like them too, but I don't want to *be* David Niven as the phantom."

"Did you have any advance warning? Did he talk about robbing a jewelry store like David Niven?"

"We had lots of story ideas about robbing jewelry stores, but they were just story ideas. At least I thought that's what they were. I guess you never know what's going on inside people. One of the things that appealed to me about Duncan was that he was calm. He was like vanilla custard. Cool. Smooth. No surprises. My head is always a mess. I do outrageous things. I've done them all my life. Duncan seemed so sane and content with his life. And now it turns out that he was as crazy on the inside as I am on the outside. And then one day he showed up at Plover's."

"Wow," I said.

"I had no advance warning," Nutsy said. "I went brain-dead. I froze. My first thought was that it was a joke. And then it got serious. He had a gun. Turned out it was a fake gun, but I didn't know that. I mean, he didn't wink at me or anything. He was totally Duncan Dare. It scared the crap out of me."

"That's because you're really a clown at heart," Lula said. "I bet you're one of those happy clowns with a smiley face and a red nose that goes *beep*."

"I didn't have a red nose," Nutsy said. "I was more of a contemporary mime."

"A mime?" Lula said. "Like one of those French guys who pretend there's a fake wall? No wonder you couldn't get a job with a circus."

"A clown is a kind of mime," Nutsy said. "For the most part, clowns are silent."

"I never thought of that," Lula said. "That's a fact more people should know about."

"Okay, I sort of get why you want to help Duncan," I said. "Explain the part about being in danger if he goes back."

"You won't believe me. No one ever believes me. I can't blame them. I'm Nutsy."

"You could try being Andrew," I said.

"Andrew and Nutsy are one and the same," Nutsy said. "Truth is, I like being Nutsy. I'm okay with it. I'm starting to get a grip on it."

"Good for you," Lula said. "I see what you're saying. I was lucky on account of I was Lula when I was born, and I never wanted to be anyone else. I've always been big and beautiful. And I got some complexity to me too."

I suppose I had a grip on being Stephanie, but I felt that it wasn't much of an accomplishment. I suspected I was a pretty easy book to read.

We were standing by the front door, and I could hear a television on in the next room. I walked in and found Duncan in his recliner.

"Hi," he said.

His voice was soft, and his eyes were slightly unfocused.

"How's it going?" I asked.

"Okay," he said. "I remember you. You came to the hospital."

"I work for your bail bondsman. You missed your court date, and you need to reschedule."

"Now?"

"When you're feeling better."

"I guess I have to go back to Trenton to do that. I want to go back anyway. I miss Sissy and my goldfish. I even miss my job. I thought I didn't like it, but now I miss it."

"Duncan Dare didn't like it," I said.

"You know about Duncan Dare? That's embarrassing. I don't know what I was thinking."

"You were test-driving a new you," I said.

He smiled for the first time. "Yeah. Duncan Disaster."

I smiled with him. "You should stick with Duncan Dugan."

"Am I going to jail?" he asked.

"I don't know. It's possible that since you were such a complete failure as a criminal, the judge will be lenient."

His eyes closed for a second. "Sorry I'm falling asleep," he said. "They gave me a pill at the doctor's office."

I left Duncan and returned to Nutsy.

"I need to go back to Trenton, and I don't have a car," Nutsy said. "The van has to stay here, so Duncan can get to the doctor. I'd like to ride back to Trenton with you if you have room for me, except you have to promise not to tell Plover I'm in Trenton."

I wanted more of an explanation from Nutsy, but this wasn't the time. I'd have to get him alone when Lula wasn't going to distract him with clown questions.

"Whatever," I said. "We'll check out of the hotel and come back to pick you up."

I looked to the front door. Beyond the door, Bob was waiting in Ranger's car. If the back seat was intact and there were no more tooth marks on the gearshift, Bob was going to get a double bacon hold-the-cheese burger for lunch.

———

We reached Jersey a little after ten o'clock that night. There'd been some long meal stops and a couple shorter snack stops and an accident on I-95. I was numb from the ass down, and I couldn't blink my eyes.

"Are we almost home?" Lula asked.

"Yes," I said. "We just left New York."

"That wasn't an entirely satisfying trip to Maine," Lula said. "I didn't get to shop for charming country crafts, and I didn't get to eat a lobster roll."

Bob had a better opinion of the trip because he'd gotten his double bacon burger.

An hour later, I turned onto Lula's street and my heart skipped a beat when I saw fire trucks in front of her apartment house. There were no flames shooting into the sky, but the air smelled smoky and the street was wet. I got closer and saw that the trucks were packing up to leave. A cop was roping the house off with yellow crime scene tape. The second-floor windows to Lula's apartment were blackened. A small clump of people stood on the sidewalk.

"That's my house!" Lula said. "Let me out. I gotta go see my apartment. All my clothes are in there. My Marilyn Monroe wig collection is in there."

"It looks like they're sealing the house off," I said.

"Marilee is one of the people standing on the sidewalk. She has the apartment under me. She'll know what's going on."

I angle-parked next to a fire truck, and we all got out.

Lula rushed over to Marilee. "What happened? I just got here. I was out of town," Lula said.

"Nobody's sure, but it looks like the fire started in your apartment," Marilee said. "Word is your apartment is toast, but the rest of the house mostly only got smoke and water damage."

"How could it start in my apartment?" Lula said. "I wasn't even home."

"Somebody was up there," Marilee said. "It sounded like the guy who comes to see you every night and stomps on the stairs. I heard him go up and then he was moving around up there. And then the fire started."

"It was Grendel," Lula said. "He's burning and pillaging. It's one of his specialties. Did he get burned along with everything else?"

"No one got burned," Marilee said. "Your apartment was empty. Everyone got out of the house."

"That's a good thing," Lula said. "I'm surprised crazy Becky in the attic was able to get out."

"They took her down in one of those bucket things attached to the fire truck," Marilee said. "She was screaming her head off. I'm thinking they drove her to the psych ward at the medical center."

"I'm sorry I missed it," Lula said. "She always puts up a good show. What about my car?"

"Your car is okay. The lot behind the house wasn't affected."

"Have you been back in your apartment?"

"No," Marilee said. "We can't go back in yet. I'm waiting for my daughter to come get me. I can stay with her tonight. They said the fire marshal will come in the morning, and then we can get back in."

"This is terrible," Lula said. "I can't believe this. I've been curating clothes all my life. I had ruby slippers that were the exact replica of Dorothy's in *The Wizard of Oz*. I had two racks of ho clothes from when I was doing erectile engineering. You can't replace stuff like that. All that stuff's got memories. And where am I going to stay? I haven't got a daughter with a house."

"You can stay with me tonight," I said. "We'll figure this out tomorrow when we get to see what's left of your apartment."

We all got back into the car, and I drove around the last fire truck and stopped at the cross street. "Where should I take you?" I said to Nutsy. "Are you staying with your parents?"

"I can't," Nutsy said. "They already had their car blown up because of me. I can't go home. And I'm sure Duncan's house is being watched. And probably Sissy's. Drop me off at the bridge. There's a homeless encampment there."

"Omigod," I said. "I'm not going to drop you off at the bridge. You can stay with me too."

While I was saying this, I calculated how much alcohol I had in my apartment. There was no way I was going to get through this sober.

CHAPTER FIFTEEN

Bob and I slept in my bed. Lula took the couch. Nutsy slept on the floor. At one o'clock Lula came into my bedroom.

"Are you awake?" she asked me.

"I am now," I said.

"I can't sleep out there with him," she said. "He snores and he talks in his sleep. If you and Bob move over, I can fit in here. I won't take up much room. I'll stay way over here on my side of the bed."

Ten minutes later, Bob and I were wide awake, and Lula was snoring like a buzz saw. Bob got up and went into the bathroom to sleep. I was left with Lula.

I dragged myself out of bed at six in the morning, staggered into the bathroom, and stood in the shower until the water ran cold. If it was necessary to sleep with Lula one more night, I would have to kill her. I got dressed, and Bob and I made our way past Nutsy to the kitchen. His socks, shoes, and assorted clothes were spread around the room. Plus, he'd helped himself to a late-night snack. Crumbs, wrappers, empty beer bottles, and cereal boxes were mixed in with the clothes on the floor. And he was snoring. I'd have to kill him too.

I poured some dog kibble into Bob's bowl and stared into the fridge. I was tempted to go for the margarita mix and vodka, but I pulled myself back from the edge of the cliff and went with coffee and a frozen waffle. I toasted the waffle and added a slice of American cheese, which instantly turned to molten yellow sludge.

I took Bob for a walk, and when I came back everyone was still snoring. Good thing I didn't have any bullets for my gun. I taped a note to the fridge door, telling Lula and Nutsy that Bob and I were going to my parents' house and that they should call me when they woke up if they needed a ride somewhere.

My mom and Grandma were at the front door when I pulled up in the Explorer. They were holding white bakery bags and boxes. I knew the Sunday routine. Early Mass and then a stop at the bakery.

Every morning my father was in the kitchen at six o'clock. He had a bowl of cornflakes with a banana, half a glass of orange juice, and a cup of coffee. At six thirty he stuck a sign that said TAXI to the roof of his Honda, and he left to make his commuter pickups. Except Sunday. My father slept in on Sunday. On Sunday, my father got up after the bakery bags arrived and the smell of fresh brewed coffee drifted up to him.

"Just in time," Grandma said to me when I joined them in the foyer. "They had those mocha and vanilla shortbread cookies that you like. Fresh baked. And we got almond croissants, powdered jelly doughnuts, a cream cheese coffee cake, and bear claws. The bear claws are for your father, but we got extra."

My mom got coffee going, Grandma set out the pastries, and I kept a tight leash on Bob so that he didn't go nuts and eat everything. My dad ambled in, put two bear claws on a plate, took a mug of coffee from my mom, and carted it all into the living room. He had Sunday shows to watch.

My mom, Grandma, and I sat at the little kitchen table.

"What's new?" Grandma asked me.

"There was a fire in Lula's apartment last night. It looks like it didn't spread to the whole house, but there's a lot of smoke and water damage throughout. Lula wasn't home at the time, so she's okay."

"That's terrible," my mom said. "Can she still live there?"

"I don't know. She spent the night with me. We'll take a look at it later this morning."

Grandma helped herself to a slice of the coffee cake. "What's happening with Nutsy?"

"I found him and then I lost him," I said.

Not a total lie. It was just that I lost him in my apartment. Sometimes Grandma had a hard time with keeping secrets, and I didn't want to put Nutsy in jeopardy.

"The word on the street is that Plover is going a little wacko," Grandma said. "Looking very nervous. Hired a new security guard and this one is armed."

I could believe it. I had twelve text messages from him demanding action on Nutsy. The last one said, *Get him or else!* I had no clue what *or else* referred to.

I took a seat at the table and grabbed a jelly doughnut. Sunday is usually an odd day for me. The office and the courts are closed, but Lula and I frequently work anyway. Lots of times it's because we haven't got anything better to do. Most of the time it's because we need the money. And some of the time it's because we actually have a viable lead.

"Do you have any other fun news?" I asked Grandma.

"Veronica Shidig died. Aneurysm."

I didn't know Veronica Shidig.

"Anything else?" I asked her.

"It's been a slow week. The best part was your mother chasing after Nutsy."

"He cheated by cutting through that lot," my mother said.

"You were a maniac," Grandma said to my mother. "You were awesome. You were like a NASCAR driver."

"I agree," I said to my mom. "You were awesome."

"I took the mirrors off the Camry," my mom said.

"Just like NASCAR," Grandma said. "Those guys are trashing cars all the time. They just pit and put some tape on the broken parts and keep going. If I was younger, and I had a driver's license, I'd want to be a NASCAR driver. Some people want to be astronauts, but an astronaut just sits in a cushy seat and gets blasted into space. A NASCAR driver has skills and guts. Only way you could make a race more exciting would be to have the drivers naked. Now, that would be something."

We all thought about that for a minute. Naked NASCAR drivers.

"The Romans used to have naked sporting events all the time," Grandma said. "Those were the days."

The conversation stopped when my father came in for a jelly doughnut and to refill his coffee mug.

"What's for dinner tonight?" he asked.

"Roast chicken and apple pie," my mom said.

This has been the answer for as long as I could remember. Roast chicken on Sunday, pot roast on Friday. The rest of the week was up for grabs.

I was on my second jelly doughnut when my phone rang. Lula wanted to go back to her apartment and Nutsy wanted to get his Yamaha.

"I have to go," I said. "Things to do."

My mom put the shortbread cookies in a plastic baggie and gave them to me. "I know you like these," she said.

I hugged my mom and Grandma. Grandma gave Bob a kiss on the top of his head, and I left.

Lula and Nutsy were waiting at the building's back door when I drove into the lot. Lula got into the front with me and Nutsy got into the back with Bob.

I drove across town and dropped Nutsy off at Sissy's house. Nutsy went straight to his bike, removed the cover, and took off for who-knows-where. I didn't see anyone in the vicinity doing surveillance. I assumed Nutsy was safe.

"Considering he's a clown, he isn't a barrel of laughs," Lula said. "Of course, he said he's more of a mime, and they're sort of creepy."

Next stop was Lula's apartment house. There was still sooty water in the gutters and the crime scene tape hadn't been removed. A lone car was parked in front of the house. The fire marshal was working early. Probably had plans for later in the day. I parked behind the fire marshal's car, and Lula, Bob, and I got out.

I ducked under the yellow tape and walked through the open front door.

"Hello?" I yelled.

Jeremy Gorden looked down at me from the second floor. "Oh God," he said. "It's you."

"This wasn't my fault," I said to him.

"I know. I know," he said. "It's never your fault."

"My coworker Lula lives in the second-floor apartment. Is it safe for her to come up?"

"Yes. Be careful on the stairs. They're slippery."

Lula, Bob, and I joined Jeremy on the second floor and Lula stepped into the charred mess that was her apartment.

"It looks to me like it started with a small incendiary device in the living room," Jeremy said.

"So, this is arson," I said. "How did the device get into her apartment?"

Jeremy shrugged. "I don't know. My guess is someone broke in and set the device on the floor. No way to know for sure because the door was destroyed by the firefighters."

Lula went to her closet. "Where's all my clothes?" she asked. "There's no clothes in here. No shoes. No nothing. There's not even any clothes ashes."

"No one has been in here as far as I can tell," Jeremy said. "The tape was intact when I got here this morning."

"My clothes are missing," Lula said. "Someone stole my clothes and set my apartment on fire. I know who it was too. It was Grendel."

"Who's Grendel?" Jeremy asked.

"He's an ogre and a demon," Lula said. "He's got an obsession with me, and he has anger-management issues. Usually, he lays waste to the mead hall, but lately he's been stalking me."

"The Mead Hall? Is that a new bar?" Jeremy asked.

"It's in Denmark," Lula said. "Its official name is Heorot, and it's the seat of King Hrothgar's rule. You'd know all about this if you played Beowulf."

Jeremy looked at me and grimaced. "Okay then," he said. "I guess that solves the mystery. I have to file my report. The structure seems safe. I'm going to have the tape removed. The department will get in touch with the rest of the tenants."

"Thanks," I said to Jeremy. "Have a good rest of the day."

"Hunh," Lula said when Jeremy disappeared down the stairs. "He didn't believe me."

"No one believes you."

"Stupid Grendel," Lula said.

"Here's the plan," I said to her. "It's Sunday, but I have a key to the office, so you're going to get your car and drive it to the office. Then you're going to call one of those fire restoration companies and make arrangements for them to clean up your apartment. I'm sure they work on Sunday. Then you're going to call your insurance company and ask to have an appraiser show up before the restoration people get there. Then you're going to figure out where you'll live until your apartment is okay."

"What about Grendel?"

"Leave him another note. Tell him you want your clothes back."

"Yeah, that's a good idea. I need a pen and a sticky pad."

"One thing at a time," I said.

Ranger called.

"It looks like you're checking out Lula's building," he said. "How bad is it?"

"The fire was mostly limited to Lula's apartment. Her apartment is trashed. The rest of the house has water and smoke damage. Jeremy said it was arson."

"Did you bring anyone back with you?"

"I left Duncan Dugan in Maine, but I brought Nutsy back with me. It was his choice. He's currently camped out at my place, along with Lula."

"Have you informed Plover that Nutsy is in town?"

"No."

There was silence on the other end.

"Are you smiling?" I asked him.

"Maybe a little," he said.

Lula went to get her car out of the building's parking area, and I drove to the office. It's always weird for me to open the office. It's Connie's job. She's supposed to be there when I arrive. The coffee is supposed to be waiting for me. The doughnuts are supposed to be waiting for me. The lights are supposed to be on.

Lula arrived a few minutes after I unlocked the door and switched the lights on.

"This is weird," she said. "This isn't right. Connie is supposed to be here. This feels wrong."

My phone buzzed. It was Connie.

"I just heard about the fire at Lula's apartment building," she said. "Are you in Maine? Did you hear about the fire? Are you in Trenton?"

"We're in Trenton. We rolled in late last night. The fire trucks were getting ready to leave when we got there. It was a real punch in the gut for Lula."

"Was she able to get in to see the damage?"

"The building was crime taped, so Lula spent the night with

me. We went through it this morning. Her apartment is a mess. The structure is still there but everything is charred."

"What about the rest of the building?"

"Water and smoke damage. We're at the office. She needs to call her insurance company."

"That's horrible. I know she loved her apartment. I'm coming to the office. I'll be there in a couple minutes."

"Connie is coming in," I said to Lula.

"That's real nice of her," Lula said. "She makes better coffee than you."

Ten minutes later Connie arrived.

"I got a lot to do," Lula said to Connie. "Stephanie has a list for me, but I'm all flummoxed and I can't remember anything."

"Pull a chair up to my desk," Connie said. "I'll help you."

God bless Connie.

"I'm heading out," I said. "Let me know if you hear from Grendel."

I drove by the Manley house. Nothing happening there. No Yamaha parked in the driveway. The next drive-by was Duncan's house on Faucet Street. No sign of life at number 72. Two blocks away I stopped in front of Sissy's house. I sat for a couple minutes and drove around the block to the alley entrance. I took the alley and paused in front of Sissy's garage. The garage door was open, and the garage was empty. Sissy was probably out with the Kia Rio. Nutsy's Yamaha wasn't parked in Sissy's yard.

Curiosity took me to Plover's Jewelry next. I cruised down King Street and parked a block from Plover's store. Bob and I got out and walked down the street. Even on a Sunday, it was a fairly busy section of town. Four blocks of office buildings interspersed with stores and restaurants. A middle school was one block over. Panhandlers hung out on corners, but I didn't see any hard-core drug users or dealers. At least none who were lying on the ground in an overdose or peddling heroin by shouting out sale prices.

I paused in front of Plover's and looked at the window displays. I caught a glimpse of the security guard through the front door. He was armed and in uniform, looking very official. A narrow alley ran down one side of Plover's and connected with the service alley behind the store. Bob and I turned at the corner and walked down the service alley. It was standard fare. Employee parking, dumpsters, and loading zones. Not attractive, but I didn't have to kick rats out of my way either. We returned to King Street, and I tried to imagine the robbery. According to the police report, Duncan ran out of the store, ran half a block, and jumped into his car and sped away. When the police finally stopped him, he didn't have the bag of jewelry. He said he dropped it as soon as he got out of the store, but the bag was never found. There were people on the sidewalk when Duncan ran out. One of them could have taken the bag, but there were problems with that theory. The police were immediately on the scene. People were detained and questioned. No one saw anyone make off with the big black garbage bag full of jewelry.

"What do you think?" I asked Bob. "Who has the jewelry?"

Bob didn't have any ideas, and I didn't have any ideas, so we went to the car and sat there for a while. I called Nutsy but he didn't pick up and his mailbox was full. No surprise there.

"Obviously I need to talk to Nutsy, and it's my bad that I didn't do it sooner," I said to Bob. "I'm not buying into the *I can't tell you my big dangerous mystery* thing. I don't mind if you listen in, but I didn't want to force him to talk in front of Lula. Lula has a tendency to lose focus. I was afraid in the middle of Nutsy's confession, Lula would have asked a clown question."

I didn't want to go home to Nutsy's mess on my living room floor, and I didn't have any good reason to go to the office, so I took a leisurely drive back to Sissy's house. I thought there was a good chance that at some point in the day, Nutsy would show up to retrieve the things he'd left behind in his rush to get to Maine.

I drove down the alley behind Sissy's house. The garage was still open and empty. No Yamaha.

"We have to be sneaky," I said to Bob. "If Nutsy wanted to talk to me he would have called back. He knows Ranger's SUV, so we won't hang out here."

I parked on Orchid Street, one block away, and Bob and I walked down Sissy's alley and found a comfy place to wait behind Sissy's garage. An hour later I heard the Yamaha *putt-putt* down the alley and park in Sissy's backyard. Luck or dogged persistence, whatever you wanted to call it, was still working for me.

Bob was immediately on his feet, happy to see an old friend. I released his leash and he rushed at Nutsy. Nutsy was happy to see Bob, not so much to see me.

"Do you have a key?" I asked him. "I don't think Sissy is home."

"She's at her sister's house. She goes there for lunch and then she stays and plays with her niece and nephew. It's a Sunday ritual. And yes, I have a key."

I followed Nutsy into the house. We walked through the kitchen and living area, into the guest room.

"We need to talk," I said to Nutsy.

"I don't want to talk," Nutsy said, picking clothes up off the floor, throwing everything onto the bed.

"We can have a friendly conversation, or I can bring Ranger in, and he can encourage you to talk," I said.

"Ah, Ranger," Nutsy said. "I know about Ranger. Everyone knows about Ranger."

"Really? What about Ranger?"

"Tough guy. Smart. High-tech security expert."

Yep. That was Ranger.

"I can't help you if I don't know the problem," I said. "Let's start with the bag of jewelry. Where is it?"

"I have it," Nutsy said.

"Wow."

"Yeah, well it's not exactly what it seems."

"How about if you start at the beginning."

"It's hard to tell what's the beginning," Nutsy said. "The beginning was when I decided to write stories. But that's not the beginning of the bad stuff. Writing stories was good. It was like being a clown. When you're a clown you're trying to entertain, to tell a story. And you're in disguise. You aren't yourself. You're the clown. When you write a book it's sort of the same thing. You give the world a piece of you. You write a story that you hope will entertain and enlighten. And you can do this in disguise by using a pseudonym. A pseudonym is like clown makeup. It protects you from the pain of rejection. So, I started to write these stories and I acquired a small group of readers online. It was perfect. I had a day job at Plover's. I didn't need to sell my stories. I just wanted a couple people to read them and enjoy them."

"And one of the readers was Duncan," I said.

"I don't know how he ambled onto my site, but he became a regular. After a couple months, we met for coffee, and we became friends. His life intrigued me. He made sure that the buttons were round and perfect. He was happy with this. At least I thought he was happy. We decided to write a story together about a guy like him who turns into a guy like David Niven in the old *Pink Panther* movies, a master jewel thief. I told you this before."

"It doesn't matter. Keep going."

"Okay, fast-forward to the day of the robbery. I was standing at the door, half-asleep because the job was so boring, and all of a sudden Duncan comes in. He's dressed in black, he's got a gun, and he calmly walks over to Plover and says, 'Stay very calm. This is a robbery. No one will get hurt if you put all of the jewelry in this bag.' And he hands him a large black plastic garbage bag. He's wearing a stupid black mask like Zorro, the kind that kids wear at Halloween. It's obviously Duncan and I'm dumbfounded. I don't know if Duncan is pranking me, if I'm dreaming, or if this is real. It all goes very fast from here. Plover panics and starts shoving all the jewelry into the bag. In minutes the shop is cleaned out, Duncan nods at me and smiles and walks out of the store. Meanwhile, Plover has pushed the button under the counter to call the police.

"Poor Duncan gets out of the store and has a moment of sanity and thinks, 'What the holy hell did I just do?!' So, he drops the bag and runs. He gets into his car and is in a blind panic trying to get away, hoping it was all a bad dream and didn't really happen."

"So how did you get the bag of jewelry? Did you just pick it up off the ground?"

"No. This is where it gets complicated."

"*This* is where it gets complicated?" I said.

"Yeah. Plover was pissed off that he was robbed. He said I just stood there like a dope and did nothing. And he was right. I just stood there like a big dope. Anyway, he fired me. I couldn't blame him. The next morning, he reported the missing tray of diamonds and he accused me of taking it."

"Did you take it?" I asked him.

"No! The police came to question me and after they left, I decided I'd go talk to Plover. I wanted to tell him that I didn't take the diamonds and that I'd like to have my job back. I thought I'd wait until he was closing up for the night. He had a routine. He hung the Closed sign in the front door and then he went into his office in the back and did paperwork for an hour or so. I thought this would be a good time to talk to him, so at nine o'clock I parked my bike in the alley. Plover's back door was open, and the lights were on inside. I went up to the back door and saw that Plover was arguing with two homeless guys. I sort of knew them. They hung at the corner all the time, harassing people for money. One of the homeless guys was standing back, close to the open door, and he was holding a big black garbage bag. The other homeless guy was yelling at Plover. He said if he didn't get a million dollars, he was going to expose Plover and go to the police with the jewelry."

My voice went up an octave. "He was trying to blackmail Plover for a million dollars?"

"Yeah," Nutsy said. "So Plover shot him."

"Are you serious?"

"Swear to God. Plover pulled a gun and shot the homeless guy. The one holding the bag sort of stumbled back, and Plover shot at him and missed."

"Both these men were unarmed?"

"Yeah," Nutsy said. "No guns, no knives, no nothing. At least none I could see. Plover squeezed off another round at the second homeless guy, and the guy turned and ran and slammed into me in the dark. He said, 'Fuck this,' and he shoved the bag at me, and he took off. So, I'm standing there like a dope again, and I see Plover walk up to the guy on the ground and shoot him two more times. The guy's body kind of jumped a little and that was it. Then Plover looked out the door and saw me standing there with the bag. He fired two shots at me, and I ran to my bike and drove off as fast as I could. I swear I was a mile away before I realized I was still holding the bag. I was in such a freak-out that I didn't even know I'd been shot. I got home and saw the blood when I got off the bike."

"You were shot?"

Listening to this story, I was pretty freaked out now, too. I hadn't expected anything like this. I wasn't even sure that I believed any of what Nutsy was saying.

"He got me on my arm." Nutsy took his sweatshirt off and showed me the wound on his upper arm. "I'm lucky Plover isn't a good shot when he's more than three feet away," he said. "The bullet tore through some flesh but it missed bone and muscle. I went to the ER and got it stitched." He grinned. "That's one of the good things about being Nutsy. The ER is used to me coming in with weird injuries. They don't ask a lot of questions anymore."

"So, you're in danger because Plover knows you saw him kill someone?"

"That's part of it. He also knows I have the bag of jewelry."

"Why didn't you go to the police?"

"There's no body. There's no proof that any of this happened.

The police would just as easily think I was part of the robbery and I scooped up the bag of jewelry. I'm already a person of interest. They would think this was another one of my stupid stunts."

"Has Plover been in touch with you?"

"He called but I didn't pick up. Then he texted and said he wanted to arrange a meeting. I figured he wanted to kill me like the homeless guy, so I didn't reply. Then he started calling my parents. That was when I moved out. And then their car blew up."

"Is that when you and Duncan decided to go to Thailand?"

"That was just talk," Nutsy said. "We don't have any money. We can't go to Thailand."

"You have the bag of jewelry."

"It's all fake. I wondered about the blackmail attempt, so I had the jewelry checked out. It looks good but it's junk. Plover wasn't upset that he was robbed. He was in a panic because if the jewelry was found and turned over to the insurance company, he'd be exposed as a fraud. He'd be ruined, and he'd go to jail. The diamonds in the safe were probably fake too, so he had to get rid of them in case he was investigated."

"Wow."

"Exactly," Nutsy said.

"What are you going to do if you can't afford Thailand?"

"I need to find the second homeless guy. He's my witness to the murder, and he can testify to the fact that I wasn't involved in the robbery. Duncan dropped the bag just like he said, and I think the homeless guys immediately grabbed it."

"That's why you came back here? To find the other homeless guy?"

"Yeah."

"What about Duncan? Why did you have to get him out of the hospital?"

"I made the mistake of crashing with Duncan when I vacated my parents' house. It was stupid of me because Plover found out and decided that Duncan and I must have worked together on the robberies. I guess he figured Duncan was the weak link, because he hounded him, demanding that he return the jewelry, threatening to kill him and his family if he went to the police. I moved out after a couple days. Another bonehead move on my part. If I'd stayed with Duncan, he might not have tried to kill himself."

"Maybe you should have given Plover the jewelry."

"That's what Duncan said. Duncan wanted me to give Plover the jewelry, but I thought the jewelry was our insurance policy. Plover needed the jewelry. He couldn't kill us as long as we had the fake jewelry."

"So, Duncan cracked under the pressure and decided to end it all," I said.

"Maybe not so much the pressure from Plover," Nutsy said. "We talked about it in Maine. I think mostly it was the failure. For once in his life Duncan took a chance and went bold and it was a complete screwup. He was crushed."

"He didn't seem crushed when I talked to him."

"He had an epiphany. He almost died and when he came out of surgery, his first thought was that he was happy to be alive. He told me he didn't need to be a slick jewel thief to feel alive. He said he just needed to breathe. Pretty fucking profound, right?"

"Tell me about the hospital."

"I got a call from Duncan. He was barely coherent. Babbling. I could hear the terror in his voice. He was out of the ICU and had been moved to a private room and he told me that Plover had walked in. Plover was dressed in scrubs like a hospital worker, but Duncan knew it was Plover. He said Plover never said anything, and he didn't know what Plover was going to do because a nurse came in right then to check vitals. Plover told her he was in the wrong room and left. I guess I panicked, but all I could think of was getting Duncan out of there and someplace safe. So, I got Sissy and her van and we rolled Duncan out and took him to Maine."

"That's quite a story."

"Yeah," Nutsy said. "Nutsy Manley pulls off another hare-brained stunt."

"This time it was probably a good idea," I said.

"I guess," Nutsy said, "but not as spectacular as some of my others."

Nutsy had gathered up all his belongings. He checked his watch and looked toward the door.

"We should leave," he said. "Sissy will be home soon."

"Where are you going now?"

"I don't know," he said. "I have to keep looking for the homeless guy, and I'm sure you don't want me in your apartment. Next thing Plover will be after you too."

"Get rid of the bike so you aren't so easy to spot, and you can stay with me. I'm going to help you. I don't know why. I'm not sure I even believe you."

"It was our intimate moment when we were at Louise Kutka's party in eighth grade," Nutsy said. "We have a bond."

"I'm helping you in spite of our intimate moment," I said. "I have to go to the bail bonds office now. Try to keep a low profile and pick up when I call you."

CHAPTER SIXTEEN

Lula and Connie were finishing lunch when Bob and I walked in.

"We got all my problems solved," Lula said. "Except for my clothes. I need to go to the mall and get some essentials."

"Have you had lunch?" Connie asked me. "There's some pasta salad in the fridge."

I got the salad and pulled a chair up to Connie's desk. "Have you been in touch with your neighbors?" I asked Lula. "Maybe one of them rescued your clothes."

"I talked to all of them but crazy Becky. No one has my clothes. What's new with you?"

"Not much. I ran into Nutsy. He was getting his stuff from Sissy's house."

"That's too bad," Lula said. "I was hoping he'd stay with Sissy. That would have been a better arrangement. He already had a bedroom in Sissy's house. He kind of cramps my style when he's living with us in your apartment."

My heart stopped dead in my chest for a full thirty seconds. "Are you staying with me? I thought you and Connie solved all your problems."

"We did," Lula said. "Figuring out living arrangements until my apartment is fixed up was easy. I told Connie we're like two peas in a pod in your apartment. There's no reason to look any further. And by the way, what were you planning for dinner? Nutsy finished off your peanut butter. And I don't think there's any more bread or beer. Maybe a glass of wine would be nice for tonight. Personally, I like white because if you spill some it doesn't leave a stain. We could celebrate being together. Just like sisters. Do you have cable? I have my favorite shows. Most of them we can stream but sometimes there's something on cable."

I finished the pasta salad and stood. "Gotta go. Things to do."

"Me too," Lula said. "What time is dinner?"

"There's no dinner," I said. "I don't cook."

"Yeah, but you defrost."

"I don't defrost," I said. "Sometimes I toast. And frequently I dial. That's as complicated as it gets."

I have nothing against cooking. I have pots and pans. I watch cooking shows and I buy foodie magazines. I actually like food a lot. It's just that I can't get motivated to spend hours in the kitchen when the only other creature eating my food is a hamster. He's happy with a grape. I suppose I could find joy in fixing dinner for Lula and Nutsy, but if I feed them real meals, they might want to stay longer. I like them, but not in my apartment.

"Okay," Lula said, "I'll be in charge of dinner. I'm excellent at dialing. Dinner is at six o'clock."

Bob and I left the office and got into Ranger's SUV. I settled myself behind the wheel, took a calming breath, and called Nutsy.

"Hey," he said.

"Where are you?"

"I'm leaving Sissy's house. I swapped out my bike for Duncan's Kia Rio. Sissy's okay driving my bike. She's done it before."

"Not perfect but good enough. Let's find the homeless guy. Pick a meet spot."

"The coffee shop on Broad and Twenty-Third Street."

Nutsy was already there when Bob and I arrived. He was sitting at an outside table, and he was looking nervous. I left Bob with him, went inside to get a coffee, and returned to the table.

"You can relax," I said to Nutsy. "Plover isn't sniper material."

"He might have hired someone," Nutsy said. "A hit man."

"Do you have reason to believe this?"

"It's what happens on television."

"Tell me about the homeless guy. What does he look like? Have you seen him since his friend was killed?"

"He was a little past middle-aged. Maybe late fifties. Hard to tell with homeless because they have hard lives, and they age. A white guy but weathered and tan. Sort of faded brown hair. Ponytail. Maybe five foot ten. Shorter than me. Medium build. He was usually in sneakers and baggy pants and a T-shirt and sweatshirt. Mostly clean-shaven."

"That describes half the men in Trenton."

"He had a spider tattoo on his hand. Both homeless guys had the spider tattoo."

"That's helpful."

"They were always on the corner, outside the jewelry store, but I haven't seen them since the one guy was shot."

"Have you talked to anyone else in the area who might know them? Other panhandlers, crazies, drug dealers?"

"A hooker knew them as Marcus and Stump. Stump is the one who was killed. He was taller than Marcus and he had gray hair that looked like steel wool. Frizzy. She said they weren't customers but she talked to them sometimes, and sometimes they showed up for the evening food truck."

"Did you talk to the food truck people?"

"Sure, but they didn't know much. They just hand out sandwiches and soup. It's not like they're social workers. They remembered Marcus because of the spider tattoo, but they haven't seen him lately."

"Have you been watching the food truck?"

"I was for a while. No Marcus."

"Have you looked at the group of homeless under the bridge?"

"Yeah, no Marcus," Nutsy said. "I went to all the shelters and the soup kitchen. No Marcus. It's like he's vanished."

"Are you sure Marcus and Stump were homeless? Some of the professional panhandlers make decent money."

"I don't know. I never talked to them when they were on the corner. They looked homeless."

I capped my coffee and stood. "Let's drive around and see if you spot him. Sunday isn't prime time for begging, but we'll cruise the hotspots."

———

I gave up the hunt at four o'clock. I dropped Nutsy off at the Kia and handed Bob over to him.

"Take Bob for a walk before you take him up to the apartment," I told Nutsy. "I need to stop at the market."

A half hour later I rolled the loaded shopping cart to the Explorer. Bread, beer, peanut butter, deli meat, sliced cheese, frozen enchiladas, a couple bags of cookies, milk, OJ, boxes of assorted cereals, several bottles of white wine, bags of chips, salsa, hot dogs, rolls, a couple boxes of Kraft mac and cheese, and a bunch of other stuff. It was more food than I'd bought in the last six months. Was I a good hostess, or what?

I loaded the bags of food in my building's elevator and called upstairs for help. I knew Lula and Nutsy were there. I'd parked behind their cars.

"I got food coming at six o'clock," Lula said after we got all the bags into the kitchen. "I went with sushi and pad thai for our first celebration dinner. We can cut up the frozen enchiladas for hors d'oeuvres."

In clown mode, Nutsy pantomimed eating hors d'oeuvres and drinking wine.

"You're freaking me out," Lula said to Nutsy. "Get a real beer for cripes' sake."

Nutsy mooned her, and then Lula mooned Nutsy.

I cracked open the wine, poured myself a large glass, and took my wine into my bedroom.

Lula's shoes were lined up against one wall. Her newly purchased clothes were hanging in my closet and her undies were in a plastic bin on top of my dresser. Two blond wigs on Styrofoam heads were also on the dresser, and one of the pillows on my bed was sporting a neon magenta silk pillowcase. A fluffy white rabbit with floppy ears was propped against the magenta pillow.

I chugged half the wine and called Morelli. "Tell me you're at the airport and on your way home," I said. "The trial is over, right? Today was the end of it?"

"Sorry," he said. "It's a weekend. Nothing happens on a weekend."

"Then why aren't you here? Why didn't you come home for the weekend?"

"The department doesn't pay me to come home for the weekend."

"So, you couldn't buy your own ticket? What do I hear in the background? Is that music?"

"I'm at a bar."

"Omigod, you're at a bar. I'm here with two morons mooning each other in my kitchen and you're at a bar."

"Is something wrong?"

"Yes! *Everything* is wrong. I can't find the homeless man, I've got men's underwear and socks in my laundry basket, I just spent five hundred thirty-seven dollars and forty-seven cents on food, and I don't like sushi."

"I'm having a hard time hearing you," Morelli said. "The music just amped up."

"What kind of music is that? Are you at a titty bar? Here's the thing, I might need to move into your house for a couple days."

"My house? Anthony is living there."

"Your brother is living in your house?"

"It just happened. His wife kicked him out again. It never lasts long. In a couple days they'll get together, and she'll be pregnant."

"I'm dying here," I said to Morelli. "You're at a titty bar and I'm facing another night of sleeping with Lula."

"We have a bad connection," Morelli said. "I thought you said you were sleeping with Lula. I'll call you later when I'm back in my hotel."

Lula yelled at me from the living room. "Hors d'oeuvres are ready. They exploded a little in your microwave, but we can clean it up later."

I drank the rest of my wine and went out for hors d'oeuvres.

CHAPTER SEVENTEEN

At 1:03 a.m. I dragged myself out of bed, put a sweatshirt on over my pajamas, and found my way to the front door in the dark. Bob was right behind me. I grabbed my messenger bag, and Bob and I exited the apartment.

"I couldn't take it anymore," I said to Bob. "If I'd stayed in there any longer, I would have smothered Lula with her magenta pillow. I need sleep."

Bob's tail was down, and he looked like he had bags under his eyes. He needed sleep too. We left the building and got into the Explorer, and I drove to my parents' house. Lights were off. I looked at the time on my phone. Crap.

"We can't crash here," I said to Bob. "Everyone's asleep. I'd scare the bejeezus out of them if I walked into the house."

I couldn't go to Morelli's house. Anthony was there. I could try a hotel, but I had Bob with me. I'd have to find a dog-friendly hotel. I drove past Connie's house. Lights were off there too, and she lived with her mother, who was a bit of a nightmare. I had one option left. Ranger.

It was eerie driving through the city. Not many cars on the road. No pedestrians. A few men sleeping in doorways of stores and office buildings. Light pooled under streetlamps, but the buildings were black.

I turned onto Ranger's street and idled in front of his office building. A light went on at the entrance to the underground garage. I was driving a fleet car, and I was a blip on one of the control room screens.

I sucked in some air and dialed Ranger.

"Babe," he said.

"Hi!" I said. All cheery. "How's it going?"

Ranger disconnected and the gate to the garage opened without the use of my key card. I parked in one of his spots by the elevator, Bob and I got out, and the elevator door opened. We stepped in and we were whisked up to Ranger's private floor. Ranger was waiting at the door to his apartment. Beyond him the lights were dim. He'd probably been asleep when the control room awakened him. He was wearing a T-shirt and sweats. He looked at me and he looked at Bob.

"There's a story here," he said.

Ranger's apartment had been professionally decorated by someone who'd listened when Ranger told her what he wanted. Cool. Serene. Subtly masculine. Comfortable. A short hall led to an open-concept living room, dining area, and small, state-of-the-art kitchen. Beyond the living room were Ranger's office, bedroom, and bathroom. Ella made sure that his one-thousand-thread-count percale sheets were ironed, his pillows were sleep inducing, his bath towels were fluffy, his kitchen was stocked, his clothes were lint free, wrinkle free, and a perfect fit. Ella and her husband lived in an apartment on the first floor.

I followed Ranger to the kitchen. "Do we need to talk?" he asked. "Do you need food? Wine?"

"I need sleep," I said.

"I'm listening."

"I don't have the energy to go into detail. Lula and Nutsy are living with me. Nutsy is on the couch and Lula has taken over my bedroom. If I stayed in my apartment a moment longer there would be blood all over the floor and it wouldn't be mine."

"This would explain the sweatshirt over the pajamas, but it doesn't explain the pajamas. I've never known you to sleep in pajamas."

"I sleep in pajamas when it's cold and when Lula is sharing my bed. She's a bed hog, and she snores like a rhinoceros. Poor Bob went into the bathroom to try to sleep." Tears started to leak out of my eyes. "They've taken over my apartment. I like them but I can't live with them."

Ranger cuddled me into him and kissed me just above my ear. "But you can live with me?"

I nodded and sniffed up some snot.

He wrapped an arm around me and moved me toward the bedroom. "We'll figure this out in the morning."

I shucked my sweatshirt and slipped into Ranger's bed. The sheets were smooth and cool. The comforter was just right. The pillow was perfect, and it wasn't magenta satin. Ranger slid in next to me and Bob jumped up onto the bed. Bob turned around twice and curled up at our feet.

"This is a first," Ranger said. "I've never slept with another man's dog."

———

Ranger was long gone when Bob and I woke up. I zipped myself into my sweatshirt and took Bob out for a short walk. When we returned to Ranger's apartment, Ella had set breakfast out for Bob and me. There was a bag of organic beef-flavored kibble for Bob plus matching food and water bowls. My breakfast consisted of smoked salmon, deviled eggs, a toasted bagel with cream cheese, a selection of pastries, a fruit plate, and coffee.

A change of clothes had been placed on the bed. This wasn't the first time I'd unexpectedly stayed with Ranger. Ella knew all my sizes. I showered and got dressed, and Bob and I went down to the fifth floor. I stepped out of the elevator and Lula called.

"Thank goodness you answered," Lula said. "Are you okay? Where are you?"

"Bob and I are at Rangeman. Breakfast meeting."

"I got up and you weren't in the apartment. And then I got to the office, and you weren't there either, so I was afraid Grendel stole you just like my clothes and stuff."

"I haven't seen Grendel," I said. "What's going on with Nutsy?"

"He was still sleeping when I left."

"I have some business to take care of here, and then I'll be in the office later this morning."

"Okey dokey. I might go shopping and get some houseplants to brighten the apartment up."

"I'm not good with houseplants," I said. "They always die."

"No problem. I got a green thumb. You know what else might be good? An aquarium."

"No! No aquarium. I do not want an aquarium."

"Salt water is best. The best fish live in salt water."

"No aquarium. No, no, no, no."

I hung up, and Bob and I walked down the hall to Ranger's office. Bob bounded in and rushed up to Ranger for ear ruffles and head scratches.

I sat in the chair by Ranger's desk. "Lula is stuck in my house. I don't know how to get rid of her."

"You could tell her to leave," Ranger said. "That usually works."

"And then there's Nutsy."

Ranger leaned back in his chair a little. "Tell me about Nutsy."

Twenty minutes later, Ranger had the whole picture.

"Do we believe him?" Ranger asked.

"Good question. I believe some of it. He's got a bunch of stitches where he was shot. And it kind of holds together if you know Nutsy. He claims to have the bag of jewelry. I think we should check it out."

"I don't have anything on my schedule until this afternoon. Let's start with the bag of jewelry. Tell Nutsy we want to talk to him."

Nutsy was still in my apartment when I called.

"Don't go anywhere," I said. "I'm downtown, but I'm on my way home."

We took my fleet car with Ranger driving. He was in Rangeman black fatigues and windbreaker. I was in black jeans, a pink fitted

V-neck T-shirt, and an extra-small Rangeman fleece jacket. Ella enjoyed dressing a girl for a change.

"What's in this for you?" Ranger asked me. "What have you got to gain by proving Plover committed a laundry list of crimes?"

"Nothing," I said. "What's in it for you?"

"Nothing," Ranger said.

"But we're going to do it?"

"I don't like unfinished business," Ranger said.

"And there are the cats. If something terrible happens to Nutsy's mom, who will take care of the cats?"

————

Nutsy was watching television and eating Froot Loops out of the box when we walked in. He looked at Ranger and all color drained from his face. Ranger took the remote off the coffee table and shut the television off.

"I told Ranger everything," I said to Nutsy. "He's going to help us."

"Stephanie said you had the jewelry evaluated. Do you have that in writing?" Ranger asked Nutsy.

"No," Nutsy said. "I had Big Al look at it."

Big Al ran a pawnshop on Broad. It was next door to one of Vinnie's rivals, Tip Top Bail Bonds.

"Big Al would know," Ranger said, "but I'd like to see the pieces."

"It's all in Duncan's attic. We put everything into a box marked 'Christmas decorations.'"

"Clever," Ranger said. "Let's take a look."

Ranger took the scenic route to Duncan's perfectly organized house so we would have a chance to check out the beggar dudes. It was still too early for prime-time begging and we didn't see Marcus. We parked at the curb and walked to the front door. Ranger had us inside before Nutsy could find his key.

"How does he do that?" Nutsy whispered to me.

"I haven't a clue," I said.

We walked through the house and Nutsy released the stairs that led to the attic. He climbed the stairs and returned with the "Christmas decorations" box.

Ranger opened the box and we all looked inside. The jewelry was in a jumble. Some pieces were wrapped in tissue. Some were scattered. An earring here, a ring there.

"This is a mess," I said.

"You should have seen it when it was in the garbage bag," Nutsy said. "The few pieces that might be worth something we wrapped in the tissue paper. It's not like they're actually real, but we thought they were pretty."

"We need to have this professionally evaluated and cataloged," Ranger said to Nutsy. "In the meantime, I think it would be interesting to have you pay a visit to Plover."

"He'll shoot me!"

"Not with his security guard looking on. Not during business hours. And not in front of Stephanie. She was hired to find you. She's going to bring you to Plover to prove she found you. She's going to collect her finder's fee. She's going to tell Plover that you're unarmed and would like to talk to him. Then she'll tell you that she'll be waiting outside."

"What will I say to him?"

"In a quiet voice that the security guard can't hear, you'll tell Plover that you have his jewelry, and you know he wants it back. Tell him that terrorizing your family isn't a step in the right direction because it makes you angry. And when you're angry you're not in the mood to negotiate."

"Yeah, that's good," Nutsy said. "What else?"

"That should be enough. You don't want to do a lot of talking. He'll ask you what it is that you want. Tell him you want two hundred thousand. And you want him to leave you alone."

"Do you think he'll do that?" Nutsy asked.

"No," Ranger said.

"What about the security guard?" Nutsy asked. "What if *he* shoots me?"

"He isn't going to shoot you," Ranger said. "You aren't armed, and you aren't threatening anyone. And he'll know that Stephanie is waiting for you outside the store. The guard can remove you from the store but that's the extent of his power."

"I guess that'll be okay," Nutsy said. "If I yell, you're going to come rescue me, right?"

"Right," Ranger said.

Ranger cut across town and pulled into the Rangeman garage. We met Tank, Ranger's second in command, on the fifth floor. Tank served in Special Forces with Ranger, and he lives up to his name.

Ranger handed the Christmas box over to Tank. "Give this to Kevin Mealy for an itemized assessment and send Sal to my office with a wire. I want the Cobalt N317."

"Do you want it to feed into your cell phone?"

"Yes."

We followed Ranger across the room to the cafeteria. Nutsy

and I got coffee, Ranger and Bob got water. Sal was waiting with the wire when we got to Ranger's office.

"This is high-tech but simple," Ranger said to Nutsy. "It's a wireless wire. It's about the size of a quarter with a sticky pad on the back. We'll put it on your chest under your shirt. If you get nervous and sweat, it should still stick to you. I'll be able to hear everything that's going on, and if things go south, I'll step in."

"Should I try to get him to incriminate himself?" Nutsy asked.

"No," Ranger said. "It wouldn't hold up in court. This is just for your safety."

I knew this wasn't true. That is, the part about it not being legal evidence was true, but the part about Nutsy's safety was only partly true. Ranger wanted to hear how Plover responded to the threat. Ranger had doubts about Nutsy's version of the crime.

On the way out Nutsy stopped and looked in at the control room. "This is unreal," he said. "This is Tom Cruise stuff. I could set a book here and sell it to the movies."

Ranger cut his eyes to him. "No."

Plover's store was a short distance from Rangeman. We parked half a block away and Bob and Ranger stayed behind. After Nutsy and I were in the store, Ranger and Bob would move a little closer. The Cobalt N317 was sexy but it didn't have great range.

Nutsy walked beside me, looking nervous.

"Are you okay?" I asked him. "This isn't going to be a big deal. Plover is going to behave."

"It's not Plover who bothers me. It's Ranger. He's even scarier than I imagined. And his office building is a fortress. He probably has one of those searchlights on his roof like Batman."

"The searchlight was on the roof of the Gotham City Police Department. It was used to summon Batman."

"Whatever," Nutsy said. He suddenly gasped and looked down at his chest. "He can hear me, can't he! Crap!"

"Don't worry about it. Everyone thinks he's scary."

"Except you."

"He's just scary on the outside. Inside he's a big gooey marshmallow."

I struggled not to laugh when I said it. I knew Ranger was listening and would be horrified. And then the horror would turn to amusement, and he'd plan his revenge.

It was still early for jewelry shopping and there were no customers in the store when Nutsy and I entered. The security guard was standing just inside the door. He nodded and smiled. Plover was at his desk. He looked up and sucked in some air.

"It wasn't part of the deal, but I thought I'd bring Andy with me," I said to Plover. "Actually, it was his idea. He wanted to talk to you."

"Arrest him!" Plover said to his security.

"Whoa, wait a minute," I said. "He's unarmed, and he hasn't committed a crime."

"He stole my diamonds," Plover said.

"That's your opinion. The police investigated and didn't charge him. Your security guard has no grounds for action. I found him for you. That was the extent of our arrangement. I'd like my finder's fee."

"Invoice me and I'll mail it to you."

"That doesn't work for me," I said. "I want it now. Cash."

Plover went to his cash register, counted out a small stack of bills, and handed it to me.

"Andy would like to talk to you," I said to Plover. "I'll wait outside. I brought him here, and I need to take him to his vehicle when you're done talking."

I left the store and stood just clear of the door. Ranger and Bob were tucked into the alleyway.

After five minutes the door opened and Nutsy walked out. He looked at me and rolled his eyes.

"We're getting picked up in front of the Cake Bakery two blocks from here," I said to him. "Let's go for a stroll."

"I can't believe all this happened because I wrote a story," he said. "My life made more sense when I was doing ridiculous stunts. Or being a clown."

"How did it go with Plover?"

"Great. He grabbed me and got right up in my face and said he would kill me and my parents and my grandmother and all my mother's cats. Good thing I was prepared for that. I got to use the lines about it making me angry and that I wasn't in the mood to negotiate. And his comeback was that there was no negotiation. So, I said, 'Does that mean you don't want your fake jewelry back? Because right now it's with a friend in a box addressed to your insurance company.' And then he said he didn't have two hundred thousand dollars. So, I said, 'How about a hundred thousand dollars?' And he thought about it for a beat and said he would need a day to come up with the money. So, I'm supposed to call him tomorrow at noon."

We got to the Cake Bakery, and since I didn't see Ranger and the Explorer, I scooted inside and bought a cake. I came out just as Ranger parked at the curb.

Nutsy sat in back with Bob, and I got in front and kept the cake box on my lap.

Ranger pulled into traffic. "You can remove the medallion," he said to Nutsy. "It cut out for about three minutes. All I heard was static."

"That must have been when he grabbed me," Nutsy said. "I told him I had his jewelry, and I knew he wanted it back, and he grabbed the front of my shirt and went psycho."

"What's the bottom line," Ranger said.

"He bargained me down to a hundred thousand dollars and said he needed a day to raise it. I'm supposed to call him tomorrow at noon."

"I'm going to drop you off at Stephanie's apartment," Ranger said. "I want you to stay there. Do not go out."

"Sure," Nutsy said. "No problem. Only thing is I could use some ice cream. Butter pecan or mint chocolate chip. Chocolate is good too."

We made sure that Nutsy was safely locked away in my apartment with a gallon of ice cream, and Ranger drove out of my parking lot.

"I missed a piece of the conversation at Plover's," Ranger said. "Did Plover really grab Nutsy or did he intentionally block the transmission?"

"I don't know," I said. "I couldn't see them. I was outside."

Ranger turned onto Hamilton Avenue. "I have to get back to Rangeman. I have meetings until four. After four we can look for Marcus. Do you want to hang in my apartment until then?"

"No," I said. "I'll come back at four. I should check in at the office."

"And eat the cake you bought?"

"Yes. And eat the cake."

———

I'd gotten a twelve-layer carrot cake with a massive amount of cream cheese frosting. I put the cake on Connie's desk and handed Lula and Connie each a fork, and we dug in. Bob was deprived of cake due to his lactose issue.

"This is an excellent cake," Lula said. "It has the perfect ratio of sponge layer to frosting. I might want to bake a cake like this. Now that I have an oven, I could see if I want to be a pastry chef. It could open up a whole new profession for me. I could end up on one of those cake-baker shows. They like having voluptuous but classy women like me on those shows. Especially if you can bake a cake."

Halfway through the cake I put my fork down. "I can't eat any more," I said.

"That's 'cause you're an amateur," Lula said. "You don't know how to pace yourself. You just jump in and gobble. I practice mindful consumption."

"It looked to me like you were gobbling," Connie said.

"Okay, but it was mindful gobbling," Lula said.

"Did I miss anything this morning?" I asked.

"We got a new FTA," Connie said. "Your old friend Simon Diggery."

Simon Diggery is a professional grave robber. He's wily but relatively harmless. He lives in a decrepit trailer with his fifty-pound pet boa constrictor, Ethel, and sometimes with his cousin, Snacker.

"What did he do this time?" Lula asked. "Did he get caught digging someone up again?"

"Drunk and disorderly, destruction of personal property, and attempted car theft," Connie said. "He crashed the Wimmer funeral, and then he tried to escape in the hearse. It was only attempted car theft because he passed out behind the wheel before he got out of the cemetery. There was minimal damage to the hearse, but Simon ran over Henry Greetch and cracked his tombstone."

Connie handed me the paperwork.

"Looks like he's still at the same address," I said.

"Does it say anything about Ethel?" Lula asked. "Not that I'm afraid of snakes or anything, but I'd take extra precautions if Ethel is in Simon's broken-down trailer."

"What precautions would you take?" Connie asked.

"I wouldn't go in the trailer," Lula said. "Although last time Ethel was up a tree and that wasn't good either."

I tucked the Diggery file into my messenger bag and stood. "Are you riding along?" I asked Lula.

"Absolutely," she said. "Someone's gotta protect Ranger's car when you go into the trailer to root out Diggery."

CHAPTER EIGHTEEN

It was a thirty-five-minute drive to the unimproved dirt road that led to Diggery's trailer. The area was wooded and sparsely populated. There were a couple yurts, a hut patched together with sheets of corrugated metal, a couple bungalows that had seen better days. And Diggery at the end of the road.

"This is real country living on this road," Lula said when we passed one of the yurts. "If I lived here, I'd have a chicken. I always wanted a chicken."

"A little red hen?"

"Exactly. You gotta admire their work ethic. And I hear they make good pets."

We reached the end of the road and Diggery's trailer came into view. The area had been cleared of trees so that the trailer sat on an island of dirt. A rusted Ford F-150 pickup was parked close to the trailer.

"Looks like he's home," Lula said. "And he got a different trailer."

The trailer wasn't new, but it wasn't a disaster either. I parked on the edge of the makeshift driveway and called Diggery.

"Yo," he said.

"Hey, Simon," I said. "It's Stephanie Plum. You missed your court date. I'm in your driveway. I came to help you get rescheduled."

"I know where you are," he said. "I can see you. Go away."

"Looks like you got a new trailer."

"Yeah. So what?"

"It looks nice."

"I came into some money."

"Is Ethel in there with you?"

"Ethel died. She was old. I got Ethel Number Two now."

"How big is Ethel Number Two?"

"Big enough to eat a cow. You're disturbing my afternoon and you're trespassing. You should leave before I have to shoot you."

"You wouldn't shoot me. We're old friends."

"We aren't friends," Diggery said. "We're business associates."

I got out of the car and waved at him. "I'm coming in," I said.

"The hell you are," Diggery said. "I got a lock on the door of this trailer. And besides that, Ethel Number Two might eat you."

"Ethel only eats when she's hungry and I'm betting on her not being hungry."

"Well then she'll squeeze you until your eyes pop out of your head and you have a bathroom accident."

"That would be unpleasant. How about if you come out here to talk."

"I don't want to go to jail."

"Court is still in session. I'll have Connie meet us at the municipal building and you'll get rescheduled, and I'll bring you back to your trailer."

"Can I take Ethel?"

"No."

"She don't like being left alone."

"Will she fit in a cage?"

"Hell no. She barely fits in my trailer."

"Turn the television on for her. I hear that works sometimes."

"I guess I could do that. You got any incentives for me to go with you?"

"Lula is with me."

"That's not an incentive. She scares the crap out of me."

"What do you want? Cheeseburger? A dozen doughnuts? A couple lottery tickets? A bucket of chicken? A six-pack of beer? Bottle of whiskey?"

"I'm heavy into whiskey these days."

"You got it."

"Okay, but you got to wait a minute, and I'll put some clothes on."

"You don't have any clothes on?"

"I like the freedom of nakedness and it saves on the laundry. And Ethel don't mind."

I guess that's the advantage of living with a snake.

I got back into the car. "He's getting dressed," I said to Lula.

"He has to wear something special?"

"Pretty much."

Five minutes later Diggery came out. He locked his door and walked to my car.

"There's a dog in here," he said.

"That's Bob," I told him. "Would you rather sit with Lula?"

"I'd rather sit in front with you. Not that I have anything against dogs, but Ethel might not like it."

"Yeah, we wouldn't want her to squeeze you in the middle of the night because she was jealous," I said.

Lula got out and sat in back with Bob, and Diggery got in next to me.

"This is a nice car," he said. "You must have come into money too."

"Tell me about the money," I said.

"It's business related," Diggery said. "I can't talk about it because I'm officially retired."

I called Connie, she met us at the municipal building, and an hour later, Diggery was rescheduled, and we were on our way back to his trailer. I stopped at the liquor store on Broad so Lula could get him some whiskey.

"Don't drink this bottle all at once and crash another funeral," I said to Diggery.

"I didn't crash the funeral," he said. "I was taking an early morning stroll and I saw they had the canopy up for the funeral and thought it would be a good place for a nap. I had a couple nips from my flask, and I was half-asleep when these people came rushing at me. I panicked and mistook the hearse for my pickup and accidentally ran off the car path."

"So, the translation is that you were out all night looking for a grave to rob. You got drunk and passed out at the Wimmer grave site, and when the funeral director tried to remove you, you got into the first vehicle you saw, and it happened to be the hearse."

"I guess that could be another interpretation of events," Diggery said.

"I might have a job for you. I need to find a body."

"A dead body?"

"Yep."

"I'm your man."

"I'm looking for a homeless guy who goes by the name of Stump. He was shot multiple times four weeks ago. Average height. Frizzy gray hair. Had a spider tattoo on his hand. Got dumped somewhere."

"That's a tough one. Where was he shot?"

"King Street. At night. Behind Plover's jewelry store."

"That gives me some ideas. If the shooter decided to drive the body out of town I'm lost. If he wanted a quick shallow grave, I know some spots. Problem is Stump's gonna be pretty decayed after a month. The hand with the tattoo might be eaten away by now. Ideally, I need something metal to look for. The bigger the better."

"Understood. I'll get back to you on it."

———

I met Ranger at four o'clock and we cruised the downtown area.

"It's been a month since Stump was shot," Ranger said. "If Marcus is still in Trenton, he might be feeling safe enough to come out of hiding. We have some contacts in the homeless community. I have one of my men talking to them."

We rode around for a half hour and Ranger got a call.

"We have a lead," he said. "Marcus surfaced a couple days ago. My man hasn't seen him, but his source said Marcus is hanging between the Catholic church on French Street and the train station."

"If he's back to panhandling, this is a good time to look for him. It's rush hour for the commuters. Prime time for beggars."

Ranger left the downtown area, drove to the train station, and parked.

We all got out and walked toward the station. We didn't see anyone who fit Marcus's description. There was a scrawny guy selling roses. Beyond him there were a couple hookers. They didn't know Marcus, but Ranger was offered a freebie. We crossed the street and saw a guy standing on the corner. He looked desperate and down on his luck and he had a piece of torn cardboard that he was using as a sign. He was slim and weathered, and he had a ponytail.

We walked toward him, all casual. A man and a woman and a goofy big dog. We stopped and read the sign. NEED WORK. HELP A VET. GOD BLESS. The hand holding the sign had a spider tattoo.

I smiled at him. Friendly. "Marcus?"

He looked at me, and then he looked at Ranger and you could see the alarm bells going off in his head. He dropped his sign, grabbed a woman standing behind him, waiting for the light to change, shoved her at Ranger, and took off into traffic. Ranger moved the woman aside and ran after Marcus, dodging cars that were screeching to a stop and swerving to avoid an accident. Bob yanked the leash out of my hand and ran after Ranger. I ran after Bob. Marcus was clearly no match for Ranger. Ranger is in prime shape and fast. He was within two feet of Marcus when Bob launched himself into the air and planted his two front feet on Ranger's back. Ranger hit the pavement with Bob on top of him.

When I got to Ranger he was on his back with Bob looking all happy at his side.

"Omigod," I said. "I'm so sorry. Are you okay?"

"Do I look okay?" Ranger asked.

"No. You have a lot of blood on your face. I think it's dripping out of your nose."

I reached into my messenger bag and found some tissues.

"Bob thought you were playing with him," I said. "He loves to chase things."

"He's not sleeping on the bed tonight," Ranger said. "And you aren't wearing pajamas."

I helped him up. "You almost caught Marcus."

"Almost doesn't count."

I drove back to Rangeman, and by the time I parked in the garage, the blood had stopped dripping from Ranger's nose.

"You're kind of scary looking," I said. "Your shirt is splattered with blood."

"I've looked a lot worse," Ranger said. "I'm fine. Everyone in my building is either retired military, police, or has been incarcerated. This won't be the first time they've seen a bloody shirt."

"Do you want me to help you get upstairs?"

"Not necessary, but I'd like you to come back tonight. We need to talk."

"You keep saying that, but we never talk."

"Life keeps interfering," Ranger said.

"Can Bob sleep on the bed?"

"Yes. But I don't want to see you in pajamas."

Fair enough. I could sleep in sweats or jeans or a suit of armor.

———

Nutsy was watching television when Bob and I entered the apartment. He was surrounded by chips bags, dirty dishes, and empty soda cans. Lula was in the kitchen, drinking wine out of the bottle.

"I just had a fright," Lula said. "Grendel almost got me. After I left the office, I went to my apartment to check things out. The tape is gone from the building, and nobody is living there yet, but you could see that people had been working to clean things up. I stepped inside to look around, and there was this horrible growl sound and Grendel jumped out at me. And then he said my name, and he reached for me, but I was already running out of the house."

"You actually saw Grendel?"

Lula took another hit from the bottle of wine. "Yeah. It was dark in the house, but I could see that it was Grendel."

"What did you do? Did you call the police?"

"No. I was in a state. I got in my car and took off, and when I drove away, I could see the outline of him standing in the doorway. He had a big bag in one hand, like a black garbage bag. I figured it was a sack that he was gonna use to kidnap me. And he was shaking his fist at me with the other hand. I tell you, my heart was racing, and all I could think of was getting back here in one piece. And here I am." She looked around the kitchen. "I need food. I used up all my calories. I don't suppose you brought pizza home with you? Maybe a meatball hoagie or a pork roll sandwich?"

"Nope. No takeout," I said, "but there should be sandwich stuff in the fridge."

Lula looked in the fridge. "It's bare in here. I think Nutsy got hungry."

"Not my problem," I said. "I did my hostess thing and now you guys are on your own."

"I don't think Nutsy has any money," Lula said. "And I spent all my money on beautification of our apartment."

I looked into the living room. There were a lot of green plants positioned around the room and a bunch of colorful pillows on the couch.

"Hey, Nutsy," Lula yelled. "Get away from my pillows with those chips. If I see chip crumbs on my new pillows, I won't be happy. And for God's sake clean up your mess. It's like you're a farm animal. And put some pants on. I don't give a rat's ass even if you are a clown. I don't have men sitting around in my house in their undershorts. Have some class."

"I need information on Stump," I said to Nutsy. "What was he wearing the night he was shot? Did he have a belt with a buckle? Was he wearing jewelry? A watch?"

"Who's Stump?" Lula asked. "Why was he shot?"

I brought Lula up to speed on Marcus and Stump.

"That's too bad about Ranger's nose," Lula said. "He had a perfect nose. I hope he's not disfigured. And it explains the bloodstains on your T-shirt."

"I didn't get to see much of Stump," Nutsy said. "He had his back to me. And I never paid a lot of attention to what he was wearing."

"Seems to me we need to find Marcus," Lula said. "We should go to the train station and see if he's still there. And we could order something from Pino's as long as we're out."

"I'm game," Nutsy said. "I'm tired of sitting here."

I changed my shirt, Nutsy put pants on, and we piled into the Explorer.

"This is good," Lula said. "It helps me to get my mind off Grendel."

"I'd like to see Grendel," Nutsy said. "It's not every day that a character out of a video game comes to life."

"According to Stephanie, he was real before the video game," Lula said. "And you only want to see him because he isn't after your body."

"I'm thinking he must fall into the zombie category," Nutsy said.

"I don't like that thinking," Lula said. "I'm not in favor of zombies. Bad enough he's a demon."

"You don't really think he's come alive from a video game, do you?" Nutsy asked.

"I guess not," Lula said. "It's like when you see a clown and he's all done up so that you don't really know what's under the makeup and funny clothes. All I know is that this thing is scary, and he looks like Grendel."

I drove around the train station and headed for the Catholic church on French Street. After an hour of searching with no results, Lula took matters into her own hands and ordered takeout for all of us from Pino's.

"We should find out where the free food is being handed out,"

Lula said, tucking into her meatball sub. "It looks like Marcus got spooked off the street today, but he might come out for soup and a sandwich."

I'd had the same thought. He'd frequented the food truck that fed the hungry in the King Street area. That was no longer convenient to him, but I suspected there was food given out by the Catholic church. I finished my chicken Parm and headed back to French Street.

I was a block from the church when I saw a small group of men huddled around a van.

"That's one of the vans that gives out food," Lula said.

"And I see Marcus," Nutsy said. "He's off to the side with a drink and a sandwich."

I drove past the van and parked around the corner, out of sight. I wanted to sneak up on Marcus, but there was the risk that he'd recognize Nutsy or me. And he'd definitely remember Bob.

"You go in first," I said to Lula. "Keep him occupied so Nutsy and I can get close to him."

We walked around the corner and didn't see Marcus.

"Maybe someone knows him," I said. "He must be crashing somewhere nearby."

"I'll go mingle," Lula said. "I'll use my finesse to fish out information."

"I've tried talking to these people," Nutsy said. "They don't give up anything, and some of them are unhinged."

"Yeah, but that's because you're you. I'm Lula. Leave this to me," Lula said, adjusting her girls, giving them some fresh air to the point where her too-tight shocking-pink scoop-neck sweater barely covered her huge protruding nipples.

Here's the thing. We all have skills, and we have an obligation to use them to the best of our ability. Some people are whizzes with math. Some people are musical prodigies. Some people can bake cakes. Some people can change a tire. Lula has breasts.

Nutsy watched Lula sashay over to the group of men. "Does she know what she's doing?"

"Yep," I said. "Stand down."

Ten minutes later, Lula returned. She had a ham and cheese sandwich on wheat and tomato soup in a cardboard cup.

"His name is Marcus Ulman," she said. "He smokes a lot of dope and drinks whatever he can get his hands on, but he doesn't do anything hard. He's been on the street for at least ten years. Lost his job when the condom factory closed. Wife left him. Has kids but doesn't know where they are. Used to hang with Stump but nobody's seen Stump and Marcus isn't talking about it. Sometimes he crashes in a crack house on the next block. Apparently, he has friends there. Third floor."

"Okay," I said. "Let's take a look at the crack house."

"Isn't that dangerous?" Nutsy asked.

"Not usually," I said. "Mostly it's just sad."

We found the house and I didn't want to involve Bob, so I left him on the sidewalk with Lula. Nutsy and I walked three flights up and knocked on the only door.

A wasted woman with straw hair and acne-pocked skin answered the door.

"Yuh," she said.

"Is Marcus here?" I asked.

She made a motion with her head that said to come in.

The truth is that I was flying on bravado here, and I was

terrified. I was usually tagging along behind Ranger on this sort of mission. Once Lula and I had stumbled into an apartment guarded by an alligator, but that wasn't a normal happening.

I stepped in and looked around. There were mattresses and quilts and sleeping bags on the floor. All soiled and haphazardly placed. All dumpster rescues. The smell was a mixture of stale French fries and human suffering. We stepped around the mattresses and found Marcus at a table in what might have been the dining room. He had a bottle of beer in front of him and he was eating his sandwich.

"Hi, Marcus," I said. "Remember me?"

"And me," Nutsy said.

He looked at me and then at Nutsy. "What do you want?"

"Information," I said.

"I haven't got any," Marcus said.

"Maybe we should have brought Lula," Nutsy said.

"I bet you'd like something better than that beer," I said to Marcus. I pulled a twenty out of my messenger bag and held it out to him. "I want to know about Stump."

"I don't know anybody named Stump," he said.

He reached for the twenty, and I pulled it away. "Tell me about Stump."

"Fuck you," he said.

It smelled really bad in the apartment, Nutsy looked like he was going to lose the Taylor pork roll he'd had for dinner, Lula and Bob were waiting on the sidewalk, and I was expecting a call from Morelli.

"I apologize ahead of time," I said to Marcus, "but it's turning into a very long day, and if I lose this opportunity, I might not be able to find you again."

"Fuck you and fuck him too," Marcus said.

I took my stun gun out of my back pocket and gave Marcus a bunch of volts. Marcus face-planted into his sandwich and slumped out of his chair.

"We need to get him out of here. Which end do you want?" I asked Nutsy.

"Holy crap," Nutsy said.

I grabbed Marcus by the back of his shirt and dragged him to the door. There were seven other people in the crack house and none of them paid any attention to me dragging Marcus. I got him into the hall and looked at the three flights of stairs.

"Are you going to help, or what?" I asked Nutsy.

"What should I do?"

"Grab his feet and don't let go. We have to wrangle him down these stairs."

I was in a full-on sweat by the time we reached the street, and Marcus was coming around.

"Cuffs!" I yelled at Lula.

"I got them in my bag," Lula said, searching through her faux–Louis Vuitton tote. "They're in here somewhere. Here's my gun."

"I don't want to shoot him," I said. "I want to cuff him!"

Marcus had passed the twitching stage and was flailing his arms.

"I found them," Lula said. "Hold him still."

Nutsy grabbed an arm, I grabbed the other arm, and we managed to cuff Marcus.

"Now what?" Lula said.

"Get him in the car and help me strap him in."

"Being that he isn't a felon or anything, this might be construed as kidnapping," Lula said. "Not that I'm worried or anything."

"My story is that he's drunk and high and we're doing an intervention," I said.

"That's just what I was thinking," Lula said. "He'll be thanking us later."

Nutsy went into the back, next to Marcus. We tried to get Bob into the cargo area behind the rear seats, but he wanted none of it, so he sat up front on Lula's lap.

"Usually, we take people in cuffs to the police station," Lula said. "Where are we taking this guy?"

"I don't know," I said. "I didn't totally think this through. I guess we take him to my apartment."

"He's not sitting on the couch," Lula said. "I got new throw pillows on the couch."

"We'll only keep him long enough to talk to him about Stump. Then we can take him back to his crack house."

"Okay," Lula said. "I guess I can live with that."

"He's drooling," Nutsy said.

"They do that sometimes after they've been zapped," I told him. "It's no big deal."

Morelli called and I put in an earbud so he wouldn't broadcast to everyone in the SUV.

"I miss you," he said. "This is turning out to be longer than I expected. How's Bob?"

"Bob is great," I said.

"How are you?"

"I'm good. My nose is feeling better, and the swelling and bruising is almost gone from my eyes. I kidnapped a guy just now and I'm taking him to my apartment. Then I'm heading to Rangeman for the night."

There was a moment of silence. "Do you want to have phone sex?" he asked.

"It would be awkward," I said. "I'm in Ranger's car with Lula, Bob, Nutsy, and the guy I kidnapped."

"Okay, well maybe later."

I hung up and Lula looked over at me. "I didn't hear it all, but I'm thinking he didn't believe a word you said."

"Not a word," I said.

"I'm here in the middle of it, and I don't believe it," Lula said.

I checked Marcus out in my rearview mirror. He was looking much more alert.

"I didn't do it," Marcus said.

"What didn't you do?" I asked him.

"I didn't do anything," he said. "Whatever you think I did . . . I didn't do it."

"We know what you did," I told him. "And we don't care."

He looked at Nutsy. "I know you. You're the doorman at Plover's."

"Yeah," Nutsy said. "And you handed the bag of jewelry off to me after Plover shot your friend."

"That was you? It was dark and I was freaked out. After Stump got shot it was all a blur. I just wanted to get out of there. I figured Plover was going to shoot me too." He looked down at his hands. "Why am I in handcuffs? Are you taking me to Plover?"

"No," I said. "We aren't working for Plover. We're trying to put a bunch of pieces together about the robbery."

"The jewelry is all fake," Marcus said.

"I was in the alley when you and Stump were talking to Plover," Nutsy said. "It sounded like you were trying to blackmail him."

"That was Stump's idea. It turned out we couldn't get much money for the jewelry, but Stump thought Plover would pay to get it back. He figured Plover was passing the junk off as the real thing. Like scamming customers and then his insurance company."

"How did you get the bag of jewelry?" I asked Marcus.

"We saw the guy who robbed the store run out and drop the bag. We were standing right there. And there was all this commotion with police and people on the street, and no one was paying any attention to the bag. So, we took it. We just walked away with it. We didn't know it was filled with jewelry. We would have been happy if it was filled with halfway-decent garbage."

"I want to know about Stump," I said to Marcus. "What was he wearing when he was shot?"

"Same thing he always wore. Pants and a shirt and a hooded sweatshirt."

"Did he have a belt?"

"No."

"A watch?"

"No."

"A ring?"

"No."

"A phone?"

"No."

"Any jewelry?"

"Yeah," Marcus said. "He always wore a cross that he got in Mexico years ago. It was big with stuff engraved on it."

"Did he have anything else on him that was metal?"

"He always carried a knife and fork and spoon. And he had a Swiss Army knife. Why do you want to know? Did someone find him? Is he okay?"

"He hasn't been found, but we're looking," I said.

"This is weird," Marcus said. "Who are you? Are you cops?"

"More or less," Lula said.

"Not me," Nutsy said. "I'm an unemployed doorman."

I was in my parking lot, and I had no further use for Marcus. He'd told me everything I needed to know. He'd backed up Nutsy's story, and he'd given me the information I wanted for Diggery. Eventually, the police would want a statement from him, but it seemed premature to turn him over to the police at this instant. Especially since he was wearing my handcuffs for no legitimate reason.

"Where are we?" Marcus asked.

"We're in the parking lot to my apartment building," I said. "Would you like to come upstairs and have something to eat? You didn't get a chance to finish your sandwich."

Marcus looked out at the building and looked down at his cuffs. "I'd rather just be free to go."

"Of course," I said.

Lula unlocked the cuffs.

"How are you going to get back to the church? It'll take you all night if you walk."

"I'll find a way," he said.

"I can drive you back," I said.

He had the car door halfway open. "No! I mean, thanks, but I don't need a ride."

I gave him a twenty. "Is there a way to get in touch with you if we need more information? Do you have a phone?"

"I don't have a phone," he said, jumping out, backing away. "I don't have anything."

"If you're going to steal a car, don't take this one," I told him.

And he was gone, disappearing behind an SUV, blending into dark shadows.

"Boy, he was in an awful rush," Lula said.

"Maybe because he was just stun-gunned, dragged out of his nice comfy crack house, cuffed, kidnapped, and interrogated," Nutsy said.

I got a call from Diggery.

"I've got someone for you to look at," Diggery said. "I happened to know about a shallow grave and thought I'd go investigate. I got him dug up, but I couldn't see the spider tattoo on account of the worms got to his hands, but I figure he's about the right size."

"I guess it wouldn't hurt to take a look," I said.

"It's the road before mine. It doesn't look like much of a road but there's a couple homes on it. I'm standing at the end of the road. I'm the one with the shovel. Snacker is here with me too."

"Does the road have a name?"

"Not that I know, but there's a couple mailboxes and a refrigerator at the start of the road. The refrigerator doesn't look all that bad to me, but no one seems to want it. I'd take it but I don't have room for another refrigerator."

"I'm about a half hour away," I said.

"Snacker and me will be waiting on you."

Lula was in the front seat next to me, scanning the road for refrigerators.

"It's dark as a witch's you-know-what here," Lula said. "I can't hardly see anything."

"We're coming up to Diggery's street," I said. "It's about a quarter mile away."

"There it is," Lula said. "There's the mailboxes and the refrigerator. It looks like a pretty good refrigerator. Now that your lights are shining on it, I can see it's got some rust. And there's a couple raccoons eyeing it up."

I turned down the street and crept along. The road was dirt and there were no lights. We passed a couple small bungalows that had trucks in the front yard. Diggery and Snacker were standing at the end of the road, leaning on their shovels. I pulled to the side and parked.

We all got out and said hello to Diggery and Snacker.

"This guy looks good," Diggery said. "He's about six feet and there's some gray hair left on his head."

"I don't like this," Lula said. "You know how I feel about dead people. Especially ones that had their hands eaten by worms."

"I like dead people," Snacker said. "They aren't judging. And they aren't always talking."

"I never looked at it that way," Lula said.

There was a mound of freshly dug dirt about twenty feet in front of us. I had Bob on a short leash and a Maglite in my other hand. We approached the mound of dirt and peered into the hole. I flashed the light on what was left of the body and gagged. Lula looked into the grave and gave up her meatball hoagie.

"It's not Stump," Nutsy said. "Stump had more hair. And Stump wore sneakers. This guy's wearing motorcycle boots."

"You didn't tell me about the sneakers," Diggery said.

"I told you when we first dug him up that I thought it was Papa Billy Wiget," Snacker said. "I'm just surprised they buried him with the boots on. The Wigets don't have any money. I guess the boots didn't fit any of them."

"It was worth a try," Diggery said.

Everyone backed away from the grave.

"The man I'm looking for was wearing a large engraved cross and he was carrying a knife and fork and spoon. And he had a Swiss Army knife," I said to Diggery.

"Okay, that could be helpful," Diggery said. "I don't suppose you want this person for any of your purposes."

"No, sorry," I said. "But keep looking."

We hurried back to the SUV and drove away.

"That was awful," Lula said. "Bad enough there's dead people filling up cemeteries, but now we got them at the end of a dirt road. I'm gonna have nightmares. All night long I'm going to be seeing Papa Billy Wiget with the boots and no hands. It was horrible. Whoever buried him could at least have combed his hair. What's this world coming to? I tell you I'm glad I don't have to sleep alone tonight."

"Who are you sleeping with?" I asked her.

"You, of course. It's a time like this when a person is glad to have friends. It's like we're family, right? Truth is, I never had much family. I had my mama and some aunties, but they were always working nights and half the time they were incarcerated.

When you come from a whole family of pleasure facilitators you spend a lot of time alone. Not that it was all bad, I mean my mama did the best she could for me. And as you can see, I turned out to be a superior human being."

I had to agree. Lula was a superior human being. But that didn't mean I wanted to share my apartment with her, much less my bed. On the other hand, sharing Ranger's bed raised issues that I wasn't ready to face.

I made a fast stop at Mega Mart for ice cream, and fifteen minutes later we were all back in the apartment. Lula poured herself a glass of wine. Nutsy dug into the ice cream and I called Ranger.

"How's your nose?" I asked him.

"It's back to normal. You've been doing a lot of driving."

"Lula, Nutsy, and Bob and I went out looking for Marcus. We found him in a crack house, and I encouraged him to talk to us."

"Find out anything useful?"

"He backed up Nutsy's story, and he was able to give me information that will be helpful to Diggery."

"Simon Diggery? The grave robber?"

"He's more or less retired, but it occurred to me that he was the local expert on deceased body location. So, I hired him to find Stump."

"Nice. I assume that's what you were doing on the road to White Horse."

"Yeah. Diggery and his cousin Snacker dug someone up, but it wasn't Stump."

"My life seems so boring compared to yours," Ranger said.

"It's going to get even more boring, because I'm staying here tonight. Lula is in the kitchen working her way through a bottle of wine, and I need to make sure she doesn't go for a second. Earlier this evening she was chased by Grendel and then she threw up on her shoes because Diggery's body didn't have any hands."

"Why didn't it have hands?"

"The worms ate them."

"Babe," Ranger said. And he disconnected.

CHAPTER NINETEEN

At 2:00 a.m. Lula was snoring so loud the windows were rattling. I got out of bed and went into the bathroom to sleep with Bob, but it was only minimally quieter in there.

Bob and I left the bathroom and tiptoed through the living room, where Nutsy was sleeping and snoring. We stopped in the kitchen and listened. Not much better.

"I can't take the snoring anymore," I said to Bob. "I'm exhausted. I need sleep."

I took my hooded sweatshirt off the hook by my door, and Bob and I went out and slept in the hall. I was dragged out of sleep by someone yelling. I squinted at my watch. Seven fifteen. The day had started. I opened the door and Bob and I stared into my apartment. Lula was in her pink pajamas that had pictures of bunnies, her hair looked like it had been electrified, and she was waving her arms and shouting at Nutsy.

"Grendel got her," Lula said. "I heard him come in the room last night and now he's got Stephanie."

"There's no Grendel," I said, stepping into the apartment. "I'm right here."

"Well, what was all the noise last night?" Lula asked.

"It was you," I said. "You snore."

"I definitely don't snore," Lula said. "Sometimes I might breathe heavy if I'm dreaming. And anyways I heard growling and snorting."

"Yeah, me too," I said. "It was you. It was horrible. And Nutsy isn't much better. Bob and I slept in the hall."

"Your problem is that you've got sensitive ears," Lula said.

I filled Bob's bowl with kibble and went to the fridge. No orange juice. No milk. No food. I looked in the freezer. No more ice cream.

"Somebody ate all the food," I said. "I'm done. I'm moving out. You guys are on your own. I love you both, but I can't live with you."

"I guess I understand that," Lula said. "It's hard when you're accustomed to being by yourself and then there's someone else. I'm one of those flexible people. New circumstances don't bother me."

I shuffled off to the bedroom and stuffed some clothes into a duffel bag. When I got back to the kitchen Bob was done eating, so I took his bag of food and told Nutsy to take Rex's aquarium downstairs and put it into the Explorer. I added my computer to the duffel bag and headed for the door.

"Where are you going?" Lula asked.

"My parents' house," I said.

"Good plan," Lula said. "You'll probably get there in time for breakfast. And I'm thinking your mom will do your laundry and everything. And don't worry, I'll take good care of our apartment. I'll keep beautifying it too. I got a knack for interior decorations."

"Am I getting kicked out?" Nutsy said.

"No, but I'm not buying your food anymore," I told him.

"I can deal with that," he said, following me to the elevator.

Bob and I drove to my parents' house, and there was a white Subaru SUV parked in the driveway. I idled at the curb and called my mom.

"Hi," I said. "How's it going?"

"It's going good," she said. "Your aunt Bitsy and uncle Fred arrived last night. They're staying with us for a couple nights, and then we're all going to your cousin Loretta's wedding. You sent in your reply, didn't you?"

"Maybe," I said. "I don't remember. I might have checked off *not attending*."

"You and Loretta were never close," my mom said, "but you really should be going to her wedding."

"Why are Bitsy and Whatshisname staying with you?"

"Loretta shares an apartment with two other girls. They're all nurses, and there wasn't room for Bitsy and Fred."

"I thought Bitsy and Fred lived in Mercerville."

"They moved to Florida when Loretta graduated nursing school."

I hung up and looked at Bob. "Guess where we're going."

Bob knew where we were going, and he was happy about it.

Ranger's apartment was always a nice cool temperature, and Bob's water bowl was always filled with sparkling fresh water.

I called Ranger when I turned onto his street. "Is it okay if Bob and Rex and I move in for a couple days?"

"Did you bring pajamas?"

"I'm wearing pajamas."

"Babe," Ranger said.

The gate to the Rangeman garage opened before I inserted my key card. I parked in one of Ranger's spaces by the elevator, and I was struggling with my duffel bag and Rex's aquarium when Hal appeared and took the duffel and the aquarium from me. I followed behind him with the bag of Bob food and Bob.

"Ranger is in a meeting," Hal said. "He said you should make yourself at home, and Ella will bring breakfast."

I stashed Bob's food in a corner and positioned Rex's aquarium on a kitchen counter. I gave Rex fresh water, and Ella rang the bell once and walked in with the breakfast tray.

"This was a bit of a rush," Ella said. "I'm afraid there aren't any pastries. There's just the usual assortment of granola and fruit and bagels and sides. There's fresh-squeezed orange juice in Ranger's fridge, plus milk and cream. Tomorrow I'll make pancakes with maple syrup and whipped cream. I never get a chance to make pancakes."

Ella left and I made myself coffee in Ranger's fancy built-in coffee machine. I pulled a stool up to the kitchen counter and buttered a bagel.

"This is nice," I said to Bob. "It's quiet."

I was on my second cup of coffee when Ranger walked in and helped himself to smoked salmon and a bagel.

"What's your plan for the day?" he asked.

"I haven't got much of a plan right now. I didn't get a lot of sleep, and my brain isn't working at top speed." I squinted at his face. "Why don't you have black eyes? I got hit in the nose and I looked like I got run over by a truck."

"I'm a fast healer," Ranger said. "I got the report on the jewelry. The gemstones are all very good fakes. And that means the diamonds Plover accused Andrew of stealing were probably also fakes."

"So, Plover has been selling fakes and charging real prices."

"It looks that way. We were able to access his insurance policy, and there's a large discrepancy between the value of what was stolen and what was insured. He's insured for the full value of real gemstones. As far as we know, Plover hasn't officially submitted a claim with his insurance company."

"He needs to get the fakes back first."

"Yes. He's in an awkward situation. He raises suspicion if he doesn't file a claim. If he files a claim for full value of the insured, he runs the risk of the fakes turning up. Then he's committed insurance fraud. If he files a claim for the value of the fakes and it goes public, he could be sued by half the population of Trenton."

"Should we just turn the fakes over to the police?"

"That would be a waste," Ranger said. "Technically, Plover hasn't committed a crime. He hasn't given his insurers a dollar value on his stolen merchandise, and none of his customers have come forward with a complaint for past purchases."

"I know a number of people who've bought jewelry from Plover. I could stir the pot a little."

"It wouldn't hurt to put some added pressure on him."

"He inherited the store from his father and his grandfather. Every girl in my high school wanted a Plover engagement ring. People trusted Plover. How could this happen?"

Ranger shrugged. "People make bad decisions. And people aren't always what they seem. Maybe Plover needed money, and he cheated a little, and then he got swept up in it. And now it's spiraled out of control. It appears that he firebombed a car and he shot and killed an unarmed man, so either he's a hardened career criminal or else he's desperate and willing to do anything to cover his tracks. My guess is that he's desperate."

I selected a strawberry from the fruit plate. "The homicide is a biggie, but we only have the word of Nutsy and a homeless guy living in a crack house."

My phone buzzed. It was Diggery.

"I hope I'm not calling too early," he said, "but Snacker and me thought of another shallow grave we knew about. We've got it dug up if you want to come take a look. The person in question is about the right size and he's got a knife and a fork. We couldn't find a spoon."

I cut my eyes to Ranger and found him smiling.

"Sure," I said to Diggery. "Where are you?"

"Snacker and me are in a patch of woods off Whitle Road. You'll see my truck at the roadside and then you have to follow the path. The grave isn't that far along. When you're in a hurry to bury someone, you don't want to carry the body any farther than necessary."

"Where's Whitle Road?"

"It's right next to Greenhill Cemetery. There's a number of shallow graves here, mostly for people who couldn't afford the cemetery. Not especially good for my line of work, but once in a while you get lucky, and it's a lot easier digging than in a legitimate burial ground."

"I'm about forty minutes away."

I put my phone down and stood. "Are you riding with me?" I asked Ranger.

"Wouldn't want to miss this one. I haven't seen a decayed body all week."

I changed into jeans and a T-shirt and hooked Bob onto his leash, and we all went downstairs. Greenhill Cemetery was north of the city between Trenton-Mercer Airport and Washington Crossing State Park. It seemed like a long drive to make with a bleeding body in your trunk, but it was an impulsive shooting, and Plover probably didn't have time to do a lot of research on shallow grave sites. Or hell, what do I know. Maybe he dumped all his dead bodies there. The woods on Whitle Road could have been filled with his disgruntled customers.

Ranger had no problem finding Whitle Road. It was a service road in a forested greenbelt that ran alongside the cemetery. No houses or businesses, just offshoots into the cemetery. We saw Diggery's truck after a half mile.

Ranger parked and we followed a path of tramped-down grass and shrubs that I suspected was only used by clandestine burial parties and grave robbers. Bob gave a single bark when he saw Diggery.

"Howdy," Diggery said. "I see Bob remembers me. I have a natural way with animals."

I thought it might have something to do with the way he smelled, but I kept that to myself.

"This here's the grave," Diggery said. "Do you think this could be your man? As you can see there's cutlery sticking out of his pocket. He might have had a cross necklace too, but it isn't here now. There were signs that the deceased had been previously disturbed."

"He looks short," I said.

"I told you he was short," Snacker said to Diggery.

"Sometimes it's the way they go into the ground," Diggery said. "Things get smushed together. Are you sure he's not the one?"

"His hands are intact, and I don't see a spider tattoo," I said.

"I guess that could be a game changer," Diggery said. "We had some time while we were waiting for you, so we dug up another body. We've gone high-tech. We're using a metal detector, and we got a hit farther down the path."

Oh boy.

Ranger, Bob, and I followed Diggery to the second grave.

"This looks like a woman," I said, staring into the pit.

"You never know these days," Diggery said. "She's a big one. And she's wearing a cross, so it might be worth considering."

"How do you know about all these grave sites?" I asked Diggery.

"Word gets around," Diggery said. "It's a small community of us interested in relieving the dead of encumbrances they had in life."

Snacker nodded. "Nicely put, cuz."

"I'm afraid neither of these deceased are the one we're looking for," I said to Diggery.

"Yeah, I was worried about that," Diggery said. "We'll keep digging. We got some other possibilities. Some of the ones we got left we have to do at night. I hope that's not a problem for you."

"No problem for me," I said.

We got back to the SUV and Ranger pulled me close and kissed me.

"What's that about?" I asked him.

"If you have to ask, you don't deserve to know," Ranger said.

The man of mystery strikes again.

———

I dropped Ranger off at Rangeman, and I went to the office. Connie was working at her desk, and Lula was on the couch, looking depressed.

"What's going on?" I asked. "The bakery run out of doughnuts?"

"I ate all the doughnuts," Lula said. "In spite of my apartment-decorating responsibilities, I'm mildly depressed, so I'm eating to achieve happiness. If this keeps up, I'm not going to fit into any of my new clothes."

"You never fit in your clothes," Connie said.

"Yeah, but that's by design," Lula said. "It's my persona. That's different from being lumpy." She looked over at me. "Anything new?"

"Diggery had a couple more bodies to look at. Neither of them were Stump."

"Gee, sorry I missed that," Lula said.

"I'm sure," I said. "Did Grendel make any more appearances?"

"No," Lula said. "The only zombie in your apartment is Nutsy. I've got a contractor coming to my place this morning to give me an estimate. My landlord is paying for repairs. She's got insurance on the building, and I had insurance on my furnishings, so I should be okay. I just have to keep the rebuilding expenses down to something reasonable. Maybe you could come with me in case Grendel shows up."

"Sure. What time?"

"Just about now. I was getting ready to leave when you walked in. He isn't exactly a contractor. He's more a handyman who works for people who can't afford a contractor. He helped turn my bedroom into a closet."

"Sounds like a good contact," I said.

"You bet your behind," Lula said.

———

The handyman was already on site when Lula and I arrived at her apartment house.

"There he is," Lula said. "That's Julio."

Julio was built like a fireplug. He was in his fifties with weathered skin and a leather tool belt to match. His black hair was pulled back into a ponytail. His truck had seen better days.

"It's important to check out a person's truck before you hire them," Lula said. "You never want to hire someone with a new truck. It's a sign that they don't need the job real bad, and they're going to overcharge you. Julio's truck has just the right amount of rust. Not so much that he looks like a failure, but enough to tell you he's a hardworking man. Either that or he spends his money on beer and dope instead of getting a new truck, but I haven't seen any evidence of that."

We walked through Lula's rooms and Julio took a couple pictures with his cell phone.

"The bad part is that everything on the surface is pretty much charred," he said. "Kitchen gone. Closet gone. Bathroom gone.

Living area gone. The good part is the structure seems okay. Like, it isn't as if the house is falling down. And when we fix things up, we can do it better than it was. I can give you a little kitchen. There's not a lot of room here, but maybe we can section things off to give you a space for a bed."

Lula was fanning her face and flapping her hands. "I'm gonna cry. I'm sorry. I don't mean to get so emotional. Maybe I could have a little stove so I could make a roast chicken. And I always wanted to bake a cake."

"I'll draw up a plan," Julio said. "I know someone who happened on some almost-new appliances so it might not cost you a lot."

"When can you start?" Lula asked. "I'm living with Stephanie right now. I'm sort of homeless."

"I can start right away," Julio said. "I have an opening. Usually, it's the appliances that take time, but these are available. And I can get a deal on cabinets if you don't mind slightly used. We'll give them a coat of paint and they'll be like new."

The translation of this was that the appliances were hijacked off a truck last week, and in the dark of night, the cabinets would be removed from a house that had been foreclosed on and abandoned. Not that any of this was so terrible. At least they'd be finding a good home. Besides, it was environmentally friendly, like recycling.

"This is one of those things that was meant to be," Lula said when we were back in the Rangeman SUV. "At first the fire looked like a bad thing, but now it's a good thing. I'm going to start practicing cooking as soon as we get home. I've got to be ready to have a stove. I didn't see any sign of Grendel either. There were no tufts of ogre hair sticking to anything."

CHAPTER TWENTY

I dropped Lula off at the office and I drove to my parents' house. It was midmorning and my mom's car wasn't in the driveway. I parked at the curb, let myself into the house, and yelled *hello*.

"I'm in the dining room," Grandma yelled back.

She was at the table, surfing on her laptop.

"Your father is at his lodge and your mother is at the grocery store," she said. "I stayed home so I could catch up on my socials."

"Anything fun happening?"

"The usual blah blah blah," Grandma said, "but Mitchell Zelinsky has a viewing tonight at the funeral home. It's going to be a good one. He was a big deal in the Knights of Columbus. They're putting him in slumber room number one. That means they're expecting a crowd. I thought I would wear my new blue dress. It's a copy of the dress Princess Kate wore for some shindig. I got it online. You can't go wrong with Princess Kate."

CNN, MSNBC, CBS, and Fox paled in comparison to the amount of news that was passed along the Burg gossip line. And Grandma was a premier member. Originally, I'd planned to get her to plant a rumor about Plover and fake jewelry, but now I had something better. There was only one thing that could top the gossip line, and that was a major viewing at the funeral home. A Plover rumor dropped there would spread like wildfire.

"You should come with me," Grandma said. "I could use a ride."

"Are dogs allowed?"

"I don't know. I never saw a dog at a viewing. I guess if you say he's a service dog it would be okay. He could be one of those comfort dogs. Like an emotional support dog but he could be a bereavement dog."

I looked over at Bob, not sure if he could pull it off. He'd probably be okay if I kept him away from the cookie table.

"Doors open at seven," Grandma said. "There's going to be a rush to get in, but I'll bet we could use the side door if we've got a bereavement animal with us."

"I'll pick you up at six forty-five."

I left my parents' house and drove to my apartment building. When I'd packed for my move to Rangeman I hadn't included anything my mother would consider to be suitable for wearing to a viewing.

Lula was in the kitchen when I let myself in. There were candles in jars on the counter and Lula had a spray can in each hand.

"I'm trying to decide on the scent we want in our apartment," she said. "I'm torn between Woodland Spring and Lemon Verbena. Do you have a preference?"

My preference was to have *no* scent.

"I don't know," I said. "It's overwhelming right now. My eyes are burning, and my nose is running."

"It'll be better once I make a decision."

Nutsy was on the couch with his laptop.

"Remember you need to talk to Plover at noon," I said to him. "If he wants to set up a jewelry exchange, tell him you want more money. Do whatever it takes to delay a meeting."

"No problem," Nutsy said. "I'm on it."

I ran into the bedroom and shoved heels, a black skirt, a white shirt, and a royal-blue jacket into a tote bag. It was my go-to outfit for events I hated and times I wanted to be invisible. It was unremarkably pleasant.

Lula followed me into the bedroom. "Looks to me like you're going to a viewing," she said. "You just crammed your blue jacket into that bag."

"I promised Grandma I'd go with her. I thought it would be a good place to snoop for gossip and start a couple rumors about Plover."

"Plover's not going to be happy about that. And while we're on the subject of unhappy, Connie got two FTAs in right after you left."

"Anything good?"

"I don't know. I just know they came in. I didn't have time to learn about them on account of I wanted to come home and do my scent testing."

"A woman has to have priorities," I said.

"Damn skippy."

I grabbed a couple granola bars out of the kitchen and Bob and I drove to the office.

"Hey," Connie said. "I have two new FTAs."

"Lula told me."

"Jenny Johnston. Twenty-three years old. Wasn't invited to a bridal shower so she trashed it. Shot the crap out of the heart-shaped piñata and pushed the bride-to-be face-first into the sheet cake. Didn't show up for court yesterday. Second one is even better," Connie said. "Henry Scargucci. Hijacked an eighteen-wheeler loaded with electronics and tried to sell them to an undercover cop. Also didn't show for court."

I took the two files, crammed them into my messenger bag, and called Lula.

"I'm going after one of the FTAs," I said. "Do you want to ride with me?"

"I might as well being that I decided on our scent. I'm going with Woodland Spring. It works better with your subdued color palette of gently used beige."

———

Lula parked her Firebird in front of the office and got into my Rangeman SUV. I handed the Johnston file over to her and pulled into traffic.

"Johnston is a bartender, working the evening shift at Danielo," I said. "This should be a good time to catch her at home."

Lula flipped through the file. "I like the part where she shot up the piñata. I'm sorry I missed that. I'm not a fan of bridal showers, but I'd go to one if I thought someone was going to empty a clip into a piñata."

Johnston lived in an apartment complex that was popular with singles. It had a pool, tennis courts, and a clubhouse with a bar and a gym.

"We should be living here," Lula said. "They have all kinds of facilities. I could play tennis. And I might find Mr. Right at the bar."

Finding Mr. Right wasn't a selling point for me. I already had two Mr. Rights in my life. I was conflicted enough. And while I have delusional visions of myself looking fantastic in tennis attire whacking the ball around, realistically I can't see it happening.

"That's her building on the right," Lula said. "It looks like she's on the second floor. I bet she's got a balcony that looks over the pool."

I was on the second floor in my building, and I had a fire escape that looked over the parking lot. I told myself it was retro. And honestly, I liked my stodgy no-frills building. It had a good mix of people.

I wasn't sure if this was a pet-friendly complex, so we left Bob in the SUV with strict instructions.

"I guess this is one of those situations where you're going to give her the baloney about how we're just going to get her rescheduled."

"It's not baloney," I said. "If everything goes right, it's the way it will play out."

"It never plays out right," Lula said. "These are people who don't want to go to jail."

"Humor me," I said. "It's our opening move."

"That's okay with me," Lula said. "It's okay as an opening move. You just don't want to count on it working."

I rang the bell twice and Jenny Johnston opened her door. She looked like her photo. Blond, slim, angry.

"What?" she said.

I introduced myself and told her she missed her court date.

"Oh, dear God," she said. "What a tragedy. Total disaster. Excuse me while I go hang myself in the bathroom. I think I'll use my outdated and too-small Gucci belt."

"It's not a big deal," I said. "We'll get you rescheduled, and you'll be back home in an hour. Maybe two."

"This is about the shower, right?" she asked. "Let me tell you about the shower. The bitch bride-to-be used to be my best friend. Turns out she was screwing my fiancé behind my back, and obviously she was better at it than I was because he dumped me."

"I could teach you a few tricks if you're interested," Lula said.

"I'm not interested," Johnston said. "I'm done with men. I'm getting a fish or a turtle or something."

"I guess they don't allow dogs here," Lula said.

"They don't allow anything that poops outside of the apartment."

"That's too bad," Lula said. "A dog would be a good substitute for a man. They make real good companions."

"About getting rescheduled . . . ," I said.

"Not only did this jerk dump me," Johnston said, "he took back his ring and gave it to the slime creature. He gave her *my* diamond ring. The ring we picked out together. It was a Plover ring."

Holy cow. There really is a God. And he must like me. Go figure.

"I have good news for you," I said to Johnston. "Don't tell

anyone where you got this information, but I happen to know that Plover is under investigation for selling fake diamonds."

Johnston sucked in some air. "Are you shitting me?"

"Nope," I said. "No shit. The slime creature's probably wearing a worthless ring. And it's not just diamonds. I'm told almost all of the jewelry Plover recently sold was fake."

"Holy crap," Johnston said. "This is big. This is fantastic. I love this. I'm happy again."

"And you got to shoot up a piñata," Lula said. "You got style. I admire you for that. I hope I can get to shoot up a piñata someday."

"Yeah, it was good," Johnston said. "It was loaded with Hershey kisses and the freaking thing exploded. There were kisses flying everywhere. It was awesome."

"And then you pushed the slime creature into the sheet cake," Lula said.

"It was anticlimactic to the piñata," Johnston said, "but it just seemed like the right thing to do."

"Like going downtown to get you rescheduled," I said.

"Whatever," Johnston said. "As long as I can do my shift at the bar. If I don't mention your name, I can spread this info, right?"

"Absolutely," I said. "Tell everyone."

Connie met us at the municipal building and wrote a new bail bond for Johnston. Lula went back to the office with Connie and Bob, and I went to Rangeman.

I changed into my viewing uniform and called Ranger.

"I need a ring," I said. "Or maybe a pendant. I was hoping I could borrow something from the Plover collection."

"Is this a special occasion?"

"Yes. The Mitchell Zelinsky viewing is tonight, and I want to spread some rumors."

"I have the Plover pieces in my safe. Come to my office and you can choose whatever you want."

Ranger had the trays stacked on his desk when I walked in.

"I need something that looks like I could afford it," I said.

"If they were real, you couldn't afford any of these pieces," Ranger said. "It would be more believable if you said you took it as a bribe." He selected a necklace that had a small pendant of an open hand on a silver chain. "This is a hamsa necklace. The hamsa is a protective symbol." He stepped close and his hands were warm on my neck as he placed the necklace. "If anyone ever needed a protective charm, it's you."

———

Grandma was waiting on the sidewalk when I got to my parents' house.

"I got a black scarf for Bob," she said. "We can tie it around his neck, so he looks like a real bereavement dog."

"We'll wait until we get to the funeral home," I said. "If we put it on him too soon, he might eat it."

I found the last parking spot in the funeral home lot, and Grandma, Bereavement Bob, and I slipped in through the building's side door. At the same time, the big double doors in the front were opened and the mourners stampeded in.

"I'm going to get a seat up front," Grandma said. "I'll meet you at the cookie table when the viewing is ending."

Bob and I slowly made our way around the perimeter of the packed reception room. Viewings in the Burg are not only socially mandatory for many Burg ladies but also are at the top of the list for free entertainment. Husbands attending are usually under the influence and congregate in clumps to discuss game scores and Viagra results.

Bob was an immediate hit.

"A bereavement dog!" Sue Mary Malinowski said. "What a wonderful idea. Can you rent one?"

"I don't know much about it," I said. "This one is just in training and I'm babysitting him for a friend." I put my hand to my necklace. "I wonder if I could have your opinion. I was given this necklace, and I really like it, but it came from Plover's, and I'm sure you've heard the rumors. Do you think this looks fake? It has some small gemstones in it."

Sue Mary took a close look at my necklace. "I don't know," she said. "It's very pretty. Have you had it appraised?"

"No," I said. "Do you think I should?"

"Considering the rumors about Plover, it might be a good idea."

I moved through the room.

"My goodness, what a handsome dog," Mrs. Critch said. "He looks all dressed up in his pretty black scarf." She leaned in and squinted at my necklace. "I heard about your Plover's necklace. Such a shame. He used to have an impeccable reputation, but now there are all these rumors about him."

"Do you think it looks fake?" I asked her.

"The little red gemstones don't really have the depth of sparkle one would expect from Plover," she said.

Viewings are from seven o'clock to nine o'clock, and by eight thirty I thought I'd done significant damage to Plover's reputation.

Grandma was already at the cookie table, and the crowd had dwindled. I started to cross the room and Martin Plover stepped in front of me and shoved me into an empty slumber room. His face was flushed, and his eyes were narrowed and fierce.

"You bitch," he said. "I hired you and you betrayed me."

He reached for my necklace, and I stepped away.

"Give it to me," he said. "It's mine."

I put my hand over the necklace. "No way. I've had this for years."

Bob was standing pressed against my leg. He growled very softly at Plover, and Plover kept his distance.

"You're all in this together, aren't you," Plover said. "Manley, the moron who robbed me, the two homeless stooges, and you. You were in it from the beginning."

"Not true," I said.

"Be afraid," he said. "Be very afraid. If you don't want to be the center of attention at the next viewing here, you'll give me the jewelry and walk away. Trust me, you don't want the kind of misery I'm willing to inflict. I have too much to lose."

"Why?" I asked. "You have a wonderful jewelry store."

"The wonderful jewelry store can't pay my bills. The profit margin is zip. No one wants quality anymore. Diamonds are made in factories. You can buy them on Amazon."

"You cheated a lot of people."

"No one knew they were cheated until you decided to play caped crusader. Everybody was happy because they had a Plover diamond. Now they'll all be running out, getting appraisals. What do you want? More money from me? That's the message I got from Manley. Forget it. The well is dry. You aren't the only one squeezing me. You're the least of my worries. I can eliminate you and your pals with very little effort. A bullet to the brain. A car bomb. Problem solved."

"But you don't want to do that until you get the jewelry."

"I don't need the jewelry if you and your partners are ashes. Don't underestimate me. I'm not a nice man. And just for the record, my father and my grandfather weren't all that nice either. They cheated at the store, they cheated at cards, cheated on their taxes, and cheated on their wives. They were nasty drunks in expensive suits."

"I don't suppose you want to turn yourself in to the police and confess everything," I said to him.

"I want the jewelry."

"Make me an offer."

"You give me the jewelry, or I kill you. That's my offer."

"I don't see that as being a very good deal."

"You have until midnight," Plover said. "You know my number." He turned on his heel and walked away.

"Holy crap!" I whispered to Bob. "He's freaking crazy. He looks so respectable and sane in his dark suit and white shirt and striped tie. Everything about him screams good taste and pillar of the community. And he's a homicidal lunatic."

I stepped out of the empty room and went back into the reception area. Plover was nowhere to be seen. I sucked in a couple deep breaths. My heart was pounding in my chest and my head felt like it might explode.

"Do I look okay?" I asked Bob.

Bob didn't seem alarmed. That was good. I was pretty sure I'd pulled it off. I hadn't backed down with Plover.

"I was a real hard-ass," I said to Bob. "Okay, so I'm a little shaky, but I have it under control."

Grandma was waving at me from the cookie table. Bob and I walked over to her. I grabbed a fistful of cookies and shared them with Bob.

"This was a real good viewing," Grandma said. "The makeup on Mitchell was excellent. He looked like he was going to get up out of his casket and go out to dinner. He had on a blue suit and a red tie, and that's always flattering. It's a shame you missed the ceremony from his lodge. They were in full regalia. Of course, the big deal of the night was the rumor about Plover. It went through the building like wildfire. I have to give Plover credit. He stayed cool and calm through it all. Just brushed it off and was his usual charming self." Grandma dunked a cookie in her coffee. "I don't suppose you had anything to do with the rumor."

"Who, me?" I said.

"I saw him talking to you."

"He's criminally insane."

"That's too bad," Grandma said. "He looks so good in a suit and tie. And it's not often a man at his age has a full head of hair."

CHAPTER TWENTY-ONE

I dropped Grandma off and drove to my apartment to check on Lula and Nutsy.

"How's it going?" I asked Lula.

"It's good," Lula said. "Nutsy got an Xbox, and he's downloaded some awesome stuff."

"Have you heard from Duncan?" I asked Nutsy.

"Yeah. He called me today. He's up and walking a little."

My phone rang. Diggery.

"I got a good one," Diggery said. "It's a male and he hasn't been in the ground all that long. He was buried wearing a cross necklace and he has a knife but no fork or spoon. Even Snacker thinks this one has some potential."

"Shoes?"

"Somebody took his shoes."

I couldn't imagine Plover taking Stump's shoes.

"I'll take a look," I said. "Where are you?"

"Willow Street Cemetery. It's not real big so you should be able to find us. You can't drive in at this time of the night. They got the gates closed. You have to park on the street. Give me an owl call when you get here, and I'll call back."

"Okey dokey," I said. "I'm on my way."

"What was that about?" Lula asked.

"Diggery has a body for us to look at."

"Who do you mean by *us*? Am I included in the *us*? Because you know how I feel about bodies when they're dead. Is this one dead?"

"Yeah."

"I don't suppose it's in the parking lot to a mall."

"It's in a cemetery."

"I was afraid of that."

"You don't have to go with me," I said. "Nutsy can go with me. He needs to identify it anyway."

"He's not a trained protective agent like me," Lula said. "He probably wouldn't even know what to do if zombies attacked."

"Cold water? Silver bullet? A stake in the heart?" Nutsy said.

"See? He don't know anything about zombies," Lula said. "You need a machete. You need to dismantle the brain."

"Do you have a machete?" I asked Lula.

"No," she said. "I got a nail file, and we could take one of your steak knives."

"I don't have any steak knives," I said.

"Then I guess we could take a table knife. We might be okay if it's a small zombie."

"Diggery is waiting," I said. "Let's roll."

———

Willow Street Cemetery is attached to a small white Presbyterian church with a classic steeple. It's on the fringe of the downtown area, and it's surrounded by nicely maintained modest homes. Lights were on in most of the houses. The church was clearly visible against the dark night. The cemetery was pitch-black. I parked on Willow Street, near the cemetery gate, and we walked into the cemetery.

"Hooty hoooo," I said.

"Hooo. Hooo," came back at me.

There wasn't much moon, and it was difficult to follow the unlit path. Mostly I could feel when I stepped off the cement onto grass.

"Hooo hooo."

"That better be Diggery *hooo*ing at us," Lula said.

My thoughts precisely. I'd used up all my adrenaline and bravado at the funeral home. I was running on empty, and I was every bit as freaked out as Lula.

The cement path ended, and we stopped walking. A *hooo hooo* called to us from the left. I flashed my penlight and caught sight of Diggery and Snacker standing about fifty feet away, next to a large headstone. I doused the penlight and cautiously made my way across the grass.

I had Bob on a short leash. I didn't know what was in front of us. In case there was more decomposition than Diggery had suggested, I didn't want Bob to get carried away and make off with a thigh bone.

"I'm gonna wait back here," Lula said. "It's not like I knew the deceased or something. I don't want to intrude on his current resting place."

"Good decision," I said.

Nutsy stepped forward. "I guess I'm needed here."

I looked at Diggery. "Light it up."

Diggery hit the grave site with his wide-angle Maglite.

"As you can see," Diggery said, "he's got on a cross necklace. And there's a knife lying next to him that I'm thinking fell out of his pocket when they dumped him into the ground. And there's a clump of gray hair clinging to his skull. Snacker and me think we have a winner here."

"It's the wrong cross," Nutsy said. "That's not at all how Marcus described it. And there's not much left of this dead guy but there's still a lot of his clothes, and it looks like he's wearing a suit and a tie."

"Yeah, but he's got a bunch of bullet holes in him," Diggery said. "We thought that counted for something."

Nutsy shook his head. "I don't think this is Stump."

"Bummer," Diggery said. "That's a big disappointment."

"It was a good try," I said to Diggery. "You're definitely getting closer. Keep looking. I'm sure you'll find him."

———

It was a little after eleven when Bob and I finally got to Rangeman. I parked in one of Ranger's personal spaces and went directly to his apartment. He was waiting at the door.

Bob brushed past Ranger and trotted to his water bowl in the kitchen.

"Are you hungry?" Ranger asked me.

"Starving."

He draped an arm around my shoulders and walked me into the kitchen. "Ella left a sandwich tray in the fridge when she heard you were coming back."

"God bless Ella."

Ranger took a bottle out of his wine cooler and uncorked it. "I say that a lot." He poured out two glasses and handed one to me. "I want to know about tonight."

"What about the sandwiches?"

He pulled out a plastic-wrapped tray of tea sandwiches and a plastic-wrapped tray of sliders. This was followed by a tray of miniature desserts.

I surveyed the sandwiches and didn't know where to go first. I wanted to eat everything. My first choice was an egg salad tea sandwich. I ate it in one gulp and chose a chicken salad slider next.

Ranger sat back in his chair with his glass of wine. "Tell me about tonight."

"I went to the Zelinsky viewing with Grandma, and I dropped a few hints about Plover and fake jewelry. And toward the end of the viewing Plover sort of threatened to kill me. Then Diggery called and said he had a good possibility for Stump, so Lula, Nutsy, Bob, and I went to Willow Street Cemetery to check it out."

"And?"

"Not Stump."

I laid waste to the sandwiches and sliders and moved on to the desserts.

"How serious was the death threat?" Ranger asked.

I shrugged. "Don't know. His family has an impeccable reputation in Trenton, but according to Plover, his father and grandfather weren't nice guys. Sounds like there's a legacy of cheating and worse. So, I don't think Plover would have a problem with killing me. He's killed before. Maybe more people than Stump. His problem is that getting rid of me is the tip of the iceberg. There are other people involved. There's Nutsy, Duncan Dugan, and Homeless Marcus. Does he try to kill all of us? Does he leave town, never to be seen again? He tried to intimidate Nutsy by blowing up his parents' car, and it worked to some extent but not totally. Maybe Plover would go that route again. That's a scary possibility because I don't know who he would target."

"What was his bottom line with you?"

"He said I had until midnight to give him the jewelry."

Ranger looked at his watch. "You were finishing up the egg salad sandwiches at midnight. You've slowed down with the desserts. It's almost one o'clock."

"I should have eaten the desserts first. I'm all filled up with egg salad and roast beef. And I'm exhausted. I'm not going to be able to eat the last mini chocolate mousse."

Ranger's phone buzzed. He had a short conversation and hung up.

"That was the control room," he said. "There's a problem at your apartment. Explosion and fire. They got the notice from your security system and from police dispatch. No more information than that."

I tried calling Lula and Nutsy but no one picked up.

"I need to be there," I said.

Ranger was on his feet. "Leave Bob here. I'll have someone come up to babysit him."

We took the Porsche Batmobile and reached my apartment building in record time. The parking lot was crammed with fire trucks, EMTs, cop cars, and gawkers. My stomach was filled with food but felt hollow. My heart was beating too fast and too hard. This felt like my bad. I'd tried to do the right thing, but it had turned out hideously wrong. I'd played the tough-guy card at the funeral home, and I'd ignored the midnight deadline, and now Plover was retaliating and playing his tough-guy card.

Ranger parked at the outer perimeter of the lot, and I hit the ground running. I ran past a fire truck and caught sight of an ambulance with people clustered around it. Two of the people were Lula and Nutsy. I stopped running and bent at the waist to breathe. I'd feared the worst, and this was the best. They were on their feet, and they looked okay. Rex was safe, Bob was safe, Lula was safe, Nutsy was safe. That's all that mattered.

Ranger wrapped an arm around me and swiped a couple tears off my cheek.

"I'm not crying," I said. "It's the smoky air."

Lula spotted us and started waving and yelling. Impossible to know what she was saying over the noise of the fire trucks.

We joined Lula and Nutsy and several med techs.

"Are you okay?" I asked Lula and Nutsy.

"Yeah," she said. "We're as good as you could be after your apartment's been bombed. We were lucky on account of we were in the living room playing a game on Nutsy's Xbox. Whatever-it-was came in through the bedroom window, so we had a chance to get out. We didn't even think twice. We were like, *Holy cow.* And we ran out. And then the fire alarms went off and everybody was coming out of the building, and the cops came, and the fire trucks came."

Ranger wandered off to talk to some of the first responders.

"I tried calling you," I said to Lula.

"Our phones are still inside," Lula said. "There was a crash when the window got broken and then a big *bang* and then there was a whoosh of flames, and we didn't waste time getting out of there."

"Smart," I said.

"I had it all decorated out too," Lula said. "Maybe some of it is still okay. I couldn't believe how fast the fire trucks pulled in. We were just out the back door, and we could see the trucks coming."

I was hoping the bathroom was destroyed. I hated my bathroom.

"We should have taken the Xbox," Nutsy said. "I wasn't thinking."

Ranger returned. "The fire is mostly out. It was confined to your apartment," he said to me. "This building is up to code with fire walls, and the trucks got here fast. The fire marshal will be here in the morning and we'll know more. Apparently, something smashed through the bedroom window. Most people wouldn't be able to throw a bottle grenade from down here, so it was probably mechanically launched."

The trucks were packing up to leave. The gawkers were dispersing.

"I'm homeless again," Lula said. "This is getting old. I'm going to have my cards read tomorrow. There's something wrong with my juju. I got an ogre on my ass and things keep burning down around me."

Ranger and I exchanged glances. We were having the same thought. This smelled like more than bad juju. Her fire and my fire were suspiciously alike.

"Why Lula?" I said to Ranger. "Why would she be targeted?"

"I don't know," Ranger said, "but it's hard to believe there isn't a connection."

"We can stay at Duncan's house," Nutsy said. "I have his key."

"Not a good idea," Ranger said. "I have a car coming. They'll put you in a hotel and stand watch. We'll regroup in the morning."

CHAPTER TWENTY-TWO

I was in Ranger's kitchen, getting my second cup of coffee, when Ranger walked in.

"You have cameras in here, right?" I said. "You knew I was up."

"No cameras," Ranger said. "Intuition."

"Any word from the fire marshal?"

"Too early." He got a green smoothie from the fridge.

"Omigod," I said. "Are you going to drink that?"

"Not everyone can get by on doughnuts," he said.

"I didn't have doughnuts for breakfast. I had pancakes. They were amazing."

"Have you heard from Lula?"

"No. I imagine she's plowing her way through the room service menu."

"We need to talk," Ranger said.

"You keep saying that."

"This is a different discussion. The firebomb was meant for you. Plover had no way of knowing you weren't in the apartment. He shot that thing through your bedroom window, thinking you would be asleep at that time of the night."

"He tried to kill me," I said.

"He could have waited in the parking lot and put a bullet in your brain, but he chose to put a firebomb through your window. A bullet would have been easier and a guaranteed kill."

"A firebomb is more dramatic. It's not something you would expect from a well-dressed jeweler. So maybe he's muddying the water. He still has hopes of not being found out. Okay, his fraud might go public, but he doesn't want to get charged with murder."

"It's still an odd choice," Ranger said. "I don't see Plover setting a bomb under a car or launching a bomb through your second-floor window. And whoever it was hit the mark the first time, because there wasn't any sign of other hits on the building."

"Maybe Plover didn't do any of the bombings. Maybe he has connections with a professional. Or maybe he has a partner. He said I wasn't the only one squeezing him. That I was the least of his problems."

"Let's move this to my office and see what turns up on a background check."

I took my coffee and followed Ranger through the living area to his home office. He pulled a second chair up to his desk so I could see his screen and he typed Plover's name into his computer.

I have decent search programs on my computer, but they don't compare to Ranger's. Ranger has total access.

"He has two younger brothers," Ranger said, scrolling through the information. "One is in California. Real estate broker. The other is a bonds trader in London. Plover is married to Jill McBride Plover. Homemaker. Active in a bunch of philanthropic causes. None of them involve building bombs. She's gotten a couple DUIs. They have a son. Frankie. Forty years old. Spent three years at Lafayette College. Didn't graduate. Did some time in rehab. Enlisted in the army. Got a medical discharge after two years. No details given. I could get details if I searched further but I don't think it's worth the time. Did more rehab. There's a period of unemployment where he lived at home. Worked at Pizza Hut for six months. Okay, here we go. For the last ten years he's been vice president in charge of new accounts for Ray Geara."

"I know that name."

"Ray Geara owns a chain of car washes where he launders more than cars. He also owns a bunch of politicians, and lately he's been dabbling in buying downtown real estate."

"This has potential."

Ranger closed his laptop. "I'm late for a meeting. I'll have Milos dig deeper into this. What are your plans for the day?"

"I have a miscellaneous FTA to clear off the books and I have a torched apartment to inspect."

———

My apartment was at the top of the list. The fire trucks were gone, but puddles of sooty water remained in the parking lot. The exterior of the building around my bedroom window was stained with soot. The living room windows were intact. I hoped that was a good sign.

I left the parking lot and went into the small foyer. It smelled smoky but it looked okay. I bypassed the elevator and took the stairs. The second-floor hall was a little sooty and the carpet was water soaked. Do Not Enter crime scene tape had been stretched across my door. I removed the tape and stepped inside.

There was a lot of soot and water damage, but the kitchen and the dining room seemed untouched by the fire. The living room had some fire damage, and the bedroom was charred trash. I looked in at the bathroom.

"Damn," I said to Bob. "It's not fair. Every time my apartment gets firebombed, nothing happens to the bathroom. I hate this freaking bathroom." I looked down at Bob. "I know what you're thinking. You're thinking that the fire marshal hasn't been here yet, so I could set fire to the bathroom, and no one would be the wiser. Well, here's the problem. The stuff I hate won't burn. The medicine cabinet is metal and the toilet, sink, and tub are porcelain. And I'm pretty sure the gross wallpaper is washable and fire retardant, because it survived the last fire. I'm boned with the bathroom."

I returned to the kitchen and looked in the fridge. Nothing worth taking. Nutsy had eaten everything.

"Here's the good part about the fire," I said to Bob. "It got rid of Lula and Nutsy. I have my apartment back. Not that it matters because I can't live in it the way it is."

I left my apartment building and drove to the office. Lula's car was parked at the curb, and I pulled in behind it.

"I bet you've been to your apartment," Lula said. "You smell like cooked couch and Bob's feet are wet."

"It could be worse," I said. "The kitchen and dining room

are mostly okay. Water and smoke damage but salvageable. The bedroom is a complete loss."

"How about your TV?" Lula asked.

"Melted."

"Bummer. At least you can stay with your parents." Lula sat up straighter on the couch. "Hold on! I saw that look just now. You aren't staying with your parents."

"What look?"

"You should never play poker," Lula said.

"She's right," Connie said. "You can't bluff."

"Omigod," Lula said. "You've been staying with Ranger."

"Aunt Bitsy and Uncle Whatshisname are visiting with my parents."

"This is big," Lula said. "Does Morelli know?"

"There's nothing to know," I said.

Lula and Connie exchanged looks that were the equivalent of *Are you kidding me?*

"Moving on," I said. "I thought I'd look for Henry Scargucci today. He's the guy who hijacked an eighteen-wheeler loaded with electronics and tried to sell them to an undercover cop. Now he's FTA."

"I could help with that," Lula said, "but I'd like to take a look at my apartment first. Julio said he would be there with some plans."

I hiked my messenger bag higher onto my shoulder. "Not a problem."

Julio's truck was parked in front of Lula's apartment house, and we found Julio inside Lula's apartment.

"I have a drawing," he said, "of what I can do. You have to use your imagination, but the little kitchen will be here, and we will make your closet smaller by relocating a wall that no longer exists, but your closet under my design will still hold as many clothes."

"That's okay," Lula said, "because after the fire I don't have a lot of clothes."

"Yes, but you will," Julio said. "I can see these things are important to you. You are a beautiful woman."

"That's true," Lula said. "I appreciate that you recognize it."

"We should have dinner sometime and we can talk about the design some more," Julio said.

"Are you a single man?" Lula asked.

"Yes. I have never found just the right woman."

"And you have your own place?"

"I have a little house."

"I'm all about dinner," Lula said. "I'm even free for tonight."

"Bob and I are going to wait in the car," I said to Lula. "I have some emails to catch up on."

Lula came down a half hour later. "We got everything all straightened out," she said. "He has good ideas and insurance is going to pay for some of it, and my landlord is going to pay for some of the improvements. And we're going to discuss it at dinner tonight at his house. It turns out that he likes to cook. It's a wonderful quality in a man. He said he learned to cook from his mama. Having his own house is another wonderful quality. Plus, he has an excellent tool belt. I noticed it contained a big hammer. It's always a good sign when a man has a sizable hammer."

I hadn't noticed Julio's hammer, but I felt like I was supposed to comment.

"No doubt," I said. "He had a hell of a hammer."

"Damn skippy."

Lula took the Scargucci file from me and paged through it. "Scargucci lives on Makinnon Street," she said. "And he's a car mechanic at that fancy foreign-car dealer on Route 33. Probably he's at work now."

I left Lula's neighborhood, got onto Hamilton, and followed it to Route 33. The dealership was just past the Regal Diner and the Dirty Car Wash.

"I would have dressed different if I knew we were coming here," Lula said. "I would have worn something with a little glam."

Lula was wearing a magenta wrap top that had a deep V-neck and some shimmer to it. Her giant boobs were barely contained in the top, so that there was a lot of flesh oozing out of the neckline and about a quarter mile of cleavage showing. Her skirt was black spandex and ended a couple inches below her hooha. She was wearing black six-inch FMPs and a glittery metallic magenta wig. This was her standard for casual work wear.

It was no surprise that Julio asked her to his house for dinner. He'd looked like his eyes were going to fall out of his head and roll around on the ground when he spied Lula.

I parked in the car dealer's area reserved for service, and Lula and Bob and I strolled into the six-bay garage. I asked for Henry Scargucci and was directed to the third bay.

Scargucci was average height, string-bean thin, and he reminded me of my cousin Vinnie, who looked like the human version of a ferret. He had a vintage Porsche on the lift behind him, and he was looking at data on the computer in front of him. I assumed he was reading the car's vital signs.

"Excuse me," I said. "Henry Scargucci?"

He turned and looked at me, and then he looked at Lula and dropped the wrench that had been in his hand. Hard to tell if it was over the cleavage or the hair. It would definitely have been about the skirt if she'd bent over.

"Yeah," he said, after he retrieved his wrench. "What's up?"

I gave him my name and my mission.

"We need you to come downtown with us to re-up," I said. "It won't take long. And I'd rather not cuff you in front of your coworkers, so it would be good if you could explain to your boss than you need an hour off and just walk out with us."

"Okay, I get that," he said. "I don't want to make a big deal of this. I like my job."

Ten minutes later, we were in the Rangeman SUV with Scargucci.

"You look like you're not too stupid," Lula said to him. "Why were you trying to sell hot stuff to a cop?"

"I didn't know he was a cop. He didn't look like a cop. My fixer set it up, just like always."

"Bummer," Lula said.

"Yeah, no kidding."

"Are you married?" Lula asked him.

"No," he said. "Divorced."

"Do you have a house?"

"Yeah. It's nice. The bitch wife didn't want it. She said the bathroom lighting was all wrong. She got the dog, and I got the house. It was a good deal. The dog had an attitude. She was ten pounds, and she barked all day." Scargucci looked at Bob. "Don't get me wrong. I like dogs, and you seem like a nice dog. It's just that dogs decide who they like and who they don't like, and this dog didn't like me. Peed on my side of the bed and ate my underwear. I was nice to it too, but it didn't matter."

I could see that Bob was considering the part about eating underwear. Eating underwear was one of Bob's favorite pastimes.

"Can you cook?" Lula asked him.

"I can get by. I don't have a lot of time to cook what with working at the dealership and hijacking trucks."

"I hear you," Lula said. "Cooking takes time. And you gotta have a stove."

"I like your hair," Scargucci said to Lula. "If you don't mind my asking, is it natural?"

"I got it online," Lula said, "but I got natural hair too."

"You're next door to the Dirty Car Wash," I said to Scargucci. "Is that owned by Ray Geara?"

"Yeah," he said. "They're all over the state."

"Does he buy cars from your dealership?"

"No. He's a Mercedes guy. Likes them new. Buys them from the Mercedes dealership. Sometimes we get one of his used to sell. One of his VPs buys from us. Frankie Plover. He likes flash but he has limited funds. He'll come in all excited about a Lamborghini but he's gotta feed his coke habit. Between you and me, he's kind of a whack job. I mean, I don't sell him cars. I just fix them, so what do I care, right?"

Right. But I cared. Frankie Plover had just moved to the top of my list of crazy people who might do anything.

"I could see you're a mechanic with integrity," Lula said to Scargucci.

"And you're a lady with class," Scargucci said. "When I make bail, we should get together."

"I'm all about it," Lula said.

We checked Scargucci in at the police station and called Connie to come bail him out.

"That was easy," Lula said when we were walking back to the SUV. "He was okay. I figure he might be good as a backup."

"He hijacks trucks," I said.

"Eighty percent of all the men I know hijacked a truck at one time or another," Lula said. "If I had to eliminate men who hijack trucks I'd never get to go out. And it's not like he deals drugs. We're talking about toasters and sneakers."

My phone buzzed and the fire marshal's name and number appeared on my screen.

"Yo, Jeremy," I said. "What's the word?"

"The word is that it's not as bad as the last time you got firebombed. I assume you already know this since the tape on your door has been disturbed."

"I took a quick look this morning. Is it officially safe to go in?"

"Yes."

"Do you have information on the cause?"

"It looks like it was a good old-fashioned Molotov cocktail fired from a can cannon. There were shards of what I'm guessing was a beer bottle and the charred remains of half of a can. From the amount of destruction, I'm thinking there wasn't a lot of accelerant and you didn't have a lot of fast-burning material in the room. Your bed and a chest of drawers. Once the fire got to the living room it had more to work with, but you had a citizen go in with a handheld extinguisher and then the fire department arrived."

"Thanks for the call," I said.

"Do you ever think about finding a different line of work?"

"Constantly."

I hung up and called Connie. "Do you have time to make a phone call and get someone in to clean up my fire damage?"

"Absolutely. How soon can you use them?"

"Now."

"No problem."

"Do you know how to make a can cannon?" I asked her.

"Doesn't everyone?"

"How easy is it to get parts?"

"Super easy," Connie said. "You can get a can cannon on Amazon. Thirty-nine dollars. Then you need a launcher. If you have an AR-15 lying around it works great. Or you can get an air gun from Amazon."

Lula was listening. "You could get the whole setup from Big Dick. He sells out of the back of his van on Saturdays. He parks around the corner from the farmer's market. If you want extra power, you could get a machine gun from him."

So, a can cannon is easy to get, but I figured you might have to take some practice shots before you could hit a second-floor window on the first try.

CHAPTER TWENTY-THREE

I dropped Lula off at the office and drove to Rangeman. Ranger was finished with his meeting and breaking for lunch when I stepped out of the elevator on the fifth floor. We got sandwiches and drinks and took them down the hall to his office.

"I got a report back from Milos," Ranger said. "Martin Plover and Geara are partners in the jewelry store. They've been partners for ten years."

"That's when Martin's son, Frankie, started working for Geara."

Ranger nodded. "This partnership is so complicated and crooked that it's hard to tell who's bad and who's good. Probably no one is good. Geara is a career criminal with mob ties. Martin Plover likes his drinks but falls just short of a drunk. He quietly abuses his wife. And he likes to gamble. His son, Frankie, is a creep. Drug addict. Sex addict. Delusions of grandeur. Descriptions of him range from charming to evil. From what I see, Geara keeps him on as his stooge."

"I have information that backs up your Frankie findings."

"I have Marcus in custody," Ranger said. "I thought we should keep him on ice until we need him. We picked him up this morning and he's very happy, living in one of my safe houses, getting fed and watching TV."

"Better than the crack house," I said.

"Apparently. Have you talked to Jeremy Gorden?"

"Yes. It was a Molotov cocktail launched from a can cannon. No structural damage. Connie is arranging for the restoration people to go to work."

I finished my sandwich and looked down at Bob. He'd finished his sandwich as soon as I gave it to him.

"I'm two men short tonight, so I'll be patrolling," Ranger said. "Don't be alarmed when a naked man gets into bed with you at one in the morning."

"I always find naked men alarming," I said.

"With good reason," Ranger said.

"Sometimes they're alarming in a good way."

"Babe," Ranger said.

I was flirting. Shame on me. I was spending too much time at Rangeman. I was finding it increasingly difficult to remember that I was in a relationship with Morelli. But that wasn't entirely my fault since Morelli showed no signs of ever coming back from Miami.

I stood and hiked my messenger bag onto my shoulder. "Gotta go. Things to do."

I drove to the bail bonds office and Morelli called just as I parked.

"I'm on a lunch break," he said. "I just heard about your apartment. How bad is it? Are you okay?"

"I'm fine. There's smoke and water damage throughout. The bedroom and part of the living room are gone. No structural damage, so I should be able to get back in soon."

"Do you know who did it?"

"I have ideas."

"Are you working with the police?"

"Not yet. It just happened. How's the trial going?"

"My part is done. I fly back to Jersey tomorrow night. Where are you staying? How's Bob?"

"Bob is great. I'm looking for a place to stay."

"You can stay with me tomorrow night. I already told my brother he has to vacate."

"I'm going to lose you any second," I said. "I'm out of phone battery."

This was a big fib. I wasn't out of phone battery. I was at a loss for words. I didn't know how to explain my days with Ranger. Were we sleeping together? Yes. Were we intimate? No. Even I couldn't believe that one.

I disconnected from Morelli and went into the office. Lula was sitting in Connie's chair behind her desk.

"Connie's downtown springing Scargucci," Lula said. "She said to tell you the restoration people are going to start your apartment today. And I've been temporarily promoted to acting office manager."

"Does it come with a raise?"

"No, but I've given myself an expense account. It's a shame I'm tied to this desk because with my new expense account I could go to the mall and get a dress for my big date tonight. My wardrobe is limited since everything disappeared in the fire."

"I talked to Morelli just now. He's coming home tomorrow."

"Is that good or bad?" Lula asked.

"It's good. Bob will be back home, and I can move in with Morelli until my apartment is put together."

"What about you-know-who?"

"Ranger?"

"You just gonna kick him to the curb?"

"It's not like that," I said. "Ranger has no expectations. He has a life that he allows me to share from time to time, but we both understand that we have no committed future together. His life path doesn't include marriage."

"Okay, what about Morelli? Is he gonna marry you? He's got a pool table in his dining room."

"Yeah, I'm not holding my breath for that marriage proposal either."

"How about you? Do you want to get married?" Lula asked me.

"I don't know. I was married once, and it was a disaster. Sometimes I think that I would like the security and comfort of a long-term relationship, but then I look at Rex and I think maybe he's enough. I don't have to share a bathroom with him."

"I hear you," Lula said. "If I got married it would be for health insurance. I'm not marrying anyone who doesn't have a group plan." Lula looked beyond me to the front door. "Hello, here's a cutie. He looks a little hungover but I'm pretty sure he's wearing a Rolex and Gucci loafers."

He was in his forties, thinning dark blond hair, white starched shirt with the top three buttons open. Tan linen blazer. Tan slacks that fit just right. Reasonable weight that had gone a little soft.

"Hello, ladies," he said, "I'm looking for Stephanie Plum."

"I'm Stephanie Plum," I said.

"And I'm the temporary acting office manager," Lula said.

"I'm Frankie Plover," he said. "I'd like to have a private conversation with Ms. Plum," he said to Lula.

"You'll have to take it outside," Lula said. "I got a sworn responsibility to take care of the phones here. And by the way, are those real Gucci loafers?"

"That isn't going to work for me," Frankie said. "I need a little privacy."

"I don't get to see a lot of Gucci loafers that are on people's feet," Lula said. "Mostly I only see them in the store. Are they comfortable?"

"You've been very annoying," Frankie said to me. "You've caused my father a lot of anxiety."

"Holy cats," Lula said. "I just got it. Your daddy owns Plover's."

"When do you sleep?" he asked me. "Are you a vampire? Do you haunt at night? You were supposed to be in bed when I sent you that present. How about if you walk outside with me and we go for a ride. I have a nice car. I have a Maserati. You ever ride in a Maserati?"

"Does your daddy know you're here?" I asked him.

"He's working at the store," Frankie said. "He does all the tedious stuff, and I get to do the security-related operations. I try to put a creative spin on them."

"Like car bombs and shooting bottle rockets out of can cannons?"

"I like things that go *boom*."

"Did Geara send you here?" I asked him.

"Nobody sends me anywhere," he said. "I don't take orders. I give them."

"That's not what I hear," I said. "I hear that you're Geara's stooge."

I heard Lula ease Connie's bottom drawer open, getting ready to go for the gun, just in case.

"That's not nice," Frankie said. "You should have better manners. Especially since I offered to treat you to a ride in my Maserati."

"Why do you want to take me for a ride?"

"I thought we could talk about things. I'm a businessperson and you're a businessperson. We might have some things in common."

"We can talk here," I said.

Frankie cut his eyes to Lula. "In front of chubs?"

Lula leaned forward a little. "Excuse me? Were you referring to me? Did you use that word in a derogatory fashion?"

"You're fat," Frankie said. "Own it."

"I'll own your ass after I stick my foot up it," Lula said.

"That's just great," Frankie said. "A fat girl with an attitude."

"I'm not no fat girl," Lula said. "I'm Lula."

Frankie gave a bark of laughter. "You're Lula? You're the one who lives in the pink and purple house on Micklin Street?"

"What of it?" Lula said.

"I told my moron assistant to get me the address of Vinnie's bounty hunter and she gave me yours. I didn't find out she gave me the wrong address until the following morning. Pretty funny, right?"

Lula's eyes almost popped out of her head, and I thought her hair might spontaneously burst into flames.

"You punk-ass piece of duck doody," she said. "Son of a gun. Son of a bitch. Son of a peach basket."

"I can see this isn't going down in a friendly fashion, so I'm just going to off both of you," Frankie said.

He reached under his blazer and pulled a gun. Lula bent down and came up with Connie's gun. The front door opened and a large, hairy man holding two black plastic garbage bags walked in.

"It's Grendel!" Lula shrieked. "Holy hell! It's Grendel. He's come to get me."

Lula fired off a shot that went wide of everything and put a hole and a spiderweb in the front window. Frankie put a bullet in Connie's desk, and Grendel whacked Frankie in the head with a garbage bag.

"Hey," Grendel said to Frankie. "Cut that out."

Bob and I ran behind the file cabinets. Lula and Frankie got off a couple shots at each other and Frankie ran out of the office and took off in his car. Grendel stood firm with his garbage bags.

Lula looked out from behind her desk. "Grendel?"

"Who's Grendel?" he asked.

"You are," she told him.

"I'm not Grendel," he said. "I'm Gordon Ruff. I'm your next-door neighbor."

He was almost seven feet tall with a bushy black beard and bushy black hair. He was wearing a black workman's jacket on his oversize body.

"Shania Brown is my next-door neighbor," Lula said.

"I'm subleasing from her. She went to stay with her sister in Minnesota."

"You look like Grendel," Lula said.

"I don't know anyone named Grendel. Does he live in the house too? I haven't gotten to know anyone."

"Why are you in my apartment at night?"

"My front door lock doesn't work. I keep complaining but nothing ever gets done. I found out by accident that my key works in your lock, so when I want to get into my apartment I go through your apartment and out the window onto the roof over the back stoop. Then I can get into my apartment through my bedroom window. I always tried not to wake you, but you must be a real light sleeper."

"Why didn't you just tell me?"

"I don't know. I was sort of scared of you. You shot at me once."

"How do you get out of your apartment?"

"The same way. Through your apartment. You're never home when I go out, and you're always asleep when I come home. I work the late shift at a meatpacking plant. It's a terrible job, but I've saved up enough to open my own butcher shop. Anyway, I've been trying to get in touch with you ever since the fire. I was home when the fire alarm went off. It was my day off. I couldn't get out my front door, so I went out my window, and when I got on the roof, I could see smoke in your closet, so I went in to make sure you weren't in there. Your whole front room was on fire, so I closed the closet door and grabbed all your stuff and threw it out the window. I can't help but notice your pretty clothes when I go through the closet. I figured you wouldn't want to lose it all." He held the two garbage bags out. "I got them all in here. And that includes a dress and jacket I accidentally knocked onto the floor a while back and stepped on. I had them cleaned. I finally met one of the other people in the house and she told me you work here."

Lula took the bags from him. "I'm all flummoxed. I don't know what to say. I didn't think I'd ever see any of this again."

"I got as much as I could. I got all the dresses and hair things, but I couldn't get to all the drawers. I tried airing your stuff out, but it still smells a little smoky."

"That was real heroic of you," Lula said. "I don't know how to thank you. Are you a single man?"

"Yes. I had a girlfriend once but working at the packing plant makes it hard for a relationship."

"Maybe on your day off I could take you out to dinner as a thank-you. You're living in your apartment now, right?" Lula asked.

"Yes. I have a couple big fans set up to dry out the carpet. It's not so bad. Shania's insurance company sent some people in to clean."

"We definitely got to get together," Lula said. "When is your day off?"

"Saturday," Ruff said. "I gotta go to work now, but I'm always okay for lunch, and you can drop in any time you want. I finally got my door lock fixed."

Lula and I watched him lumber down the street.

"You got to admit, he looks like Grendel," Lula said. "And he has a growly voice like Grendel."

"Do you still think he's Grendel?"

"I'm leaning toward him being a doppelgänger, and I'm willing to overlook the obvious similarities since he's not married and conveniently lives next door. You never know when you'll want to borrow something or when you'll need a place to live."

"You'd live with Grendel Doppelgänger?"

"Only if he didn't turn into a demon. I could live with an ogre, but a demon would creep me out."

A cop car sped past the office, lights flashing. Sirens were screaming in the distance.

"Something's going down," Lula said.

We walked outside and checked the street.

"I see some flashy lights by the hospital," Lula said.

Bob lifted his leg on my right rear tire, and we all went back into the office.

"We should make a list of things we need," Lula said. "I don't need clothes anymore, but I need furniture and accessories. I'm thinking about getting a little dining table with two chairs in case Grendel Doppelgänger wants to come to dinner."

"I need clothes," I said. "I brought some to Rangeman but not enough to get me through a week. And I need furniture."

"And you need a television," Lula said. "Yours got melted."

"And I need a car," I said. "I can't use the Rangeman car forever."

"That's a big-ticket item," Lula said. "Good thing you made some apprehensions this week."

Connie walked in and dumped her purse on her desk. "I got Scargucci bailed out and when I turned onto Hamilton on my way back here there was a car up on the sidewalk, smashed into a light post."

"We saw the lights," Lula said.

"I was stuck there while they got the guy out of the car. Bucky

Balog was there directing traffic, and he said the guy had been shot. Upper arm. He said it was road rage."

"What kind of car?" I asked Connie.

"Blue Maserati."

"Am I good or what?" Lula said. "I didn't think I got him."

"Did I miss something?" Connie asked.

"Frankie Plover came in and pulled a gun on us," I said. "There were shots fired and he ran out and drove off in his blue Maserati."

"I used your gun," Lula said to Connie. "Hope you don't mind."

"This has to be the first time in the history of the world that you actually hit your target," Connie said.

"She took out the front window," I said. "And Frankie put a couple rounds in your desk."

"This never happened," Connie said. "Some random took a hit from a guy needing anger management. We know nothing about it."

"Works for me," I said.

"Freakin' A," Lula said.

"Get out of my chair," Connie said to Lula. "I need to check out my gun. It probably needs an exorcist after you've handled it."

"Where are you staying tonight?" I asked Lula. "And do you know where Nutsy is staying?"

"Nutsy is with his parents. He figures if he hides and never goes out, no one will know he's there. I have options. I could crash here, or I could go to a hotel, or Julio could turn out to be the man of my dreams, or at least he could be Mr. Good Enough, and all my problems are solved. And if Julio doesn't work out, I got backups."

I slouched onto the couch and took up Lula's *Star* magazine. I wanted to be Lula. She navigated life better than I did. If something didn't work out exactly as planned, she moved on to door number two. No problem. She had backup men. I had backup men, and it gave me an eye twitch.

"Do you want to get married?" I asked Lula, returning to our conversation that Frankie had interrupted.

"Sure," Lula said.

"When?" I asked her.

"When I meet Prince Charming. Or when someone asks me, whichever is first."

"Would you marry anyone who asks you?"

"I wouldn't marry Simon Diggery. He smells like dirt and boa constrictor."

"Fair enough."

"Here's your problem," Lula said. "You got two men that's at the top of the hot chart. They got everything any woman could hope for in spades. And they got their own agenda. Nothing wrong with that as long as your agenda matches up with their agenda. Problem is that their agenda don't include getting married and you're thinking maybe you want to reexamine the advantages of matrimony. Makes sense since you aren't getting any younger."

"I'm not *that* old! And I'm not reexamining anything."

"Just sayin'. Anyways there's lots of men you could talk into marrying you if you just lower your standards. I've got my sights set on Julio right now, but I wouldn't mind passing Scargucci or Grendel Doppelgänger over to you. Of course, you don't want to be thinking about Scargucci for too long. He might be doing time soon."

I glanced at my watch. Was it too early for wine? Maybe a couple shots of tequila?

Connie was on the phone talking to the glass-replacement guy. "Accidental gun discharge," she said to him.

I grabbed my messenger bag and stood. "I need to check on my apartment," I said.

I got into the Rangeman SUV and drove to my apartment. There were restoration vans from several companies in my parking lot. I was the only one with significant fire damage but there was water and smoke damage throughout the building.

Bob and I took the stairs to the second floor and walked past the giant fans in the hallway. My door was open, and several people were working inside. An eviction notice was tacked onto my door. No surprise there. I was a disaster. It was shocking that I hadn't gotten kicked out sooner.

I asked one of the workmen when he thought I'd be able to move back in.

"Maybe tomorrow," he said. "It won't be perfect, but some of your rooms will be okay. It's going to need paint and carpet or new flooring in the bedroom and living room. I guess that's not your problem since you've been asked to leave."

"My rent's paid until the end of the month."

"At least you don't have a lot of furniture to move," he said. "As far as I can see, the only thing that didn't get burned up or water soaked is your dining room table and chairs."

"Lucky me."

"I can see you have a sense of humor. Maybe we can go out sometime. I'm free tonight."

"Thanks," I said, "but I'm already in two relationships. Maybe if you wanted to marry me."

"Lady, you just got evicted because, from what I hear, you

were firebombed. I've tried bungee jumping and I parachuted out of a plane once. I'm not a wimp, but I'm not crazy enough to marry you. The best I could offer you is a one-night stand."

"I appreciate your honesty," I said. "I'll keep you in mind if I ever need a one-night stand."

"Just call the restoration company and ask for Smitty."

I went to the cupboard in the kitchen. No tequila. I looked in the fridge. No wine. Bob and I went back to the Explorer.

"Morelli's coming home tomorrow," I said to Bob. "You'll be able to go home, and it looks like I'll be able to go home. We're happy about that, right?"

Bob looked like he was moderately happy, and I wasn't sure how I felt about anything. I drove to Rangeman and set my computer up on Ranger's dining room table. I went online and ordered a couch and a table lamp from Fast Fred's Furniture to Go. I was told it would be delivered between two o'clock and four o'clock tomorrow. I went to Amazon and bought a sleeping bag. One-day delivery.

———

Ella arrived at six o'clock and rolled a pretty glass-and-silver cart into Ranger's dining area. She set the table for two and transferred the food and drinks from the cart to the table. She was on her way out when Ranger walked in. He was dressed in Rangeman fatigues, and he was armed.

"I'm tight on time," Ranger said. "When I have this kind of schedule I usually just grab something from the café on the fifth floor, but I wanted to catch up with you. Tell me about your afternoon."

"Connie was downtown bonding someone out, Lula and I were in the office, and Frankie Plover walked in. There was some yada yada yada, and he said he was going to kill us. He pulled a gun, Lula pulled a gun, and shots were fired. By some miracle, Lula tagged him in the arm, and he ran off. He got into his car and crashed it a couple blocks down Hamilton. He told the police he was the victim of road rage."

"No other damage?"

"Lula put a bullet in the front window and Frankie drilled a couple holes in Connie's desk."

"That's it?" Ranger asked.

"I went to see my apartment. The restoration people were working there. They thought I'd be able to get in tomorrow if I wasn't too picky about the conditions. And I've been served with an eviction notice. Guess I've had one too many firebombings. How was your day?"

"Routine. I'm hoping for an armed robbery while I'm on patrol."

"After a routine day in the office, I imagine you'd like the opportunity to chase someone down and punch him in the face. Maybe throw someone out a window like the good old days."

"You're yanking my chain, but it's all true." He pushed back from the table. "I have to go. Hal is probably already in the garage waiting for me."

I collected the plates and put them on the cart. I went to the fridge and found a slice of key lime pie with a pretty swirl of whipped cream on top of it and a side garnish of raspberries and blackberries. Bob had already eaten, and Ranger never ate dessert, so I had the pie all to myself.

I was finishing the pie when Grandma called.

"You've gotta come over here," she said. "We have a disaster. Loretta's wedding is Saturday and one of the bridesmaids just got her appendix taken out. We figure you're about her size and could fit in her dress."

"You want me to be a substitute bridesmaid?"

"Yeah," Grandma said. "It's a good gig. You get to sit at the head table at the reception."

"No. No, no, no, no."

"Okay, I'll level with you. It's no picnic being here. You'd think it was the king of England's coronation. There's elaborate plans in place and a lot of hysteria going on. Your mother's been knitting and sneaking hits of Jim Beam since seven this morning. If they can't find someone to fit in that dress and walk down the aisle, all hell's gonna break loose."

Crap!

"Fine. I'll do it if the dress fits, but I want a pineapple upside-down cake out of this."

"You got it."

———

There were a bunch of cars parked in front of my parents' house, forcing me to park two doors down, in front of Mrs. Kenny's house. Aunt Bitsy, Loretta, and assorted people I'd never seen before were huddled in groups in my parents' living room and dining room. Seating charts were spread across the dining room table and seemed to be the cause of crises. Bob and I put our heads down and went straight to the kitchen. My mom was at the table, knitting needles in hand, working on a twenty-seven-foot scarf. Grandma was holding a tray with about forty sandwiches on it.

"Take this to the dining room and give it to Bitsy," she said. "I'll meet you upstairs."

Bitsy got excited when she saw me.

"Stephanie!" she said. "Thank goodness you're here." She waved her arms in the air. "Everyone! This is Stephanie. She's going to fill in for Elena and save my little girl's wedding day."

"If I fit the dress," I said, handing Bitsy the sandwiches.

"Of course you'll fit the dress," Bitsy said. "If not, we'll just take a tuck here and there."

Grandma came up behind me. "Gangway," she said. "I gotta get Stephanie upstairs."

The bridesmaid dress was laid out on my bed. It was gray satin and there was a lot of it.

"This is never going to fit," I said.

"It might not be so bad," Grandma said. "We'll just take a tuck here and there."

"It's gray."

"Loretta is kind of plain. I think they didn't want her to be overshadowed by her bridesmaids on her special day."

I shucked my T-shirt and jeans and got into the dress. The length was okay, but Elena clearly had a lot more chest than I did.

"It could be worse," Grandma said. "We'll just stuff some socks in your bra. You used to do that in middle school anyway."

"Who are all those people downstairs?"

"Seven of them are the other bridesmaids."

"There are seven bridesmaids?"

"That's why they needed you. Seven doesn't come out even when they're all lined up. And then there's the wedding planner and her crew. And there's some kind of high-level discussion going on with the reception seating and who's getting the prime rib."

"Mom looked zoned out."

"Your mother was a real trouper until this morning when we heard about the appendix and Bitsy went into a state. Bitsy was all bug-eyed and foaming at the mouth and gonna call everything off, you'd think she was the bride. And your mother picked up her knitting and she hasn't left the kitchen table since. She's like a little island of calm in a big raging storm."

"Was my wedding frantic like this?"

"No. You saved frantic for your divorce. People are still talking about it."

I went downstairs and found Bob sneaking sandwiches off people's plates. I hooked him up to his leash and we went to the door.

"Don't forget about the rehearsal," Grandma said to me. "Tomorrow at six o'clock at the church, and then there's the rehearsal dinner afterward."

———

Bob and I had a quiet dinner, we watched some television, and I did a last email check of the day.

"Things are coming together," I said to Bob. "We've got the fake jewels. We've got Marcus, the homeless guy who *didn't* get shot. We've got Nutsy. There's only one missing piece to the puzzle. Stump. We need a body."

I changed into a tank top and pajama bottoms and slipped

into bed. Bob jumped up, found the perfect sleep spot on Ranger's side, turned around four times, and flopped down.

The room was dark, and the bed was perfect, but I couldn't sleep. I was waiting for Ranger. I didn't know what to expect. And I didn't know how to respond.

"I'm confused," I said to Bob. "I'm a mess."

———

Ranger came home a little after one. I got out of bed when I heard him in the kitchen.

"I didn't expect you to still be up," he said when I walked in.

"I couldn't sleep. Are you having another green smoothie?"

"Mixed berry. Why couldn't you sleep?"

"I have things on my mind," I said. "Morelli is coming home tomorrow."

"And?"

"I'm feeling guilty. He doesn't know I've been staying here."

"Do you feel guilty because he doesn't know or because you like staying here?"

"Both," I said.

"Then I don't see where you have a problem. Give him his dog back and tell him you're living with me."

"I can't do that. I'm in a committed relationship with him."

"Where's the commitment? Is he going to marry you?"

"Maybe someday."

"Maybe never," Ranger said. "And you can do better."

"Really? Who's better than Morelli and is willing to marry me? Name one person."

"Me," Ranger said.

His eyes held mine. Unblinking. The ultimate poker face. I didn't have much of a poker face, but I was pretty good at recognizing a bluff.

"Okay," I said. "When?"

"Saturday," he said. "You and me. Vegas."

"I can't do Saturday. I already have to walk down the aisle in a hideous gray bridesmaid dress. How about Monday."

"I have a full day of meetings on Monday. Wednesday might work for me."

"Fine. As long as this Plover problem has been taken care of by then."

He put the smoothie on the counter.

"Understood. We have an engagement. Would you like a ring? I have a safe full of Plover's finest."

Brain freeze. Was it possible that I actually just got engaged to Ranger? Was I happy? Confused? Terrified? Aroused? All of the above?

"A ring isn't immediately necessary," I said.

"I'm glad to hear that, because I have a better way to celebrate the occasion. It's bedtime."

Oh boy.

CHAPTER TWENTY-FOUR

Bob and I had breakfast and headed down to the fifth floor. We walked past the control room and the café, and I peeked into Ranger's office.

"Are you busy having a routine day?" I asked him.

"The day is just beginning," he said. "I have high hopes for a disaster."

"I thought I should check up on things before I take off for the bail bonds office. Sometimes things that seem like a good idea at night look different in the morning."

"Like getting married."

"Exactly! There are things you need to consider before you marry me. Like Friday night dinners with my family, living with a hamster who runs on his wheel all night long, and the risk of having your apartment firebombed."

"Not a problem," he said.

He wasn't backing down. I wasn't surprised. Backing down wasn't in Ranger's DNA.

"Okay, then. Good," I said.

I wasn't backing down either. Truth is, there was a part of me that liked the idea of marrying Ranger. Then there was another part of me that was screaming, *Are you insane? Get a grip!*

"I'm not riding patrol tonight," Ranger said. "We'll talk when you get home."

"Perfect."

I turned and left his office. I rushed to the elevator and stared at the floor all the way to the garage, avoiding eye contact with Ranger's men. My heart was beating so hard in my chest that my vision was blurred.

Bob and I got into our SUV, and I carefully drove out of the garage and down the street. I stopped at the corner so I could catch my breath.

"I thought I was calling his bluff, but maybe he wasn't bluffing," I said to Bob. "Now what? What just happened here?"

Bob gave me a sideways glance. He knew perfectly well what was happening. He'd been there the whole time. If he could have talked, he'd have told me I was a nincompoop for even asking the question. The answer was obvious. I was going to marry Ranger. I was going to be Mrs. Rangeman.

The thought was terrifying. And hard to believe. I wasn't unhappy. Which by default left happy. Although sometimes happiness and panic feel awfully similar.

"We aren't telling anyone," I said to Bob. "I need to figure this one out."

I cut across town to Hamilton Avenue. I stopped for a light, and I looked at myself in the rearview mirror. My eyes were deer in headlights. Damn! I cruised around for an additional ten minutes until I could feel my heart rate return to normal and I was capable of blinking.

We reached the office, and I parked behind the glass-installation truck. Two men were fitting a new pane of glass in the large front window. Connie and Lula were inside, watching the replacement operation.

"That's really fast service," I said to Connie. "I'm surprised they had glass that size in stock."

"They said they keep it on hand because we get so many bullet holes."

I bypassed the doughnut box on Connie's desk and went to the coffee machine.

"How was dinner last night?" I asked Lula.

"It was excellent," she said. "He made some spicy Mexican thing in a fry pan. There was chicken and sausage in it. And his house is nice. He keeps it real neat."

"Did he get to use his big hammer?" I asked her.

"He didn't have any occasion for the hammer, but I got to see the tool that counts. It wasn't sized like his hammer, but he knew how to use it to good advantage. From my experience, which as you know is vast, I'd always take small but clever over big and dumb. Not much you can do with a big dumb tool."

Connie and I didn't have Lula's depth of experience, but we nodded in support of her point of view.

"I checked on Frankie Plover," Connie said. "He got treated in the ER for his gunshot wound and car crash abrasions. No overnight stay."

"Did they do a drug test or a sobriety test on him?"

"No," Connie said. "My sources tell me he was coherent and needed medical attention."

"This isn't good," Lula said. "He's going to be all cranky over this. He could decide to bomb the office. That would be bad since I got all my clothes and my wigs in the storeroom. I got some personal overnight sleeping arrangements made but they don't include my extensive wardrobe."

"What's happening with Simon Diggery?" Connie asked. "Has he turned up anything helpful?"

I selected a doughnut from the box on the desk. "He texted me this morning. He said he has a promising dig site, but he needs the right circumstances."

"What does that mean?" Lula asked. "No moon? Full moon?"

I did a palms-up. "Don't know." I looked over at Connie. "Any new FTAs?"

"No. The end of the week is always slow. I'm sure we'll have one or two on Monday."

"Then I'm going to look in on my apartment. The restoration people were there yesterday."

"Is it ready for us to move back in?" Lula asked.

"No," I said. "They need to dry it out. I'll let you know what I find."

I drove to the supermarket, cracked a window for Bob, and ran in and grabbed a basket full of essentials. I parked in my apartment building's lot and carted the bags of groceries upstairs. A lone workman was in my apartment, checking on the fans.

"How's it going?" I asked him.

"It's good. All of your rugs and upholstered furniture have

been cleared out and carted away, and the fans have done their job of drying things out. We'll leave the fans here for another day or two. If you're moving back in, you can turn them down when you're in the apartment and put them back on high when you leave."

Bob snuffled his crotch.

"Sorry," I said, "he has no manners."

"It's okay," the restoration guy said. "I get that a lot. It's my manly scent. Maybe we could get together for a drink sometime."

"That's tempting, but no," I said. "I'm engaged."

The restoration person left, and I put the groceries away. I would only have the apartment for a couple more weeks, and I had no reason to leave Rangeman, especially since I seemed to be engaged, but I felt compelled to stock up with waffles and peanut butter.

I walked through the apartment to my bathroom. It was ugly but it was totally intact. Much like the '53 Buick. Magically indestructible.

"I could consider this to be an act of God," I said to Bob. "It's like the big guy is telling me it's time to move on. New beginnings. That's how Lula would look at it."

I returned to the kitchen and Ranger called. "I have a franchised Rangeman facility in Virginia that's had a total security breach. I'm flying out with my tech guy. I'll give you a call tonight when I know more."

"He has an empire," I said to Bob. "And he has me."

Good thing Bob wasn't in a position to have a conversation with Morelli. News of my impending marriage wasn't something Morelli would want to hear from his dog.

———

By four thirty I had my couch set on a dry spot in the living room and my new sleeping bag unrolled on the couch. The table lamp was plugged in and placed beside the couch.

"I guess I don't need any of this," I said to Bob, "but it's like the waffles and peanut butter. It feels like the right thing to do. It's still my apartment."

I returned to Rangeman and changed into the black skirt, white top, and blue jacket I'd worn to the Zelinsky viewing. It was the only outfit I had that was appropriate for a wedding rehearsal.

I gave Bob a big bowl of dog kibble and when he was done, I clipped him to his leash.

"You have to be on your best behavior," I said to Bob. "We're going to church."

This wasn't my first wedding rehearsal, so my expectations were low. I was partnered with a guy who worked as a bartender and was super impressed with himself. His eyes were rimmed with black liner and his pants were tight across the ass. His teeth were very white, and he smiled a lot. I had used up most of my smiles earlier in the day, so I was struggling to keep up.

Bob walked down the aisle with me, strained at the leash, and snuffled Father John's crotch, leaving a drool mark on his cassock.

"So sorry," I said to Father John. "I'm babysitting. His owner has terminal cancer and is in hospice."

"God bless," Father John said. "Perhaps you could allow one of the family members to watch the dog while we conduct the rehearsal."

I gave Bob over to a boy who stepped forward. "Maybe he wants to go outside to tinkle," I said to the boy.

We resumed the rehearsal and had gotten to the part with the vows when there were loud slurping noises coming from the front of the church. Bob was drinking from the baptismal font. Everyone turned to look and there was a group gasp.

"He was thirsty," the boy said.

When we were done with the rehearsal, I called Lula. "I need help," I said. "I have to go to dinner with the wedding party and Bob is persona non grata. Is there any chance that you can babysit?"

"Sure," Lula said. "Julio is watching wrestling and as long as I get back to tuck him into bed, he'll be happy."

I met Lula in front of Casa Soupa. It was a family-friendly bar and restaurant in the Burg, not far from the church. The rehearsal dinner would be held in their private room. The menu was predetermined. I didn't care what I ate as long as it was served with some form of alcohol.

"I'll leave as soon as possible," I said to Lula. "Here are the keys to the SUV. This is a halfway-okay neighborhood. Maybe you can walk him around a little and then the two of you can go back to the SUV."

I watched Lula and Bob walk down the street and I went into the restaurant. I was at an awkward age. I was ten years older than the rest of the wedding party and at least twenty years younger than everyone else. Loretta and her fiancé were holding hands, looking overwhelmed and nervous. I'm sure that they were in love, but it seemed overshadowed by the event. I thought this is the way it was when you were young and it was your first marriage. I didn't want my second marriage to be overshadowed by the event. I wanted the event to be private and personal.

Antipasti was brought out and the toasts began. Halfway through the toasts my phone vibrated, and Nutsy's mom's number showed on my screen. I quietly excused myself and left the room. I stood in the narrow hallway and called Celia back.

"I'm sorry to bother you," Celia said, "but I'm worried about Andrew. He got a clown gig. I thought he shouldn't take it, but he was excited and said it would be okay. He was supposed to be back hours ago, and I haven't heard from him."

"Who hired him?"

"I don't know, but I heard him repeat the address when he got the phone call. It was Shirley Street. I don't know the number."

"I'll look into it," I said. "Let me know if you hear from him."

I went back to the dining room and made my excuses. I left the restaurant and found Lula and Bob standing by the SUV.

"I just got a call from Celia Manley," I said to Lula. "Nutsy got a clown gig and he's overdue to return home."

"He's got clown in his blood," Lula said. "He probably could never refuse someone wanting him to be a clown. It's too late for a little kid's birthday party, so he must be entertaining a bunch of adult clown lovers."

"Or he could be entertaining Frankie Plover."

"That was going to be my next possibility," Lula said, getting into the SUV.

"Celia said Nutsy was heading for Shirley Street."

"That's a strange place for a clown performance," Lula said. "It's mostly industrial around Shirley. Some small warehouses and stores. Although, there's a dance studio and a gym and one of those trampoline bounce places for kids. The bounce place advertises parties all the time. I know about it because it's next to a store for hair and nail techs. My friend Yolanda works there and gets me a discount."

Shirley was just past lower Stark Street. At this time of night there was no traffic, and most buildings were dark. A few of the smaller units had lights shining in windows. The dance studio, gym, and bounce thing were dark. I crept along, looking for Nutsy's Yamaha. After two blocks I came to a small one-story building that was lit and had a bunch of balloons fixed to its mailbox.

"Hunh," Lula said. "I bet there's a clown in there."

I idled in front of the building for a moment and a text message dinged on my phone. Unknown caller with a photo of Nutsy in a clown costume. He was strapped to a straight chair. His face was bruised and bleeding. He was slumped over, possibly unconscious. There was another ding. *Congratulations. You found us. Join the party.*

"Are we going to join the party?" Lula asked.

"Eventually," I said. "Are you armed?"

"Do bears do it in the woods?" Lula said. "Are you?"

I reached under the driver's seat and unlatched the gun box. I took out a Glock 19. "Yep," I said. "I'm armed."

I wouldn't ordinarily walk into a situation like this with just Lula and Bob as backup. Unfortunately, Ranger was in Virginia and Morelli had just landed at Newark. And I didn't feel comfortable relying on 911. I didn't want a bunch of first responders thundering in with lights flashing.

I texted a message to Morelli. *I'm in a situation. Let me know when you roll into Trenton.*

I drove around the block, getting a feel for the area. I pulled it up on Google Earth on my cell phone and got a bird's-eye view. The building was freestanding with a small swath of ground around it. Morgan Plumbing was behind it and there were several other small freestanding buildings on either side of the balloon building. I parked two doors down and ran around to the back of the SUV. This was a Rangeman fleet car equipped with standard cargo. The standard cargo included a first aid kit complete with an AED, ankle shackles, knives, batteries for Maglites and stun guns, flash-bang grenades, and smoke bombs. The only things missing were an Indiana Jones–style whip and a *Star Wars* lightsaber.

I grabbed a knife and the flash-bangs and smoke bombs and brought them up front. I gave half to Lula, and I shoved the rest in my pockets and messenger bag.

"I'm all about this," Lula said. "I'm ready to kick ass. I'm in Avenger mode. It's disgraceful, what they did to Nutsy. You don't treat a clown like that."

"When we go in and things get hairy, please try not to shoot me," I said.

"I know in the past I've been off the mark sometimes," Lula said, "but things are changing for me and I'm just about at sharpshooter level now."

Lula, Bob, and I left the SUV and stayed in the shadows as we crept up to our target. Lula and Bob plastered themselves against the side of the building and I moved around it, looking in windows. Most of the rooms were dark and empty. I reached the back of the building and I saw Nutsy strapped to the chair. He was slumped over, not moving. I couldn't tell if he was dead or alive. No one else was in the room with him. I continued around to the far side of the building. The shades were down here, but there was no sign that lights were on or that people were inside. I scuttled across the front and rejoined Lula and Bob.

"I can see Nutsy," I said. "He seems to be alone, but I find that hard to believe."

"Are we going to go get him?" Lula asked. "I'm ready. I saw that picture of him, and I don't like clowns being treated like that."

"We're going in through the back door and we're going to get him out as fast as possible," I said. "If it's necessary we'll use the flash-bangs and smoke bombs before shooting."

"Okay," Lula said. "I got it. Flash-bangs, smoke bombs, and then shoot. Is your heart racing? My heart is racing."

"Yeah," I said, "my heart is racing."

Not as much as when I thought about marrying Ranger, but it was up there.

We inched our way around to the back of the building and I went to the back door. I looked in the window. Still only Nutsy in the room. I tried the door. Unlocked. Not a good sign.

Lula and Bob were close behind me.

"On the count of three," I said. "One, two, three."

I opened the door, we tiptoed in, and I immediately went to Nutsy. His color wasn't good, but he was breathing. He was taped to a flimsy kitchen chair, and I decided it would be easier to transport him on the chair. I tipped it over and dragged it toward the door. Lula ran over to help, and that's when Martin Plover walked in from the front of the house, gun drawn. Frankie came in through the back door.

"Set the chair down and back away from it," Martin said. "Now!"

"Jeez, don't get your shorts in a bunch over it," Lula said. "This man is a clown. Have some respect."

A third guy came in from the front of the building. He had a large steel barrel on a hand truck.

"We haven't got enough barrels," he said, looking us over. "I only brought three. What are you going to do with the dog?"

"We'll turn him loose," Martin said.

"You'll get into big trouble for that," Lula said. "We got leash laws in Trenton."

"This is going to be fun," Frankie said.

"Shut up," Martin said. "This isn't fun. It's business. And I'm not happy about it. I'm tired of cleaning up your fuckups. You're lucky one of these barrels doesn't have your name on it."

"Jeez," Frankie said. "That's harsh. I have some good ideas." He looked over at Lula and me. "The balloons were my idea. And I was the one who texted you."

"I liked the balloons," Lula said. "They were a good touch. We would have had a hard time finding the house without them."

"It sounds like you want to put us in the barrels," I said to Martin. "Do you think we'll fit?"

"We'll make you fit," Martin said, still scowling at his son. "I knew you and your sidekick would eventually come looking for Manley. It's what you do, right? It turns out that killing is the easy part. Disposal is the hard part. I don't mind digging one shallow grave at a time. Three is too much. So, we'll pack you all up in the barrels, and Daryl will put the barrels in his truck, drive them to his boat, and dump them offshore. Very clean."

"I'm not getting in no barrel," Lula said. "I've got plans for the rest of the evening."

"You're going in first," Martin said.

"The hell I am," Lula said.

She reached into her tote bag and was pulling out her gun when Martin shot her. Bob ripped the leash out of my hand and lunged at Martin, clamping his teeth onto Martin's wrist, shaking it like it was a dog toy. The gun fell out of Martin's hand and skittered across the floor. I threw down a flash-bang in the direction of the gun, squeezed my eyes shut, and put my hands over my ears.

The instant the flash was over I grabbed my stun gun and tagged Martin. The barrel guy was staggering around, disoriented, and I managed to take him down too. Frankie had attempted to run out the back door but was blinded by the flash-bang and had crashed into Nutsy, still strapped to the chair. I cuffed Frankie and left him sitting on the floor.

"I'm dying," Lula said, sprawled on her back. "I've been shot. It's all over. Tell Julio I'm sorry I couldn't make it for the end of *Smackdown.*"

"I don't think you're dying," I said to her. "I don't see any blood. I think you fainted. It looks to me like he shot your purse."

"Are you kidding me? Damn him anyways. That's a Gucci knockoff."

"Do you have cuffs in there?" I asked her. "I only had one pair with me, and I put them on Frankie."

Lula sat up and found a pair of cuffs in her bag. The barrel guy's fingers were starting to twitch, so I used the cuffs on him. I gave the stun gun to Lula and told her to give Martin Plover more volts if he moved. I ran to the SUV, got another set of cuffs and a roll of surgical gauze, and returned to the building. Martin's wrist was bloody and mangled from Bob's giant canines, so I wrapped it in gauze and then cuffed him.

Bob was sitting in the middle of the room. He looked dazed and he was drooling. I put my arm around him and gave him a kiss on the top of his head.

"Sorry," I said. "I didn't want to shoot anyone, so I went with the flash-bang."

My phone buzzed in my pocket. It was Diggery.

"I think we finally found him," Diggery said. "The address is a little dicey so I'm hoping you can get here quick."

"Where are you?"

"I'm in a fancy neighborhood. Just look for the big white house on Lasso Way. It's got one of those circle driveways and my truck is parked one house away. We're in the backyard. The missus of the house is passed out in bed, like always. The mister is out, and I don't want to be here when he comes home."

"Lasso Way sounds familiar," I said. "Who owns the house?"

"Martin Plover."

"Don't worry about it," I said. "He isn't coming home any time soon. I'm on my way. Don't go anywhere."

I called Morelli.

"Where are you?" I asked him.

"Route 1. I should be home soon. Forty-five minutes, maybe."

"I have something you need to see. It's on Lasso Way. I don't have the exact address but it's Martin Plover's house. Can you do a detour?"

"Are you going to be there?"

"Yes."

"Then I'll do a detour."

The two Plovers and the barrel guy were gaining function, mumbling and rolling around.

"What are we going to do with these idiots?" Lula asked me.

"I don't want to leave them here," I said. "And I don't want to wait for the police to show up. I guess we take them with us."

"It's going to be a tight fit in the SUV," Lula said. "Especially with Nutsy and his big clown feet."

Nutsy had his head up and his eyes open, looking like he was trying to pull himself together.

"I can call Rangeman and ask them for help," I said.

"Or I can call Julio," Lula said. "He isn't far from here. I could have him bring his truck."

Fifteen minutes later we had the three men in the back of Julio's pickup. We walked Nutsy to my SUV and put him in back with Bob.

"What the heck were you thinking?" Lula said to Nutsy. "Who has a party out here?"

"Lots of people," Nutsy said. "I've done parties here before. Mostly at the bounce thing. And besides, there were balloons on the mailbox."

"That was Frankie's idea," Lula said. "He's real creative that way."

"He's a crackhead lunatic," Nutsy said.

"How'd you get all beat up?" Lula asked him.

"Frankie," Nutsy said. "He was the only one here when I arrived. He opened the door and sucker punched me. And then I think he hit me over the head with something because I blacked out, and when I came around, I was strapped to the chair. He was trying to get me to tell him where you were and where the jewelry was, but I didn't know, and I couldn't think right. Then his father came in and yelled at him and told him to go help with the barrels. Martin didn't care about where you were. He figured you'd come to him. And he was right."

"It was lucky that you were living with your mother, and she thought to call Stephanie," Lula said.

"It was probably Sissy who thought of that," Nutsy said. "She talked Duncan into coming home. She drove him back yesterday. We're all hiding at my parents' house."

"I can't see Duncan getting a harsh sentence," I said. "After the way everything has played out, he might just get community service."

"Whatever it is, Sissy will be there for him," Nutsy said.

"That's nice," Lula said. "It's almost a happy ending. It would be good if you had a happy ending now."

"That's the best part," Nutsy said. "A publisher made an offer for a collection of my stories. I didn't get much money for it, but it's a start."

CHAPTER TWENTY-FIVE

I led the parade to Martin Plover's house on Lasso Way. The three men were handcuffed, and Julio had wrapped them in duct tape as a further precaution. We left them in the truck and walked around to the backyard, where Diggery and Snacker were standing guard over an open grave.

Julio made the sign of the cross. "Holy mother," he said.

"Snacker's finally happy about this one," Diggery said. "He meets all the criteria. He even has some tattoo left on his hand. I should have thought of this first off. After all those others didn't work out, I got to remembering about when you first hired me. You said the shooting took place behind Plover's jewelry store. And it was right after Plover was robbed. In the beginning I was using that as my jumping-off spot, but then a couple days ago I thought what if Plover was the shooter. Or maybe his kid was involved. Snacker had a run-in with the kid in a bar once and he said the kid was scary. So suppose the Plovers were involved somehow. If you're an amateur or if you're short on time, where do you put fresh kill? In your own backyard, right? This backyard is nice and private too. It's got a big hedge going around it. And it's got flower beds, so the ground is easy for digging."

Nutsy was standing beside me with his oversize clown shoes hanging over the edge of the grave.

"What do you think?" I asked him. "Could this be Stump?"

Nutsy nodded. "I'm pretty sure it's Stump. The size and the clothes and the hair that's remaining are all right. And the tattoo looks right."

I heard a car door slam in the front of the house and moments later Morelli came up behind me.

"What have we got here?" he asked.

"Stump," I said. "The last piece to the puzzle."

"I didn't dig him up," Diggery said to Morelli. "I'm retired. Snacker and me were just called as professional authorities."

"Understood," Morelli said. "I appreciate your help." He turned to me. "Do we know who dug him up?"

"Some random," I said. "Might have been a pack of dogs."

"Yeah, we'll go with dogs," Morelli said.

He spied Bob pressed against my leg and he got down on one knee and hugged Bob. Bob looked like he was going to burst with happiness. Morelli looked pretty happy about it all too.

"There are three men duct-taped in the back of a pickup truck in front of this house," Morelli said. "I'm pretty sure one of them is Martin Plover."

"There's a bunch of bullets buried in Stump, and they should match the gun Martin keeps in his store. I have two witnesses who saw him shoot an unarmed homeless man."

"Stump is the unarmed homeless man?" Morelli asked.

"Yep."

"I also have the jewelry that was stolen from the store. All fake. And there's a small building on Shirley Street that contains three steel drums that were meant for Lula, Nutsy, and me. Bob saved the day on that one. He deserves a steak for dinner tomorrow."

"You've been busy," Morelli said.

"It started out simple and sort of mushroomed."

"I'm going to call this in," he said. "In ten minutes it's going to be a circus here. Anyone who doesn't want to be part of the circus should leave."

"I'll tell Diggery."

"Come back after you send him away."

Two hours later, Morelli had the full story, the two Plovers and the barrel guy were in custody, Nutsy had given his statement and been driven home, and Lula had gone home with Julio. The ME was still working to move the body. Mrs. Plover slept through it all.

"I'll need the jewelry," Morelli said.

"It's in Ranger's safe. He's out of town but I'll have it transferred over to you when he gets back."

"How long will he be away?"

"I'm not sure. I just spoke to him, and he thought a couple days."

"This isn't the way I'd imagined my first night back," Morelli said. "I was looking forward to a quiet night at home with you and Bob. Miami was a nightmare."

"I'm sorry I got you involved, but I didn't want anyone else untangling this. If you hadn't been on your way back to Trenton, I probably would have put Plover on ice somewhere until you returned."

I looked over at Bob. He was curled up next to one of the lights that had been brought in to illuminate the crime scene.

"It's past Bob's bedtime," I said to Morelli.

"Mine too," Morelli said. "Take him home for me. I'll tell the ME I'm leaving, and I'll meet you at the house."

"Is your brother there?"

"No. He left yesterday. He's back with his wife."

I walked Bob to my SUV and drove him to Morelli's house. It was less than a mile from my parents' house, in a very similar neighborhood. It was a small two-story, three-bedroom house with living room, dining room, kitchen on the ground floor.

The living room had guy furniture bought as a package. A big, comfy couch and two recliner chairs to match. Saddle-brown leather. A large square coffee table that could easily fit four extra-large pizza boxes plus a couple six-packs of beer on it. And a state-of-the-art, massive flat-screen television.

Ranger's living room was cool and serene. It was a quiet place to collect yourself. Morelli's living room was a noisy collection point for family members and friends. Both men spent their day dealing with violence, lawlessness, and chaos. Their manners of renewing their positive energy were miles apart. I was somewhere in between. They were black and white and red. I was gray. Ironic that I would be walking down the aisle at Loretta's wedding the day after tomorrow wearing gray.

I parked at the curb, and Bob and I went to the door. Bob was obviously excited. His ears were up, his eyes were bright, and his tail was furiously wagging. Bob liked me . . . but not as much as he liked Morelli. And this was clearly his home. I was less enthusiastic. I'd once thought that this could be my home, but it didn't happen, and now I was going to marry Ranger. And I was going to have to tell Morelli.

I unlocked the door and Bob rushed in. I switched the lights on and followed Bob to the kitchen. I filled his water bowl, went to the fridge, and got myself a beer. The kitchen was unusually tidy. This meant that after Morelli's brother left, his mom came in and cleaned. Morelli had a cleaning person who came in once a week, but no one cleaned like Mama Morelli. Except Ella. The difference being that Mama Morelli cleaned up after her sons, and her sons weren't exactly neat freaks. Ella cleaned up after Ranger, and Ranger didn't leave toothpaste in the sink or fast-food wrappers and empty beer cans spread throughout his apartment.

I heard the front door open and shut. Bob gave a woof and took off to greet Morelli.

"He missed you," I said when they came into the kitchen.

"And I missed him." Morelli reached out and drew me close. "And I missed you," he said. "All the time. Every moment."

"Even when you were in the titty bar?"

"Especially in the titty bar. The pole dancers were all eligible for Medicare. It was the only place I could get a beer and a burger without walking a mile. My hotel didn't have room service. The city of Trenton doesn't provide a per diem that covers the Ritz-Carlton."

His lips brushed across mine, his hands moved under my shirt, and he kissed me. The kiss deepened and I felt the heat start in my chest and rush through my belly to points south. I've known Morelli for almost my entire life. I played choo-choo with him when I was five. I was the tunnel and he was the train. He didn't get to see much more than my cotton undies but it was still a memorable experience. I gave him my virginity when I was in high school. And here I was, all these years later, still hopelessly attracted to him and in love with him. A voice that sounded a lot like Jiminy Cricket whispered in my ear that I was also in love with Ranger and was about to marry him.

"There's something I need to tell you," I said to Morelli.

"Me first," he said. "When I was in Miami, I realized that I hated being away from you. I don't want to live like this anymore. I gave the pool table to my brother. He's making a rec room in his basement. I want a dining table. I want kids of my own. I want to get married."

My heart stopped dead for several beats. I didn't see this one coming. "Excuse me?"

"I want to marry you."

Oh boy! Holy crap!

BONUS MATERIAL

Thirty Quotes from Thirty Books

I'm not someone who likes to look backward, but the publication of the thirtieth book in the Stephanie Plum series sent me on a quick trip down memory lane. I asked my longtime readers to identify their favorite lines from Stephanie's previous adventures and picked a few of my own, and now I'm happy to share with you thirty quotes from Stephanie & Co. that still make me smile.

Janet Evanovich

#1 "I shot that sucker right in the gumpy." —*Grandma Mazur*

#2 "You've got a hell of a gene pool, babe." —*Ranger*

#3 "Tell me you don't have legs sticking out of that car." —*Morelli*

#4 "You can't be a fucking musician without fucking cursing."
—*Sally Sweet*

#5 "Trade my Firebird for that whale you drive? I don't think so. Friendship don't go that far." —*Lula*

#6 "Nice dress. Take it off." —*Morelli*

#7 "He hardly ever kills people anymore. He has cataracts." —*Vinnie*

#8 "I'm disappointed. Usually when I'm with you a car explodes or a building burns down." —*Ranger*

#9 "Ranger cut his eyes to me and the smile widened ever so slightly —the sort of smile you see on a man when he's presented with an unexpected piece of pie." —*Stephanie Plum*

#10 "Maybe I should be a cop. Do you think I'm too short?"
—*Grandma Mazur*

#11 "I need a new life, but I'll make do with doughnuts."
—*Mary Lou Stankovic*

#12 "You can entrust your loved one to a funeral parlor that takes the time to use doilies." —*Grandma Mazur*

#13 "I was ready to put out, but he got some acid reflux from the cookies and had to go home." —*Grandma Mazur*

#14 "I used to have birthday cake in the freezer for emergencies, but I ate it." —*Stephanie Plum*

#15 "Have you ever seen Ranger eat bacon?" —*Ramon*

#16 "I'm only getting one doughnut. I'm on a new diet where I only have one of anything." —*Lula*

#17 "I love your granny. I want to be just like her when I grow up."

—Lula

#18 "I'm thinking about becoming a cougar." *—Grandma Mazur*

#19 "Cupcake, you are my lunch." *—Morelli*

#20 "What kind of man comes and drinks your pinot noir, and then throws you in a dumpster? This man has no manners." *—Lula*

#21 "I got it on good authority that God wants me to get Bella for Him." *—Grandma Mazur*

#22 "I've been run over by a van, stun-gunned at least twice, injected with some sort of narcotic, and there's a good chance I've got bubonic plague. Today isn't a good day."

—Stephanie Plum

#23 "I knew it was a mistake to have that cat in the film. He was a scene stealer." *—Lula*

#24 "Let me know if you need help with the zombies. I'm good with dead people." *—Grandma Mazur*

#25 "By nine o'clock it had become obvious that Lula and I were even worse at waiting tables than we were at being bounty hunters."

—Stephanie Plum

#26 "I got good ankles. They're one of my best features. They haven't started to sag yet." *—Grandma Mazur*

#27 "Besides, no one hardly ever gets shot at a viewing. That's usually reserved for the funeral." *—Stephanie Plum*

#28 "Note to self: If you're going to go gonzo and get arrested, use waterproof mascara in case you cry." —*Stephanie Plum*

#29 "The woman is a maniac. Although, you have to give credit to someone her age who could climb over that console wearing a granny dress and handcuffs." —*Stephanie Plum*

#30 "I didn't have any antihistamine, but I found some Tic Tacs. I think they're helping." —*Lula*